W9-BSM-524

THE BRINK

Other Books by Dan Gallery

STAND BY TO START ENGINES

8 BELLS & ALL'S WELL

NOW HEAR THIS

TWENTY MILLION TONS UNDER THE SEA

CLEAR THE DECKS

DAN GALLERY

THE BRINK

DOUBLEDAY & COMPANY, INC. 1968 GARDEN CITY, NEW YORK

FIRST EDITION
LIBRARY OF CONGRESS CATALOG CARD NUMBER 68-24835

PRINTED IN THE UNITED STATES OF AMERICA

"To Herman"

THE BRINK

1

In December, during the 1970s, up near the top of the world in the Norwegian Sea, the sun peeped over the horizon only an hour before noon, and a new day began for those creatures that live on or near the surface of the earth and its oceans. The sea lay cold and empty beneath the pale northern sky.

The day is short in the Arctic at this time of year. The sun edges up over the horizon about 11 A.M. It never gets very high, and it eases down into the sea again a couple of hours later. Night lasts twenty-one hours, and the day is a half-hearted, feeble one.

This morning some Arctic early birds soared lazily over the choppy waters looking for unwary fish. Now and then a whale surfaced, let out a puff from its blowhole, and went below again. These were the only signs of life in this part of the world. There was no trace of man and his works.

But the sea was not as empty as it looked. One hundred fathoms below the surface the USS *Nemo*, our newest Polaris submarine, cruised northeast at ten knots. One third of her crew were at their stations on watch, one third in their bunks, and the other third were doing the things that Polaris sailors do in their spare time. In the roomy crew's lounge, some were writing letters, some reading or studying, and others sitting around shooting the breeze or playing games. Some were in the nearby mess room eating. They feed around the clock on these boats, and Polaris sailors eat high on the hog.

Cocked, aimed, and ready in the Sherwood Forest midship section of the boat were sixteen Polaris missiles with atomic warheads. These missiles are solid fuel rockets about three feet in diameter and thirty feet long. Their vertical launching tubes running thru the hull seem like the trunks of trees in a great forest. Sixteen of them pack more explosive power in their warheads than all the bombs dropped by both sides in World War II . . . enough to smash the sixteen biggest cities in Russia and kill perhaps five or six million people in a holocaust that would be over in a matter of minutes. Hitler's slaughterhouses, working overtime, took several years to kill that many Jews.

The *Nemo* is one of a fleet of such craft which patrol the waters of the Far North enforcing an uneasy peace in this world. Her battery of missiles is our final argument, our "instant and devastating retaliation," in case our "adversaries" ever make a false move. She is constantly alert for a flash from Washington which will tell her to cut loose hell on earth and perhaps blast civilization back into the Dark Ages.

In the crew's lounge this morning, two sailors sat hunched over a chessboard. This is a sight you seldom see on any other type of naval ship. But the crews of the Polaris boats are the cream of the crop, and everyone on board from the Skipper down to the Captain of the Head is a brain.

One of the players was a colored mess boy from the wardroom. The other was a sharp young technician from the reactor room who had a degree in nuclear physics.

"Your move, Joe," said the colored boy.

"Yeah—I know it," said Joe. "What's your hurry? We're

gonna be out here a couple of more months. There's plenty of time."

"Sure," said the mess boy, "but even if you stall that long you won't get out of the jam I got you in now."

A kibitzer said, "He hasn't got you yet, Joe. Move your castle."

"Keep your big mouth out of this," said Joe. "I'll figure this thing out for myself."

At this point the lights began to blink, a buzzer sounded, and a voice said on the squawk box, "All hands to battle stations—All hands to battle stations—"

No alarm bells clanged. No bugles blew as they do on surface ships. But all hands jumped just as if they had. In the lounge, letter writers dropped their pens in the middle of words and stomped out cigarettes, readers slammed books face down to keep their places and scrambled for battle stations. In the bunk rooms, sailors who had been sound asleep bounced out of their bunks wide awake before they hit the deck.

Any time General Quarters sounds on a Polaris boat, this may be IT. No one dallies on the way to that drill—if it is a drill.

Throughout the ship the battle watch relieved the cruising watch, who scurried off to their own battle stations. In less than a minute, 132 officers and men were at their posts and the *Nemo* was ready to do—whatever she was told to do.

In the main control room the Navigator relieved the Officer of the Deck and took the reports . . . "Reactor control manned and ready" . . . "Torpedo control manned and ready" . . . "Missile control manned and ready" . . . and so on from all parts of the ship.

The Captain took his station on the central platform near the periscopes, where he could see all that was happening. Commander Banks, class of '55, USNA, was a husky man who had played B-squad football and was known to his intimates as Spike. He had gone into the submarine service right after graduation, and got into the atomic program on the ground floor, grew up with it, and now had one of the choice jobs open to people of his time. He was obviously on his way to the top.

As he strapped on his battle phones he scanned the array of gauges and instruments on the control panel in front of him, nodding to the Navigator as the ready reports were relayed to him. Nearby, the Executive Officer was also scanning the control panel, double-checking that everything was going right.

The Captain and Exec each held a radio dispatch in his hand. It was the urgent priority message over the "hot circuit" from the Pentagon that had triggered this drill.

The dispatch contained two special authenticating words, one for the Captain and one for the Exec. The Captain had a small book, which was always in his hip pocket, with a list of key words and dates. The Exec had a book with a different list. Neither ever saw the other's book. Each checked every incoming "ATOMIC" dispatch to make sure that it included his key word for the date in question. Both had to agree that their key words checked before the dispatch could be accepted as authentic. A locked brief case accompanies the President of the United States wherever he goes, and contains the master lists of words and dates.

As the last ready reports were coming in, the Captain held up his dispatch and nodded to the Exec. The Exec held up his, nodded back, and stepped over so they could compare the two dispatches, see that they were identical, and each could check that his own key word was in the other's dispatch.

Then the Skipper flipped a switch on the squawk box and said over the PA system, "This is a drill. Prepare to simulate firing the whole missile battery. This is a drill."

Throughout the ship all hands did nearly all the things they would do if this were for keeps instead of only a drill. In most cases this involved simply watching dials and punching buttons at the right time. It was hard to go wrong on this, because precisely programmed mechanical brains monitored the whole process and automatic interlocks would stop everything and flash red lights in case anyone made a blooper. There is seldom any hitch in this final check, because everything is supposed to be cocked and ready twenty-four hours around the clock. In this case, a red light on the status board showed one missile was not ready.

"Number six is out for a guidance adjustment," said the Exec.

"I know," said the Captain. "That's the one for Sverdlovsk."

This sort of drill takes the system almost, but not quite, up to the final seconds of a firing countdown. Certain switches in the firing circuit are never closed; certain bits of final information are withheld from the missile guidance systems. The ship comes up near the surface, to launching depth. But the heavy steel doors on top of the missile tubes in the Sherwood Forest are never opened. To actually fire, both the Skipper and Exec must unlock safety switches in the circuit with different keys, to which there are no duplicates.

The drill does not go to the point where the Skipper's thumb on the firing key, or an accidental lurch against it, would launch a missile that could start World War III.

For the next few minutes a stream of reports came in over the Exec's battle phone as various stations completed and checked their parts of the job. A yeoman standing near the Exec with a clipboard and stopwatch checked each item on the final countdown sheet as it came in and scribbled the time alongside it. The Captain stood silently at his station, tapping his foot, staring at the control panel, and thinking about . . . whatever the skippers of Polaris subs think about at a time like this.

As the final report came in and the countdown reached zero (for a drill), the Exec put his key in the lock and said, "Ready to fire, Cap'n."

As he did so he punched his stopwatch, glanced at it, grinned, and held it up for the Captain to see. "New record, Captain," he said. "Two seconds better than the old one."

The Captain nodded, flipped a switch on the squawk box, and said, "Well done to all hands. New record. Very well done. Secure from battle stations."

A Polaris submarine like the *Nemo* is the most wondrous machine that man has yet devised. All the best scientific brains from Newton to Einstein have helped to make this thing possible. Packed into the sleek hull are the fruits of centuries of research prying out the secrets of what makes this universe tick. It is the crowning glory of "civilized" man's long struggle to harness the forces of nature—his masterpiece in the field of physical science.

The end product of all this is a weapons system capable of instant massive slaughter on a scale not yet seen on this earth.

After nearly two thousand years of the Christian Era and the first twenty-five years of the Atomic Age, it is a grim milestone on man's road toward learning how to run the world and to live in peace with his brothers.

The *Nemo* displaces eight thousand tons—more than a light cruiser in World War II. In the old days submarines, unlike all other naval vessels, were called "boats." But now even the submariners are beginning to call them ships.

The ship is nuclear powered, can outrun most surface ships and outmaneuver any of them. She runs deep and can stay down till her food gives out. Surface ships stumble across "nukes" only by accident, and can't hold contact when they do.

Even running submerged, the ship is in constant radio touch with the Pentagon. She has to be, to fulfill her mission. No one can tell when the Hour of Doom will strike. She must hear it when it does.

Her main contact with the world around her is by sound. One of the big facts of life in a submariner's world is that water is an excellent conductor of sound. A sub listens continuously to pick up any telltale noises coming from the depths around her, and tries to be as silent as an eel herself. Her streamlined hull has no sharp projections to make sound waves in the water. Her propeller is specially designed to prevent "cavitation"—digging holes in the water at high speed—which can be heard for miles. Even a small nick in a propeller blade generates a squeal that makes submariners cringe.

Submarines are known as the "silent" service and this doesn't mean just at press conferences. Silence is a way of life with them. It is indeed golden when your life may depend on it!

So a submarine, running under wraps herself, has an array of passive listening devices which put no energy into the water but enable her to eavesdrop on the depths around her. These depths are far from silent. The ocean throbs with the heart-beat of the world, which you can hear if you listen on the right frequency. The cracking and groaning of the earth's inner crust can be heard from places thousands of miles away. Storms and breaking waves on the surface make noises which a trained ear down below can recognize. Fish make all sorts of noises. Porpoises seem able to talk to each other. Surface ships stir up a storm of noise in the water from the hull, screws, and machinery.

A good sound man listens to these noises the way a maestro listens to a symphony orchestra. He must be able to pick out the throb of a propeller from the chorus of other sounds in the ocean the same way that Toscanini used to put his finger on an erring flute player in the midst of a crashing crescendo by the whole orchestra.

The "holy of holies" on a Polaris sub is the Sherwood Forest, the midship section housing the sixteen missiles. These are solid fuel rockets that require no long countdown like the liquid fuel giants at Cape Kennedy. For them the countdown is always "ten seconds and holding." Their guidance systems are updated and corrected automatically as the ship moves through the water so that they are always bore-sighted on their targets every minute of the twenty-four hours. By punching a few buttons and flipping a switch you can shift the aiming point of any missile from the intersection of the runways at a bomber field near the Black Sea to the place in Manchuria where the Chinese are making A-bombs. Or to the dome of St. Peter's, for that matter.

There is no horseplay or monkey business in the Forest. Everyone who works there knows that he can make a mistake that might be fatal for the *Nemo*. Maybe even for the whole United States.

It would not seem at all out of place if everyone who entered the Forest genuflected and blessed himself as he did so.

Controlling and living in this instrument of national policy are twelve officers and 120 sailors. You might think that because of the job they may someday have to do, these men would be hand-picked Gestapo types with ice water in their veins. But they're not. Except for being well above average intelligence, they are a typical cross section of American youth.

None of them would deliberately be mean to old ladies or little children. But all are skilled technicians proud of having been picked for vitally important jobs. Each is determined that when and if the Great Day comes and the Skipper has to push the button that will obliterate a lot of old ladies and little kids, his particular piece of equipment will function as designed.

The Navy teaches them a great deal about technical things. But whatever they know about history, and the whys and wherefores of life on this earth, they must pick up on their own time.

The Navy since the days of sail has trained its men to obey orders. Although these men may someday be given an order that will release the Four Horsemen of the Apocalypse—all they have to do is carry it out. The Navy sees no need to get dramatic about this. It just assumes that every man who takes the oath of allegiance means exactly what he says.

On a long cruise submerged, one day is just about the same as the next. In fact there is no real night and day. You stand two four-hour watches each day, put in eight hours sack time, and have eight hours to live it up. You live by a simplified calendar with only three days in the week—Yesterday, Today, and Tomorrow.

You might think that utter boredom would be a problem on a ship like this. But it isn't. There is a new movie every day. Several times a day there is a concert on the PA system, and the radio news from home. The game room, gym, and library are always busy.

And no matter how humdrum the routine, each man carries in the back of his head the knowledge that in the next half hour he may have a hand in changing the course of history.

Soon after secure from drill, the ship's doctor, Lieutenant Commander White, tapped at the door of the Captain's cabin. Dr. White was a general practitioner, surgeon, and psychologist, trained to handle problems that come up when you have a group of men isolated from the rest of the world for some time and under a certain amount of constant tension. He could treat anything from mumps or a toothache to broken bones, a ruptured appendix, or a fractured ego. He observed each man in the crew daily for any signs of mental trouble. There are no unimportant jobs on a Polaris sub, and any one of the 132 souls aboard could do grave harm if he went round the bend.

Each day, he dropped in for a chat with the Captain to tell him about the health of his crew, and also, of course, to have a look at the Captain, too. (Meantime the Captain was also taking a good look at him.)

As the Doctor entered the roomy cabin (roomy, that is, for a submarine), the Captain said, "Hello, Doctor. Have a seat. How's that kid that broke his ankle the other day?"

"Fine, Captain," said the Doctor, settling himself down on the leather settee. "Except we're having trouble keeping him in his bunk. He doesn't think we can get along without him and wants to be up and about standing watches. . . . That was a fine drill this morning, Cap'n. You must feel pretty good about the new record."

"Yes, it was a good drill," agreed the Captain. "The boys get better every time. I guess that if and when the Great Day comes we won't delay things much down here at our end when they decide to shoot the works."

"Not if the drill today was a fair sample," said the Doctor.

"By the way," he added, "I see by the latest radio news that your dad has just made four stars and is being ordered to London as Commander in Chief Naval Forces Europe. You must be very proud of him."

"Yes, I am," said the Skipper. "But he earned it. He's been in this Navy thirty-eight years now. He was a fighter pilot during World War II and was in all the big battles in the Pacific. He got shot down once and had ships sunk under him twice. He used to tell me and my brother some hair-raising tales when we were kids about the early days of naval aviation. He always said the Lord must be saving him for something, and I guess this new job is it."

"Your brother in the Navy too?" asked the Doctor.

"No indeed," said the Captain. "He went straight. He's a priest. In Rome now, attached to the Vatican."

"The Vatican? That's like being on CNO's* staff, isn't it?" asked the Doctor.

"In a way. He and I are going to get together for a visit with Dad in London after this cruise. . . . Doctor, how do you size up that new ensign we just got aboard, young Gateau?"

"I think he's going to be all right, Cap'n. I notice he reads a lot of deep stuff about philosophy and such. Most newcomers don't have time for that—too busy learning about what we've got on board. But this lad is very smart—seems to learn fast. I think he'll be okay."

"He learns fast, all right," said the Skipper. "I checked him out for diving the ship the other day, and he knows damn near as much as I do about it already. What I'm afraid of is he may be too smart for his own good."

"How do you mean, Cap'n?"

"He thinks too much . . . all that far-out reading he does isn't good for him. . . . You don't want deep thinkers out here."

"Hmmmm," said the Doctor. "Caesar said something about men who think too much."

* Chief of Naval Operations

"He said, 'such men are dangerous.' Now don't get me wrong, Doctor. I'm not really worried about young Gateau. But he ought to be thinking about inertial accelerometers, instead of Plato's philosophy, if he's going to be a good Polaris man."

"There's a lot to learn on these boats, all right," conceded the Doctor.

"We call 'em ships now, Doctor," corrected the Captain. "And one of the troubles with these ships is that after you learn all about them yourself and get to be skipper, they give you so many hand-picked young hot shots to help you that you got nothing left to do yourself any more. It isn't like in the old boats, where the skipper was a busy man. So if you don't watch out, you start thinking in all your spare time. And that isn't good, either."

"You seem to be holding up all right, Cap'n," said the Doctor.

"It's a great comfort to hear you say that," replied the Captain with mock gravity. "But sometimes I wonder."

"Why?"

"Well, as you know, of course, the skipper of one of these craft can do a lot more to change life on this earth than the skipper of one of the old pig boats could ever do."

"He sure can."

"We take all sorts of precautions to guard against an accidental shot on one of these drills—or at any other time, for that matter."

"That's right."

"It is inconceivable that any accident or mechanical malfunction can launch a missile. They also take great precautions in Washington to make sure that no one in the Pentagon can send an unauthorized firing message. We have a foolproof system at this end to detect it, even if they did. We also go to great lengths to guard against what you and your colleagues call a 'knowledgeable psychopath' in the crew."

"Yessir."

"But what happens if *I* am the knowledgeable psychopath, and decided to shoot on my own hook?"

"That's a tough situation, Captain," said the Doctor. "But what has to be done is clear-cut. If I'm convinced that you have gone round the bend, it is my duty to tell you that I think you are incapacitated for duty and to ask you to turn over command to the Exec and go on the sick list."

"Exactly right, Doctor," said the Captain. "But suppose I refuse. I'm a commander. You're a lieutenant commander. I'm captain of the ship. And let's suppose I haven't become a complete screwball trying to climb the bulkheads—that would make it too simple. Suppose I'm acting pretty normal so far as anyone but an expert like yourself can tell. . . . What then?"

"That makes it much tougher, Cap'n. . . . But if I'm sure you've gone off your rocker there's still no question what has to be done. I go to the Executive Officer and tell him what I think. If he believes me, it is his duty to relieve you of command. I must say, Cap'n," he added, "that this crew has absolute confidence in you. They would be very reluctant to disobey an order from you."

"Yes, I know that, Doctor," said the Captain. "That's what bugs me a little. . . . Haven't you got some sort of a do-it-yourself quiz I can give myself each morning when I get up to make sure I'm still okay?"

"No, I haven't," laughed the Doctor. "We'll just have to sweat it out together with me dropping in to report each day."

"Well, anyway, I guess we see eye to eye, Doctor. I just wanted to be sure we understood each other. You know what your duty is. And I don't want you to have any doubts that I know what it is, too. It doesn't bother me a bit to know that you're taking a careful squint at me now and then, so long as you don't get too nosy about it."

At this point the battle phone on the bulkhead alongside the desk buzzed discreetly, a pilot light began flashing, and the Captain picked up the phone.

"Captain speaking—go ahead."

After a moment he said, "Very well. I'll be right up."

Replacing the phone in its rack, he said, "They want me up in control. They've picked up screw noises closing in on us."

2

When the Captain got to the control room he found the O.O.D.* and the Navigator bending over a plotting board.

"We've picked up propeller noises, Cap'n," said the Navigator. "Twin screws, three-bladed, one-fifty rpm . . . sounds like a destroyer about fifteen miles away . . . the bearing is changing slowly."

The Captain studied the plot for a moment and then said, "Must be a Russian. Nobody else has destroyers running around in this area. Is he pinging?"

"We haven't heard anything yet," said the Navigator, "but we're watching for it."

A destroyer's sonar finds things underwater by emitting a sharp ping into the water every few seconds. This ping spreads out in all directions and if there is nothing out there but salt water of uniform density and temperature the sound wave goes on and on till it dissipates. But if it encounters something

* Officer of the Deck

else, an echo comes back. From this return echo, experts can determine the direction and distance of the something. Whether it is a submarine, school of fish, whale, a layer of cold water or one of the many other things that will return an echo, remains to be seen. Destroyers cruise around pinging continually when they are looking for something. Submarines have even better sonars than destroyers, but they don't like to use them much, because the ping they have to make betrays the sub's presence long before an echoed ping would. Submarines prefer to rely on their passive listening devices to warn them of the approach of other ships. Surface ships make lots of noise.

For the next ten minutes the *Nemo*'s passive listeners clamped on the noise from the destroyer's screws. The bearing continued to change slowly, indicating that the destroyer was passing clear of the sub. Then it stopped changing and the noise from the screws began increasing, showing that the destroyer was heading right at them.

"Hmmm," commented the Captain. "That must be an accidental change of course. I don't see how he could have spotted us . . . he isn't pinging." (Skippers always refer to another ship as "he," meaning the other captain.)

The Navigator studied the plot thoughtfully and agreed.

After a few minutes the Captain said, "Let's change course ninety degrees to the right and see what happens."

The O.O.D. gave the necessary orders to the helmsman, the boat swung ninety degrees right to the new course, and the Navigator and Captain watched the plot of the bearings coming in from the sound room. At first they began to draw aft, but after a few minutes they steadied down again.

"I'll be damned!" commented the Skipper. "He seems to be able to stay right with us."

The Navigator and O.O.D. nodded gravely.

"Are we making any noise?" demanded the Skipper of the sound room.

"No, sir," the answer came back. "So far as we can tell we're not making a sound. We checked very carefully."

"Let's get a range on him," said the Skipper. "Just one ping."

Passive listening tells you direction only, not distance of the other vessel. To get a range you have to make a ping. But it takes a very alert sound man on the other ship to pick up just one ping.

In the sound room the sonar operator triggered his set to let out one ping and listened carefully for about twenty-five seconds. Then a faint echoed ping came back and he announced, "Range nineteen thousand, five hundred yards, closing slowly."

The Skipper said to the Navigator, "He picked us up at a range of about twenty miles. I don't see how he's doing it without pinging. Keep a careful plot of this whole thing and make sure the sound room gets it all down on tape. Our Anti-Sub Warfare people back home will be interested in this."

"They'll drop everything else till they figure it out," observed the Navigator.

For the next fifteen minutes the bearing plots and the slowly increasing sound level of the screws showed the destroyer was coming right at them. The Captain glanced at the depth gauge, which showed 100 feet.

"How deep is the layer this morning?" he asked.

He was referring to the depth at which the temperature inversion in the water occurs. Ordinarily as you go down from the surface, the temperature of the water decreases at a uniform rate. But at some depth as you go down, which varies from day to day, there is a sudden change in water temperature, which causes a so-called layer. Sonar beams do not penetrate this layer. They bounce off it as if it were a tin roof. A submarine underneath the layer is safe from probing sonar beams, although it can still hear noises coming from a vessel above the layer.

"The layer is at two-fifty this morning, sir," reported the Navigator.

"Let's get under it," said the Captain. "Take her down to four hundred feet and change course ninety degrees to the left."

The O.O.D. took her down to four hundred feet, changing

course as they went. "Steady on new course at four hundred feet," he reported.

The destroyer continued to close as indicated by the increasing sound level. It soon became obvious that the layer didn't bother her a bit. The sailors on watch in the control room began exchanging significant glances, raising eyebrows, and shrugging shoulders.

"I'll be damned," said the Skipper. "These birds have got something new we don't know anything about. He isn't even pinging, at least not on any frequency that we can hear . . . but he stays right with us."

They were now joined by the Executive Officer, who had been following developments in the sound room. "All we can hear, Cap'n, is screw noises. We haven't heard any sign of a ping. I've got our best people on the phones down there now. These guys must have some brand-new way of tracking us."

As the destroyer continued to close, the Captain said, "Get me another ping on him."

Soon the report came back from the sound room: "Range ten thousand yards."

The Captain stood for a couple of minutes staring at the plot in deep thought and tapping his fingers nervously every now and then on the board.

"How about getting our torpedoes armed and ready, sir?" asked the Exec.

The Captain, lost in thought, obviously didn't hear him.

After another minute the Exec repeated his query.

"Oh, excuse me," said the Captain. Then after a long pause he added, "No, leave the torpedoes as they are. Keep the attack director manned. And keep the problem set up on it."

This order referred to the mechanical brain that keeps track of what your own ship and an enemy target are doing and of how you must aim a torpedo in order to hit him.

"Aye aye, sir," said the Exec.

"Now let's boost her up to full speed," said the Captain, "and see what that does to him."

Back in the reactor room the sailor on watch punched a couple of buttons, woke up some of the sleeping electrons in the atomic furnace down below, and shot a surge of extra power back to the engine room. Still running silent, the *Nemo* accelerated rapidly to full speed.

In the control room the officers watched the speed indicator moving up the dial. As it was settling down at top speed, the sound room reported: "Target is increasing speed; rpm is now three hundred."

By this time some of the sailors from the off-duty watch had drifted into the control room and were standing in the background watching with grave faces. The Executive Officer started to make them move on, but at a sign from the Skipper he held his peace.

"He must hear something," observed the Skipper. "I think they've made a breakthrough in some low-frequency area that we haven't gotten into yet."

"Yeah," agreed the Exec. "And at this speed, none of our surface sonars could operate at all. But it doesn't seem to bother him a bit."

After another fifteen minutes, during which the destroyer continued to close, a report came in from sound: "He's slowing down now to two-fifty rpm. He's directly astern of us . . . we estimate at two miles."

"How about that?" said the Captain in grudging admiration of this fine technical performance. "He's settling down to fly formation on us! . . . Start our sonar going, continuous pinging."

"How about turning loose a decoy, Cap'n?" asked the Exec. Submarines carry self-propelled underwater noisemakers which they can release to scurry off making noises that confuse homing torpedoes and produce phony echoes that gum up probing sonars.

"No-o-o . . . I don't think so," said the Captain. "I don't want to make any funny noises that he might misinterpret. One of those things could be mistaken for a torpedo. I want you to ping on our own sonar so we can keep an accurate plot on him."

"Aye aye, sir," said the Exec.

Then after a moment, the Captain said to the Exec, "Joe, get the Doctor and come up to my cabin."

A few minutes later, the Captain, Exec, and Doctor met in the cabin.

"Gentlemen," said the Captain, "I want you to know how I see this situation. By now everyone on board knows what's going on, and there's going to be a lot of talk about it. I don't want to aggravate things by getting on the PA system and making speeches about it, but you two can get the word around without making a federal case out of it. . . . This guy obviously has something new that we've never run into before. I don't know if we're going to be able to shake him off. I figure he is pretty sure we're not going to take any hostile action. . . . He must be, to just sit there within torpedo range. I don't think he is, either—otherwise, he would have already done it. I was a bit concerned about that for a while. An hour or so ago, when he began getting close to us, it was a rather hairy situation. That's why I didn't want to do anything that might scare him. . . . Anyway, the way the rules of this game are set up for us, he gets to make the first move. If he wants to nail us, there's a good chance that he will, and they'll never know back home what happened to us. We can do the same thing to him, but we really have no excuse for doing it; he's got as much right to be out here doing what he is as we have. So . . . any comments?"

"What you say is quite true, Cap'n," said the Exec. "But we have a right to defend ourselves if we think he is attacking us. How far do we let him go before we retaliate?"

"That's the sixty-four-billion-dollar question," replied the Captain. "There's only one reason for us being out here, or for the whole Polaris program, that makes any sense. That's to prevent an atomic war. For us to do anything that might start the war is unthinkable."

"Would you just sit tight and let him destroy us, Cap'n?" asked the Exec.

"If that would prevent an atomic war, I think I might," said the Captain. "But of course it wouldn't. If he has orders to destroy us, the Russians are already committed to the war, and if we just sat back and did nothing, it could only delay the final outbreak of war a little. If I know he means to destroy us, I'll let him have it first. But the only way we can tell that he has put something in the water that can hurt us is by listening. I'm not going to do anything that might start a war just on the basis of what might be an idle rumor coming out of the sound room."

"He's hanging on about two miles behind us now, Cap'n," said the Exec. "If he puts anything in the water it will take a couple of minutes for it to catch up with us. We're sure to hear it coming."

"Right," said the Captain. "But I'm not going to shoot just because I hear a strange noise in the water—and I hope we don't make any noises that he interprets as being hostile. . . . So there you are. We are right back where we started from."

"Couldn't we surface, Captain," asked the Doctor, "and ask him if he wants to borrow a sack of coffee?"

"Yes. I've considered that too, Doctor. Much as I would hate to do it, I will do that rather than go off half-cocked. . . . But I want to do more than just get rid of him," said the Skipper. "We've got to find out how he's doing this. I don't want to shake him off until we do. I want to keep a continuous plot of this operation, showing our position, course, speed and depth, and also his. I want continuous tapes from our sonar with time records that we can tie into the plot. I want water temperatures, salinity, and everything else that could possibly be of any interest to our ASW* experts back home."

"Yessir, Cap'n," said the Exec. "We're doing all that now."

"Now lemme see," said the Captain, glancing at his watch. "I want to get some photos of this guy to bring back with us.

* Anti-Submarine Warfare

It's dark up there now, and will be for another twelve hours. When it gets light I'm coming up near the surface to stick up a periscope and get pictures for our ONI* boys. Meantime, I'm going to keep running at high speed to the northwest and taking him further away from his base. He will have to break off eventually and go home for oil."

"We can outlast him, that's for sure," said the Exec. "What condition of readiness do you want while we're doing this, Cap'n?"

"This may go on for days," said the Captain. "We can't keep the boys at battle stations all that time. I want just the regular cruising watch, except in the sound room and torpedo room. We'll have to double the watch in the sound room to make sure we don't miss anything. And I want to keep the torpedo room manned, with two fish ready to shoot, but the tube doors closed."

"Aye aye, sir, I'll take care of that," said the Exec.

"Now, gentlemen," continued the Captain, "this is a touchy business. We've got a real smart crew and they can all see we've been caught by surprise with something we don't know anything about. One of the main things we've got to contend with is the jitters. We've just got to play it cool and sweat it out."

Until next morning the *Nemo* ran deep, ran silent, ran fast, and zigzagged to the northwest. The Russian stayed with her like a barnacle, never more than a mile or so astern. It soon became obvious to all hands that they weren't going to shake him off. This gave them all something to think about, because up to now one of the major facts of life for them had been that the *Nemo* could slip away from anything. It shook their pride and faith in the ship.

At one time, the Skipper tried reversing course suddenly. The sonar plot on the destroyer showed that the Russian caught the change within about a minute and resumed his station a mile

* Office of Naval Intelligence

astern within five minutes. The Captain then circled continuously for half an hour. This seemed to puzzle their tormentor at first, but eventually the plot showed him to be simply making a big cloverleaf pattern over the spot where the *Nemo* was circling.

During this period no one in the control room said a word. The only sound was the string of reports coming in over the speaker from sonar control. "Bearing zero four zero, range two five double oh . . . Bearing zero four two, range two five five oh . . ." etc.

The Navigator plotted these positions on his chart with the Captain and Exec peering over his shoulder. Everyone on watch in the duty section listened carefully and scanned the faces of the trio around the chart board.

Finally the Skipper said, "Okay. Let's head northwest again. Steer three one five . . . I'll be in the cabin. Let me know if anything changes."

There was no bull session in the crew's lounge that night. There were a couple of chess and checker games, some of the boys read books, and others sat around listening to a music program on the PA system, saying nothing. All of them felt vaguely uneasy, and whenever a newcomer joined the group they all looked up at him inquiringly, with a silent question, and resumed their troubled thoughts when he said nothing.

Presently an older man whose hair was beginning to gray came in and sat down. He had a genial, weather-beaten face and keen blue eyes set among crinkles that came from squinting into many an ocean gale. He was Jim Murphy, Chief of the Boat, whose actual rate was chief quartermaster.

Officially, the number two man on a submarine, as on any ship, is the executive officer and the chain of command goes down through the line officers by seniority to the lowest ensign. But, of course, on a sub the number two man so far as the rest of the crew are concerned is the Chief of the Boat. He isn't even a commissioned officer, but he is the skipper's (and exec's) right-hand man in dealing with personal problems of the crew.

He is an old-timer who has worn bell-bottomed trousers himself and is a sort of father confessor for the younger men. He knows the Navy Regulations almost by heart, but understands that they were written for those unfortunate people who wouldn't know what to do if it wasn't all spelled out for them in a book.

In the military services, discipline is supposed to be governed by the Uniform Code of Military Justice. But the lawyers haven't yet been able to penetrate the depths of the ocean with their gobbledegook. So on submarines, whose disciplinary problems are few anyway, the Chief of the Boat makes up his own code when and if needed.

Murphy looked around at the circle of sober faces, and said, "Who's dead?"

For a moment no one answered. Then Miggs, who had been in the *Nemo* since commissioning, said, "I had a hunch this deal was too good to be true."

"What's buggin' you, Mac?" asked Murphy.

"That goddam tin can up there," said Miggs.

"He ain't bothering us–so far, anyway," said Murphy.

"No, but I don't like to have him peeking over our shoulder that way."

"Sort of invasion of privacy, hunh?"

"Yeah. Everybody is getting too suspicious of each other these days. This world is getting too small to live in. Personally, I like a little elbow room and some peace, quiet, and security. But now, everywhere you go, somebody is getting ready to heave an atom bomb at you. Those damn things are dangerous."

"Don't worry about atom bombs, Mac. As long as we're down here ready to negotiate, there ain't gonna be no atomic war. You might say we're really a part of the Peace Corps."

"I ain't worried about any atomic war while we're out here. This is the safest place in the world to be when they start heaving those big pineapples. But when you get back home and go ashore, then you have got something to think about, because the Russians have got a big rocket somewhere that's aimed right at you. If they ever fire it you could get knocked flat on your ass. And if we get home after they've fired it, then you got fallout to worry about. Out here, atom bombs or even fallout can't hurt you with six hundred feet of water over you."

"So what are you worried about? We sit around out here with air conditioning and central heating, we take our bunks and mess tables along wherever we go, three good meals a day, four on and eight off, and an extra scoop of ice cream every Sunday. What the hell more do you want?"

"We don't hit any good liberty ports on this run."

"No . . . but we got a new movie every day. If you don't like this line of work, you can always ship over in the Marines next time," observed the Chief.

"The hell with that. It makes me nervous to get shot at. If I go wading around in rice paddies, I'm apt to catch cold. And it hurts my back to dig holes in the ground. But people have gotta fight, and if we keep stalling off an atomic war, they're going to have little ones like Korea and Vietnam, and you can get hurt even in those kind if you're not careful. I don't want any part of that. . . . Hell, I came in the Navy to dodge the draft and get out of military service."

"Okay. You got it made. Those little wars can't hurt you down here," said Murphy.

"No. But that snoopy son-of-a-bitch up there astern of us, maybe he can. Maybe he doesn't understand that all we're trying to do down here is mind our own business and keep our rockets ready in a perfectly friendly manner."

After a moment Murphy said, "I don't see why you guys are so broke up over this thing. . . . We've got a guy on our back that we can't get rid of. So what? . . . He ain't bothering us any . . . and I'd rather be down here where it's comfortable and air-conditioned than up there rolling around in a tin can with the wind blowing, in the North Atlantic, where it's colder than all hell."

Some of the boys nodded half-hearted agreement. Finally one spoke up, "Whaddya think he's going to do, Chief?"

"He isn't going to do a damn thing," said the Chief. "If he was, he would have done it long ago. We can't kick about what he's doing. He's got as much right to do it as we have to do what we're doing. And we've done the same thing to their subs off our East Coast. The only bad thing about this is that we don't know how he's doing it. But what the hell . . . that's no skin off our ass. We've just got to pick up all the dope we can, and turn it in when we get home. This is going to make our sonar experts sweat blood for a while after we tell them about it. But they'll come up with an answer to it. They always have."

3

Next morning at ten o'clock the Captain came into the control room and said to the O.O.D., "What's our trim now?"

"About fifty tons positive, Captain," said the O.O.D. "We have to hold her down with the planes."

Turning to the seaman at the big control wheel, he asked, "How much angle does it take?"

"About a half a degree, sir," said the lad watching the trim bubble and the depth gauge.

"Okay," said the Captain to the O.O.D., "I want to take in ballast slowly until we have slight negative buoyancy—so it takes about a degree to hold us up. I'm going up to periscope depth as soon as there is enough light up there to take pictures. I want to be heavy when we do it to be sure we won't broach and so I can get down fast again if I have to. Get the periscope camera rigged and loaded."

"Aye aye, sir," said the O.O.D., and began venting air from the ballast tanks to let water in. This is a job for experts, because you have to let the water in equally forward and aft or you throw the boat out of trim and may get an up and down angle on her. The O.O.D. watched the depth gauge, the trim bubble, the pointers on the control planes, and the after flippers as he tinkered with his vent valves, letting in just enough water to make the boat want to sink. After ten minutes the lad on the planes said, "We're heavy now. It takes about one degree to hold her up."

"Very well," said the O.O.D.

"Nice work, Jack," said the Captain. "I'll be down in the sound room for the next half hour."

The sound room on a sub is a sort of inner sanctum. It is, to a submarine, what his ears are to a blind man. When you talk down there you lower your voice. And you don't talk at all except when you've got something to say.

It is full of electronic marvels for bugging the ocean and listening in on what goes on in its depths. It has passive listeners which pick up, amplify, and analyze all sounds in the water around them. Decibels, pitch, tone quality, modulation, and Doppler are the grist for their mills. It has active sonars which send out pings in all directions and have large scopes which show bearing and distance of anything that sends back an echo. The men who work there are a special kind of expert who all have rabbit ears. When they put on their headphones and listen to the ocean they are like doctors with stethoscopes. A doctor can listen to your insides for a minute and find out things about you that are none of his damn business. A good sound man can tell you about things going on in the depths around you that are hard to believe sometimes, too.

The Captain nodded good morning to the men on watch and said to the Chief in a low voice, "What's cooking out there?"

"Twin screws, three-bladed, two hundred rpm. No Doppler. Staying right astern of us at two thousand yards. I think it's kind of choppy up there this morning. We hear a lot of pounding and the screws race a little now and then."

"Let me hear some of your tapes," said the Skipper.

The Chief handed him a set of earphones, selected a reel of tape, and put it on a machine. The Captain spent the next half hour listening to tapes and the Chief's comments on them. There was nothing whatever on the tapes but the *thum thum thum* of propellers and the other sounds which usually come out of a nearby ship. To an ordinary listener the tapes would have sounded like a Victrola record which keeps going round and round with the needle in the last groove, and won't turn off.

"Could he be pinging on some frequency we can't hear?" asked the Captain.

"Nosir," said the Chief emphatically. Pointing to the bulkhead, he said, "These dials will indicate sounds way beyond the range of human ears. You can see there's not a sign on any of them of anything beyond aural range."

"How do you think he's tracking us, Chief?" asked the Captain.

"I haven't any idea, sir. But one thing is for sure–it isn't by sound."

At eleven o'clock the Captain came back to the control room and said, "Sound General Quarters."

As the Exec took his place alongside him, he said, "I'm going up to periscope depth. I'm only going to stay up there long enough to get some pictures. If we can get a good profile view, we can be sure of his nationality and our electronic hot shots back home may be able to spot some Buck Rogers gadget that will give them a clue as to what he is doing. . . . While I'm up there I want to stick up a whip antenna and see if he is using his radar."

"Aye aye, sir," said the Exec.

When at periscope depth, the top of the conning tower is a few feet below the surface. The top of the long hull is a few feet further below. The upper end of a periscope is a little over an inch in diameter and sticks up only a few feet above the waves. A whip antenna is about as big around as a broomstick and sticks up about ten feet, but is hard to see in choppy weather. It takes very sharp eyes indeed to spot a scope or a whip antenna in a choppy sea.

A few minutes later, when all stations had reported manned and ready, the Captain took station at the periscope and said, "Bring her up slowly to thirty feet."

He kept glancing from the depth gauge to the level bubble as the ship rose slowly on an even keel. As it neared thirty feet, he put his face to the eyepieces of the periscope and stood by with a firm grip on the slewing handles.

"Steady at thirty feet, sir," said the Exec.

"Up scope," barked the Captain.

The Quartermaster punched a button and the whole long scope tube was shoved up about six feet, carrying the Captain on a small platform up with it. As soon as the top of it broke surface, the Captain made a quick sweep all around the horizon and then put his cross wires on the destroyer following along a mile astern.

"This won't give us much of a picture," he announced. "It's a dead head-on shot. But let's get a couple anyway."

While the photographer was shooting, he said to the Exec, "Have you got the antenna up?"

"Yessir," said the Exec. "He is using his radar. We've got our analyzers on it."

Then the Captain said, "I'm going to haul off to one side of him and try to get his silhouette. . . . Change course ninety degrees to the right and slow down to five knots. I'll get some good shots as he runs by astern."

"Bearing one three five–range nineteen hundred yards," said the loudspeaker from the sound room.

The O.O.D. put the rudder over, the ship swung right, and the Skipper swung the scope to the left to hold his cross wires on the target.

In a few moments he said, "Profile is opening up nicely now. That's a Russian destroyer. Stand by on the cameras."

"Bearing one five zero–range one-seven-double-oh yards–closing," said the loudspeaker.

"Stop the engines," ordered the Skipper. . . . "Watch your depth control as we slow down. I want to get a couple of good close-ups of him as he goes by astern and then submerge again . . . boy! Look at that spray he's throwing up," he said with his face glued to the eyepiece, as the destroyer plowed into a wave.

"Bearing one five five, range one thousand yards," said the squawk box.

"Oh-oh!" said the Skipper a moment later. ". . . He's swinging right!"

"Bearing one five five, range eight double oh, closing fast," said the loudspeaker.

"Son-of-a-bitch!" yelled the Skipper. "Take her down! Crash dive! Full speed ahead! Down scope! Sound Collision Quarters!"

"Bearing one five five, range five hundred yards," said the sound room.

The destroyer was coming right at them, at twenty knots.

"Ahead full speed, left full rudder," barked the Skipper.

Things were happening fast now throughout the boat. Watertight doors were slammed and dogged down tight, buttoning the boat up so that one flooded compartment wouldn't sink her. Water was pouring into all ballast tanks, with air belching out of the vents. The controls on the planes were at full negative, and the lad on the flipper controls had them against the stop in the nose-down position.

Everything possible was being done to urge the boat downward. But eight thousand tons doesn't jump at the crack of a whip. It moves ponderously, and starts slowly.

"Bearing one six oh, range three hundred," intoned the speaker.

An ominous sound now was becoming audible all through the boat, building up in volume . . . the THUM-THUM-THUM of the destroyer's propellers beating in through the hull, without the help of any sonars or amplifiers. As the depth gauge began creeping downward, the sound was building up into a crescendo . . . THUM swish, THUM swish . . .

"Range one hundred yards," said the loudspeaker, with a note of alarm in the voice this time.

In a few more seconds, sounds like the roar of a great waterfall filled the boat. As the destroyer raced by a few feet overhead, it was like an express train going over an underpass. . . . The racket began decreasing and the sound room said, "Two hundred yards . . . range is increasing."

"Close all vents," barked the Skipper. "Blow main ballast! Stop her at four hundred feet!"

This was a large order, because the *Nemo* was gathering momentum on her way down, now, and once you get eight thousand tons moving, it's just as hard to stop as it was to start. As the sweating sailors threw switches, opened valves, and wrestled with control wheels, the ship steadied at 450 feet. "Nice work, Mr. Gateau," said the Captain to the O.O.D. "That was a close one."

"That bastard tried to ram us, Cap'n," said the Exec. "I think we ought to let him have it."

"No!" said the Skipper. "Why should he try to ram us? If he wants to sink us he has other ways to do it that won't smash up his own ship, too. That was accidental. I think he just lost track of us for a minute and started to circle."

"I guess you're right at that, Cap'n," said the Exec.

"Destroyer has circled around and taken station astern of us again," said the loudspeaker. "Range two thousand yards."

"Steady at four hundred feet now, Cap'n," reported the O.O.D.

"Very well," said the Skipper. "Secure from GQ. Unbutton the ship. Course north. Speed fifteen."

Turning to the chief electronics man nearby, he asked, "Did you get anything of interest out of his radar?"

"Yessir," said the Chief. "He has it going constantly. Frequency is fifty-two hundred megacycles, pulse repetition rate five-fifty pulses per second, and sweep rate is once around the horizon every twenty seconds. Nothing new or startling about it."

"Good work, Chief," said the Skipper.

Later the Skipper, Exec, Navigator, and Doctor were conferring in the cabin, with the plot of all operations since the first contact laid out on the table before them. After rehashing the whole business and studying all the data, the Captain said, "It stumps me. . . . It's quite obvious he knows where we are all the time almost as well as if he can see us . . . but I haven't any idea how he is doing it."

The Exec and Navigator nodded gravely and the Exec said, "That goes for me too, Cap'n."

"Gentlemen," said the Doctor after a pause, "for me to put in my oar on a thing like this is just a little bit like trying to teach your grandmother how to suck eggs."

"That's a conservative statement, I'd say," replied the Captain. "But sometimes grandmothers aren't as smart as they're supposed to be. What's on your mind, Doctor?"

"This is just a shot in the dark, Cap'n—thinking out loud. But I don't think even Dr. Einstein himself would know all about everything that goes on inside that reactor of ours. We've got it heavily shielded to keep in all the kinds of radiation that we know anything about. Everyone on board wears special badges, which I check every day to see if they are getting too much radiation. But the atomic scientists are finding new kinds of particles and new rays every day—things we never heard of before. It seems to me just possible that our reactor is putting out something we don't know about yet, which gets through the shielding. Maybe the Russians have found out about it and know how to detect it."

"Hmmmm," said the Captain. "Maybe your grandmother isn't such an expert at sucking eggs after all. Now that you mention it, I feel sort of stupid for not thinking of this myself. Of course it's possible. Improbable—but possible. Two days ago if anyone had told me a destroyer could ride herd on us without pinging, I would have said they were crazy. But what you are suggesting, Doctor, is no more improbable than what this guy is actually doing to us. . . . What do you think, Joe?"

"I think it's damn well worth exploring," said the Exec. "The question is—how do we do it? Shut down the reactor and see what happens, of course. If we could lie on the bottom with everything shut down, that would soon give us the answer. But the water is too deep here. . . . How long do you think we can just sort of float around in neutral buoyancy, a couple of hundred feet down, with everything shut down?"

"I dunno," said the Skipper. "You've got to be very lucky to hit exact neutral buoyancy in a boat this size. And with our elastic hull squeezing or expanding as we change depth, you can't hold it if you do hit it. And once you start up or down with no headway on, it's hard to stop . . . but wait a minute, now! We've got a sharp layer here. . . . I remember during the war, in the *Grampus*, they got away from a Jap destroyer in the China Sea where it was too deep to lie on the bottom by lying doggo on top of the layer for twenty-four hours. If we settled down on it real gently, we might be able to lie on top of the layer here."

"I think we can, Cap'n," said the Exec.

"Do you follow what we're talking about, Doctor?" asked the Captain.

"I'm afraid I don't," said the Doctor.

"The temperature difference in water above and below the layer," explained the Captain, "makes a difference in the water density. It often amounts to four one-hundredths of one percent. That doesn't sound like much, but for a displacement of eight thousand tons it's three tons difference."

"I follow that all right, Cap'n."

"Suppose we are one ton heavy in the light water above the layer. Then we would be two tons light when we sink into the heavy water below it."

"I follow that, too," said the Doctor.

"So if we settle down real gently into the layer we may just stop and float there, halfway between the heavy and the light water."

"Sounds almost like walking on water," said the Doctor.

"That's about what it is," said the Captain. "It's like keeping a patient just barely alive while you take his heart out and tinker with it . . . but if we're lucky, maybe we can do it. . . . Let's have a shot at it tomorrow, Joe. I want to get some sleep now. I didn't get much last night."

That evening in the crew's lounge, none of the usual games got started, and discussion of world events centered on the near miss by the Russian destroyer.

"How close do you think that guy came to us?" asked an engineer of Hilton, one of the sonar men.

"I dunno," said Hilton. "But it was the loudest screw noise I've ever heard. Even with the volume turned all the way down, it almost blasted my ears off in the phones."

"Hell, you didn't have to have phones to hear him," said the Engineer. "We heard him through the hull way back in the reactor room."

"How much water does a destroyer draw, Chief?" asked one of the yeomen.

"About sixteen feet," said Murphy.

"Well," said the yeoman, "we were at fifty feet when he went over us, so he musta missed us by over thirty."

"Now wait a minute," said Hilton. "Our depth gauge is in the keel. The top of the hull is thirty feet above that and the top of the sail is ten feet above that. He passed over our bow. If he had been a hundred feet further aft he would of hit the sail."

"Would he have sunk us if he did?"

"Hell no," said Murph. "But he might have sunk himself. The plates of our pressure hull are three or four times as thick as his. He would have torn a lot of gingerbread and fairing off of us, but if he got down to the pressure hull it would of ripped him wide open. And it wouldn't of done more than put a dent in us."

"It sounded like he was ripping us wide open when he went over us," said the Engineer.

"Aw, we knew in the sound room he wasn't going to hit us," said Hilton smugly. "It wasn't as bad as it sounded to you guys. He didn't even scrape any paint off of us. Water does funny things to sound," he explained. "It amplifies and distorts it. It takes many hours of listening before you get your ears tuned to sort things out right. But once you get the hang of it you can really tell what's going on around you just by listening."

"How do you do that, kid?" asked Murphy innocently.

"It's hard to explain," said Hilton. "It's like learning to recognize somebody's voice. It's resonance, tone quality, pitch, frequency, and a lot of other stuff that you only learn by practice and lots of it. But a good sound man can tell you whether he's getting an echo back off a layer of cold water, a school of fish, or a metal plate. Fish make lots of funny noises and sometimes sound like machinery. But with enough practice you can tell the difference."

"Yeah," said Murph, who had gotten just the lead he was angling for. "I know what you mean. I saw a good example of that sort of thing when I was in destroyers on my first hitch, before I came into submarines. One day we were cruising along near Hawaii and we sighted a couple of mating whales on the surface about half a mile away."

"Whaddya mean, 'mating whales'?" asked a listener.

"I mean a momma and a poppa whale going at it right there on the surface where we all could see it."

"Boy! That musta been something to see," exclaimed several.

"It was," said the Chief. "The whales go to it as if they enjoy it. And a hundred tons of passionate blubber can stir up a hell of a commotion in the water."

By now all other discussion in the lounge had stopped, and everyone was hanging on Murphy's words.

"Everybody on the bridge," continued Murph, "grabbed a spyglass or a pair of binoculars. People on deck manned all the guns and trained them out so they could watch through the gunsights. Pretty soon word comes up on the squawk box from the sound room, 'Unidentified echo bearing oh four five, range twelve hundred yards.' That's right where the whales were."

"Yeah," said Hilton judiciously. "You'd get a real good echo off anything as big as a couple of whales. But a good sound man shoulda been able to tell you more than that."

"They did," said Murph. "I'm coming to that. Everybody on the bridge was so interested in watching what the whales were doing that nobody bothered to pass the word below to the sound room about it. They just said, 'bridge, aye aye,' and kept on watching.

"Then, so help me," said the Chief, "half a minute later word comes up on the squawk box from the experts in the sound room: 'We hear screw noises!!'"

4

Next morning as the Captain came into the control room the Exec said, "Good morning, Cap'n. I think I've got her very close to neutral buoyancy."

"We'll soon see," said the Captain.

"I've been working on it for four hours," said the Exec, "but we haven't touched the planes for ten minutes now and our depth has been two hundred feet, plus or minus five."

"That's good, Joe. . . . Where's our friend?" asked the Captain.

"Two thousand yards directly astern. Staying with us like a shadow."

"Okay," said the Captain. "We might as well go to work. How deep is the layer this morning?"

"Three hundred, sir," said the Navigator.

"Let's start slowing down and working our way down to three hundred," said the Captain. "I want to stop the engines at two-eighty and try to settle down on the layer with no headway on her. . . . Does the reactor room know what we're going to do?"

"Yessir. I've given them a full briefing. All unnecessary lights and machinery are already shut down. They are all set to shut the reactor down completely."

"All right, start easing her down," said the Skipper. . . . "And pass the word for all hands to stand fast till we finish this job."

For the next half hour the *Nemo* slowed down gradually, and finally stopped her prop at 270 feet and coasted to a stop at 280.

Everybody stared at the depth gauge to see what was going to happen. If it started up, they would have to let a little more water in.

While they were slowing down, the Russian had begun to close in and overrun them. Then he slowed down, too, and finally stopped, lying to about five hundred yards away. The sound room kept control fully informed as to what he was doing.

After they had stopped the engines and been hovering for about five minutes, the Exec walked over to the depth gauge, tapped it with his fist, and peered closely at the hand on the dial. "We're settling, Captain," he said rather smugly. "We have very slight negative buoyancy–just what we want."

"Nice going, maestro," said the Captain. "Shut down the reactor."

Back in the reactor room, the Chief Engineer put out the atomic fire. He could start it up again in a hurry if he had to. He had enough steam in the boiler to keep a small generator running for another hour.

"Tell the sound room to watch the keel thermometer now and let us know when we get down to the layer," said the Captain.

For the next ten minutes the ship settled slowly to a depth of 310 feet, where the sound room reported: "Entering layer. Temperature has changed eight degrees."

Five minutes later the sound room said, "We hear screw noises. Destroyer is going ahead slow."

"I think he's lost us," said the Skipper.

"Hmmm," observed both the Navigator and Exec.

A few minutes later the sound room said, "Range one thousand yards. He seems to be circling to the right."

"He's trying to make up his mind what to do now," observed the Skipper.

The depth gauge was holding steady at 310 feet. The *Nemo* was sitting on the layer, half in it and half out.

Twenty minutes after they shut down the reactor the sound room reported: "Range twenty-five hundred yards–*HE HAS JUST STARTED PINGING.*"

"By God," exclaimed the Captain. "We've got it! It is the reactor."

Every face in the control room now wore a broad grin.

"Range two thousand yards. He's coming back," reported the sound room. "He's still pinging."

"All right now," said the Skipper, "I'm satisfied we've solved this riddle. But we're going to have to convince a lot of sour-bellied skeptics when we get home. We've got to nail this thing down now, and bend the nails over."

"This explains the 'ramming' incident," observed the Exec.

"Sure it does," said the Skipper. "I stopped the engines when we sheared out to get his profile! That was the first time we stopped the reactor since he got on us. He just lost us for a few minutes, and that turn toward us was accidental. We started up again very shortly, so he never did get around to pinging on us."

"Range fourteen hundred yards," said the sound room. "He's slowing down again now. Still pinging."

"Tell the Engineer to start his reactor," said the Captain. In half a minute the reactor was cooking again and a few seconds later the pinging stopped.

After a few minutes the Skipper said, "Shut down the reactor." Within a minute the Russian was pinging again.

"Now . . ." said the Skipper, "I'm going to sink under that

layer and see what that does to him. . . . Let's see, if we sink about ten feet a minute for an hour we'll get down around a thousand. That's as deep as I want to go. So we'll have to start the reactor again after an hour. I want to trim the boat about twenty degrees nose up as we are going down, so when I shoot the power to her we'll be damn sure we're going up."

The Exec and Navigator nodded enthusiastic agreement with this plan and got to work on it.

Twenty minutes later, now slightly heavy, the ship had sunk through the layer, and the Russian's sonar beams were bouncing off the cold water and dissipating in the distance without producing any echoes. Five minutes later the sound room reported, "Screw noises have started again. He seems to be circling."

"At this rate of sinking we can keep going down for an hour," said the Captain. "You'd better juggle your ballast a little to trim her down aft," he added.

"If it's okay with you, Captain, I'd rather use personnel," said the Exec. "I hate to disturb our actual buoyancy."

"Right," said the Skipper. "That's a much better way."

The Exec flipped a switch on the squawk box to the crew's lounge and said, "Send six men aft to the rudder room."

"Range fifteen hundred yards," said the sound room. "He's making one hundred rpm and going north."

The Captain glanced at the depth gauge and said, "We can keep this up for at least another half hour. I'll bet we've got him wondering now what the hell we're doing."

Soon the weight of six men all the way aft was making itself felt and the boat was tilting down by the stern. When the angle reached fifteen degrees the Exec got on the squawk box to the rudder room and said, "Six men to the forward torpedo room on the double."

The six pieces of live ballast scrambled five hundred feet through the boat, uphill, to stop any further nosing up. As the last one, a newcomer in the crew, reached the torpedo room he gasped to one of his pals, "What the hell are they trying to do to us, anyway?"

"We're just trimming the boat without having to pump any water around. Six of us moving the length of the boat gets the same leverage as shifting ten tons twenty feet. We'll have to haul ass back to the lounge room in a minute and then you can go back to sleep again."

"Well I'll be a cast-iron son-of-a-bitch," observed the first lad.

For the next hour the screw noises kept receding, the pinging continued, and the range on the Russian opened out to twenty thousand yards.

As the depth gauge eased down toward 950, the Captain said, "Start the reactor. Tell them to give us full speed ahead as soon as they can."

In the reactor room, flipping a few switches brought the sleeping atoms back to life. In half a minute, the *Nemo*'s great five-bladed propeller began kicking over again, exerting many tons of force and urging the boat forward. On account of the twenty-degree uptilt, a good many of these tons were also lifting. The boat stopped sinking and began coming up.

Almost immediately word came from the sound room: "He has stopped pinging . . . rpm of screws is increasing . . . it's two-fifty now."

"You see," said the Captain. "He picked us up right away, as soon as the reactor fired up. He'll be back on our tail shortly. . . . Level her off at three hundred feet, course north, speed fifteen."

"Aye aye, sir," said the O.O.D.

As the ship picked up speed, the planes became effective again for controlling depth, and they had no trouble leveling off at 305 feet. The normal lights came back on and word was passed unfreezing personnel. The lad on the plane control had to heave around with his big wheel for the next ten minutes as a heavy rush of men to the "head" (gents' can) disturbed the balance of the boat. Then everything settled down again to routine cruising, with the Russian hanging on a mile astern.

Soon after secure from the "Doggo" operation, all hands not on watch crowded into the crew's lounge to explain their versions of how they had outsmarted the Russian. Everyone was full of the fact that they had won the battle of wits and found out how he was tracking them. For the time being, the fact that he was still on their back was small potatoes.

Chief Murphy came in and said, "In case any of you guys don't know it, I want to tell you there was some mighty fancy submarine handling this morning."

"Yeah," agreed another old-timer. "The Skipper must have whale blood in his veins."

"The next thing is to get him off our back. . . . That may not be so easy," said Murphy.

"We could stick a fish into him with one of those atomic warheads on it," observed one naval strategist. "He'd never know what hit him. And neither would anyone else. He would just disappear off the face of the earth."

"Yeah," said the Chief. "That would sure get rid of him. But it's a sort of unneighborly way to do it."

"Chief," said a wardroom mess boy, "I was reading a book the other night about the Battle of the Atlantic that told about a trick the German sub skippers used to pull to get away from us. Maybe we could use it."

"What was that?" asked the Chief.

"It's a stunt they pulled when our people caught them on the surface at night by radar. They would leave a radar decoy on the surface and submerge. Our people would follow the decoy all night, and the sub would be long gone in the morning."

"Yeah! I remember that," said the Chief. "They used to secure an aerology balloon to a block of wood so it would drift along about ten feet above the water. They'd tie a bunch of tin foil to the balloon so it would give you exactly the same kind of radar return as a periscope or a conning tower. Destroyers would charge around at high speed all night, scattering ashcans all over the ocean—which didn't bother the balloon a bit. They couldn't see the balloon at night, and nobody is going to turn a searchlight on when he thinks the other guy is peeping down his throat with a periscope. Then, when the sun came up, they'd find a pie-faced goddam balloon grinning at them. So they would bust the balloon with twenty millimeters and go on about their business. Half the time the destroyer skippers wouldn't even report it, because it made them look foolish."

"Do you think we could do that, Chief?" asked the colored boy.

"I don't see why not," said the Chief. "Of course it wouldn't really spring us loose, because he would get back on us again as soon as we started the reactor. But it might tell us something. . . . And I know damned well our skipper would love to pull something like that on the Russian. . . . I'll suggest it to him."

A little later the Chief tapped on the door of the Captain's cabin. "Hello, Murph," said the Skipper as the Chief came in. "What's on your mind?"

"I've got a suggestion to make, Cap'n. Brown, the mess boy, thought of it . . . The old radar decoy stunt that the Germans used to pull—with an aerology balloon tied to—"

"Hell yes!" interrupted the Captain. "I remember that one well. I know several distinguished flag officers now who fell for it during the war, when they were destroyer skippers—this is the perfect setup for it!"

"I'll break out a balloon from the storeroom and rig up a decoy if you say so, Cap'n."

"By all means!" said the Skipper. "Go right ahead. Leave us not shilly-shally about this thing. We can surface at the beginning of the next dark period and wait till his radar locks on us. He keeps it going all the time, so that shouldn't take long. As soon as we know he's got us on radar, we shut down the reactor, turn the decoy loose, and sink slowly like we were doing this morning. He doesn't use his sonar when he doesn't have to, so I don't think he'll turn it on. He'll just stay with the decoy."

"Yessir," said the Chief. "There's fifteen to twenty knots of wind up there, so the decoy will drift downwind pretty fast—maybe about ten knots."

"Yeah," said the Skipper. "Don't make the float too heavy, or the wind will shove that balloon down onto the water. Make it just heavy enough so the balloon can't lift it. Then it will skip along on the surface pretty lively."

"Yessir, Cap'n," said the Chief tolerantly. "I know how to rig it. You don't have to worry about that."

"Of course not," said the Captain apologetically. "Sometimes I forget I'm not the only seafaring man aboard this craft."

"This is going to be the most fun I've had with my clothes on for a long time, Cap'n," said the Chief.

"That goes for me, too!" said the Skipper. "Ask the Executive Officer to step in here."

As the Exec came in, he observed, "I can see by that gleam in your eye something is cooking, Captain."

"Right you are," said the Captain. "You remember how Admiral Halsey used to have a Dirty Trick Department on his staff? Well, we got one on this ship, too. . . ." And he explained what he wanted to do.

"I don't see how it can miss, Cap'n," said the Exec, his eyes lighting up. "We'll have twenty hours of darkness after we turn that thing loose. It will drift maybe two hundred miles before sunrise. We may get him clear off our back with it."

"I doubt that very much," said the Captain. "I don't think we can keep the reactor shut down long enough."

"How deep are you willing to let her sink, Cap'n?"

"A thousand feet."

"We might string that out three or four hours if we're lucky," said the Exec. "And of course we don't have to use the reactor to come up. We can blow ballast."

"When we get down that deep, I don't want to fool around blowing ballast to come up. I want to have a good angle on the boat like we did this morning and blast her up fast when I decide to come up."

"Aye aye, sir, Cap'n," said the Exec. "We're still in neutral buoyancy. I can bring her up with the planes whenever you say. When we turn loose the decoy and shut down the reactor we'll still have enough headway to pull her down with the planes. After that we play it by ear."

"I want to come up three hours from now. That will be an hour after dark . . . and, oh yes, there's one other little matter. Take her up now to periscope depth and get one quick peek at the wind. Yesterday we were directly upwind of him on this course. That's no good because the balloon would drift right at him. . . . He might come so close he'd see it. I want to be directly crosswind from him when we release it. So after you get the wind direction, change course slowly until we are going directly crosswind. That will give him a chance to settle down astern again before we release the balloon."

"Aye aye, sir. Will do."

"And just one more thing," said the Captain. "This was Brown's idea and I want to cut him in on it. Tell him he'll be Murphy's helper when we release the balloon up on the sail. Tell him he's going to need warm clothes and gloves up there."

An hour after sunset, the Captain, Chief Murphy, and Brown assembled in the upper conning tower station just below the hatch that opens up onto the top of the big vertical fin sail. Murphy had a deflated balloon with a bunch of tin foil tied to it. About twenty feet of stout cord attached the balloon to a balsa-wood float. Brown was lugging a helium tank about the size of a scuba diver's oxygen bottle. Murphy and Brown had inflated the balloon once to find out how much helium it took to not quite lift the balsa-wood float. All were warmly dressed, wore life jackets, and safety belts which could latch into ring bolts around the sail in rough weather.

The Captain leaned over the voice tube to the control room below and called down to the Exec, "Okay. Bring her up."

In a few minutes the Exec called up, "Breaking surface now, Cap'n . . . nothing in sight through the scope . . . sound room says target bears dead astern, two thousand yards . . . he *is* using his radar . . . wind abeam."

Two husky sailors heaved on the hand wheel, unlocking the hatch, and threw it open. The Captain—by longstanding submarine custom—went up first, followed immediately by the others.

It was a black, cold night, with a spanking breeze and a choppy sea. The *Nemo* had been riding as steady as a church in the calm water a few hundred feet down, but she now began to heave, pitch, and throw up clouds of spray from the bow. Murphy and Brown got busy inflating the balloon, while the Captain checked the wind. It was thirty degrees on the port bow. Since the ship was making fifteen knots, this meant the actual wind was almost directly abeam—right where he wanted it. It was too dark to see the destroyer a mile astern.

"Almost ready, Cap'n," said Murphy as the helium hissed in and the balloon swelled to its five-foot diameter.

"No hurry. Take all the time you need," said the Captain.

In a minute Murphy said to Brown, "That's enough. Disconnect. Now get that sheet in place," he added, crouching over the balloon and holding it below the shielding around the top of the sail so the wind couldn't get at it.

Brown handed Murphy two corners of the sheet and drew the rest of it over the balloon, holding two corners himself so they held the balloon down under the sheet.

"Any time you're ready, Cap'n," said Murphy.

The Captain picked up the carefully coiled line in one hand and the float in the other.

"Stand by," he said.

Murphy and Brown rose to their feet, holding the balloon down with the sheet. Murphy was on the upwind side. The Captain tossed the float over the lee side of the sail to starboard, and let the cord run out of his hand.

As the coil neared the last loop, Murphy yelled to Brown, "Let go!"

Brown let go his two corners of the sheet. Murphy held

onto his. The balloon flipped out and took off free and clear. It jerked the float up out of the water as it came to the end of the slack, but then dropped it into the water again. The balloon, riding ten feet above the waves, sailed off downwind towing the float very nicely at about ten knots.

"Well done," said the Skipper. "A real seaman-like job. Get below, you two."

The Skipper took a last look around, popped down the hatch himself, and pulled it down behind him. The two waiting seamen grabbed the wheel and locked the hatch.

"Take her down," barked the Skipper down the tube.

As soon as he hit the floor plates of the control room, the Captain said, "Stop engines. . . . Secure the reactor. . . . Try to hold her at sixty feet."

"Did you get a good launch with the decoy, Cap'n?" asked the Exec.

"Perfect," said the Captain. "It's probably making seven or eight knots downwind with the balloon riding nicely about six feet over the waves."

"Don't you think he may smell a rat when we seem to be making eight knots with the reactor shut down?" asked the Exec.

"Could be. We'll find out very soon. He's still getting a good blip on his radar, so he has no reason to think we've submerged. He doesn't know what kind of auxiliary power we've got for running on the surface. It would be perfectly logical for him to assume we've got a small diesel that kicks us along at eight knots."

"I guess it would be," said the Exec. "As long as he doesn't start pinging, we may get away with this."

"Let's watch this from the sound room," said the Captain to the Exec. Turning to the O.O.D., he said, "We've just about lost our headway now. She should start sinking very slowly if we've been lucky on the buoyancy. If she should want to come up, take in a little more ballast. I want to sink as slowly as possible."

"Aye aye, sir," said the O.O.D.

In the sound room the *Nemo*'s own sonar was shut down, of course, so the only information they were getting was from passive listening. As the Captain put on the head set they handed him when he came in, the THUM swish, THUM swish of the destroyer's screws was coming in loud and clear.

"One hundred rpm," said the sound man on watch. "Two hundred held him steady at two thousand yards astern when we were making fifteen knots."

"That checks very close," observed the Skipper. "That balloon is making about eight knots and it takes half as many rpm's to keep station on it as it did to do it on us at fifteen knots."

"Do you want me to get a ping on him now and then?" asked the sound man.

"No indeed," said the Skipper. "We've got his rpm curve calibrated close enough now to plot him as accurately as we need to, just as long as we can hear him."

After ten minutes, during which the bearings taken in the sound room showed the Russian to be definitely moving south and there was no sign of a ping out of him, the Skipper said, "I think we've got it made. He's going to stay with that radar blip from the decoy as long as we keep our reactor shut down. If we can delay starting it long enough, he may be clear out of range when we do."

"What do you figure that range is, Cap'n?" asked the Exec.

"I don't know. But I believe he picked us up originally at about twenty miles, so let's say that maybe thirty miles is his outer limit."

"Sounds reasonable," said the Exec.

"It will take our decoy four hours to drift thirty miles. We are at a hundred-foot depth now, and I won't go any deeper than a thousand. So that means we've got four hours to sink nine hundred feet. That's two hundred and twenty-five feet an hour. We've got to be lucky to keep it that slow."

"I think we will do it," said the Exec. "I had her so close to neutral buoyancy that one barnacle falling off would make a difference," he added smugly.

Suddenly there was a long, low whistle out of the loudspeaker and a chirruping noise, followed by a series of sharp beeps.

"Porpoises," said the sonar man. "A couple of them just found us and they're talking it over."

"They're very gabby and curious animals," observed the Chief. "Just watch. In a minute they'll call a whole school over."

Confirming what the Chief said, there was a lot of shrill whistling, followed by the excited chatter of new arrivals.

"They're supposed to have a language of their own," observed the Captain. "Scientists back home are making tape recordings and trying to learn it."

"Too bad they ain't here now with their recorders," said the Chief as the chattering and chirruping increased.

Soon the racket sounded like feeding time in the bird house at the zoo. It didn't take a language expert to know that the ideas being expressed were curiosity, surprise, pleasure, and amazement—like a bunch of kids at a circus parade.

"They don't seem to be a bit afraid of us," observed the Skipper.

"They're not," said the Chief. "They play around us for hours sometimes, making so damn much racket you can hardly read the sonar through it."

"Listen to that!" said the Exec as a twittering chirrup came in. "A little one saying 'Hey, Ma! What's that?'"

Soon there came an awed squealing twitter with a rising inflection and a loud "gloop" at the end of it.

"Did you get that?" chuckled the Chief. "One of 'em just said 'Boy oh boy! Look at that big son-of-a-*BITCH.*'"

"That's exactly what he said," agreed the Skipper. "You ought to send a tape recording and translation to those scientists."

"No need to translate that last one, Cap'n," said the Exec. "Anybody who speaks English could tell that's what he said."

"Let's go back to control," said the Captain.

An hour after submerging, the depth was three hundred feet. The Russian's bearing was almost downwind and he still was not pinging.

"I think we're going to be able to hold off on the reactor about four hours, Cap'n," said the Exec. "We pulled her down with the planes a hundred feet before we leveled off, so we've only sunk two hundred since we lost our headway."

"Yeah," said the Captain. "But don't forget as we go deeper, the hull gets squeezed and we don't displace as much water. Our negative buoyancy will increase. But it looks pretty good so far. . . . Let's get an up angle on the boat now with your live ballast system, like we did yesterday."

At the end of the second hour they were only down to five hundred feet. The Exec passed the word to the crew's lounge, "Eight men aft to trim ship," and said to the Captain, "We're at five hundred now and at the rate we're going it will be another two and a half hours before we get to a thousand feet. I think he'll be out of range by then."

"We shall see," observed the Captain.

"Bearing is now due south," reported the sound room. "Holding steady. Screw noise gradually decreasing; rpm is still one hundred."

A minute later the sound room said, "We just heard a burst of gunfire. . . . It sounded like about ten rounds of twenty-millimeter, bearing due south."

"There goes the old ball game!" said the Skipper. "He probably turned on a searchlight and he's busting the balloon now. He's probably so damn mad he's almost busting a gut, too. He'll start pinging in a minute."

"Yeah," said the Exec. "Two hours since submerging. He's only seventeen or eighteen miles away. I'm afraid he'll spot us."

"Probably will," agreed the Skipper.

A moment later the sound room said, "Destroyer has started pinging."

"We'll know in another minute," said the Skipper.

The next report from the sound room was: "Destroyer is increasing speed—rpm three hundred."

"Get me one ping on him," said the Skipper.

Soon word came back, "Range three two oh double oh—bearing due south—three hundred rpm. Pinging constantly."

"Sixteen miles," said the Skipper. "Get me another ping in five minutes."

For the next five minutes, using only passive listening, all that the sound room could tell was that the bearing was constant, the rpm noise was about the same, and the sonar kept pinging. After the second ping the sound room reported: "Range two seven oh double oh—bearing south—three hundred rpm."

"Looks like he's got us again, Cap'n," said the Exec. "He's headed this way at thirty knots. I guess we might as well start the reactor again."

"No. Not yet," said the Captain. "We're under the layer now, and I don't think he's getting any echo off us. Naturally he is heading back for the spot where we submerged. He should be about over us in twenty more minutes. Let's sit tight and see what happens."

For the next twenty minutes the sound room reported "bearing south—screw noise getting closer." Finally the screw noise could be heard through the hull again, as it had been two days before during the "ramming" incident. This time it didn't get nearly as loud, because the Russian passed at least six hundred feet overhead, and kept going at thirty knots for another ten minutes.

As he passed overhead, the Skipper said, "That shows he is not getting through the layer and doesn't have us on sonar."

The outside pressure squeezing the hull was making the boat sink a little more rapidly now.

Ten minutes after the can passed overhead, the sound room reported, "Bearing is changing to the right–destroyer seems to be circling."

"I think we've milked this act just about as much as we can, now," said the Skipper. "If he's as smart as he ought to be, he must know we can't be far from where we turned that decoy loose. He's starting to circle that spot now. I'm going to let him go on another five minutes and then I'll start the reactor. I think he'll stop pinging almost immediately as soon as I do."

Five minutes later the Skipper said, "Start the reactor. . . . Bring her up to two hundred feet. . . . Course north, speed fifteen."

Within seconds the pinging stopped, and fifteen minutes later the Russian had taken up his familiar station dead astern at two thousand yards.

"Well, Joe," said the Captain, "I'm satisfied that he's tracking us by means of our reactor. How about you?"

"No room whatever for any doubt about it," replied the Exec.

5

In the Captain's cabin that night the Skipper, Exec, and Doctor were reviewing events of the past few days.

"How is the crew taking this, Doctor?" asked the Captain.

"Pretty well, Cap'n," replied the Doctor. "I've been watching everybody closely for signs of the jumping jitters and I haven't seen any. All hands are still doing their jobs well. I see nothing to worry about yet."

"I don't either," said the Captain. "I suppose I've got more reason than anyone to worry and I'm getting adjusted to it. But I do have a funny feeling, like the one in a nightmare when you are walking down the street stark naked with everybody looking at you. I can feel that guy up there staring at me, even when I get in my bunk and turn out the light."

"Like a guy peeking over your shoulder in a poker game?" observed the Doctor.

"Yeah," said the Captain. ". . . If you're aiming a gun at one of your neighbors, you don't like to have any of his brats looking over your shoulder while you're doing it."

"I hadn't thought of it that way," said the Doctor. "But that does sum it up pretty well. . . . What do you think we would do, Cap'n, if this situation were reversed? Suppose the Russians had a fleet of Polaris subs and kept them stationed fifty miles off our East Coast? How would we react to it?"

"We would raise hell about it, of course," replied the Captain. "I think our government would be forced to protest to the Russians. They would reply and say, 'Well, you're doing the same thing to us.' And the upshot would probably be an agreement—for whatever it was worth—to keep our subs a thousand miles or so from each other's shores. We might even agree that any sub found inside those limits would be sunk."

"We've had our subs up here for a couple of years now. Why do you think the Russians haven't protested?"

"For several reasons, the main one being that they are a lot more realistic about such things than we are. Until they get a fleet of Polaris boats themselves, they are in no position to negotiate. Besides, until this guy got on our back they couldn't prove anything or do anything about it, even if they knew about it. Now that they are able to find us and track us, they may protest. They may even threaten to sink any Polaris boats they find in the Arctic or Norwegian seas. But I don't think they would dare to carry out the threat, because this could start World War III and they know we will blast them off the map if that happens. They can knock us back a couple of hundred years too, but it will be the end of them. So I think if we have guts enough to stand up to them on this and insist that what we are doing is allowed by international law, we will get away with it—until they get Polaris boats too. Then we will have to change international law. This situation is a lot like when they put the first Sputnik up. It came over the U.S. a couple of times a day, which was a flagrant violation of our air space under international law, just like our U-2 was of theirs. But we were caught flatfooted and it was a couple of months before we could put anything in orbit. There was nothing we could do about it without looking silly. So we just swept it under the rug. Now it's an accepted fact of international law that you can fly satellites over anybody's backyard, although we still draw the line at U-2's. . . . After all, Rule Number One of international law is still very strictly enforced."

"What's that, Cap'n?" asked the Doctor.

"Might is right. Despite two thousand years of Christianity, the UN, and what have you, that's still the way this world is run. . . ."

"We made them take their missiles out of Cuba," said the Exec, "and we had our Polaris boats on regular patrols up here when we did it."

"Yes—but we had pictures of their missiles in Cuba. They couldn't prove we were up here."

"What would you do," asked the Doctor, "if you were in command of that tin can up there, Cap'n?"

"I think if I were a Russian and didn't believe in God or a hereafter, I would sink this ship. There's a good chance that our people back home would never find out what happened to us. We would simply disappear, leaving nothing but an oil slick. So far as anyone would ever know, it could be just another *Thresher* or *Scorpion* disaster. This is why that guy up there worries me. If I were in his shoes, believing what he is supposed to believe, I think I would shoot the works. . . . Now, the next item on the agenda is to get him off our back. Joe, when you go forward, tell the Navigator to bring me the chart showing the bottom in this area. I want to have a look at it."

"Aye aye, sir," said the Exec. ". . . If you're thinking of lying on the bottom, it's way too deep for that, Cap'n."

"I'm not thinking of that at all," said the Captain. "But by this time tomorrow we're going to be rid of that guy."

"What are you going to do? Let him have it, Cap'n?" asked the Doctor.

"Definitely not," replied the Captain. "But I'm going to make him disappear off our sonar scopes and we're going to disappear off whatever he is watching us on."

"How are you going to do that, Cap'n?" asked the Doctor.

"Just stick around, Doctor. You'll see," replied the Captain smugly. "You may have some interesting psychological reactions to observe among the crew tomorrow."

Early next afternoon the Captain took station on his platform in the control room and surveyed the dials on the bulkhead in front of him. The ship was running a hundred fathoms deep, making high speed, and heading due north. The control room is always quiet, but today the silence was tense and brittle. Every few minutes the silence was broken by the speaker from the sonar room intoning the bearing and distance of the shadowing destroyer, which was hanging on a mile astern. It's hard to make a report of bearing and distance sound obscene, but the sonar operator almost did.

"Tell sonar to keep a sharp lookout for surface echoes ahead," said the Captain.

"Aye aye, sir," replied the O.O.D., and passed the word to sonar.

For the next half hour the silence was broken only by the routine reports from sonar. Then the sullen voice in sonar changed pitch and said, "Sonar contact dead ahead. Fourteen miles—can't make out what it is yet."

"Very well," said the Captain.

Five minutes later the report came through: "Range on new contact twenty-seven thousand yards, bearing dead ahead. Contact is spread over an arc of five degrees and looks like land."

"All hands to battle stations," said the Captain.

Throughout the ship, as fast as they were relieved by the regular battle watch, the members of the cruising duty section scurried off to their battle stations. As the Exec took his place alongside the Skipper and buckled on his battle phone, he said, "What's up, Cap'n?"

"You'll see pretty soon," said the Captain.

All through the boat hatches were dogged shut, special circuits were energized, and ready lights began popping on in the control room. After a minute the Exec said to the Captain, "All stations manned and ready, sir."

"Very well," said the Captain. "I want to steer a weaving course now, twenty degrees each side of north."

"Aye aye, sir," said the Exec, passing the necessary orders to the helmsman.

As all hands were well aware, a weaving course disconcerts the mechanical brain of the attack director in a surface ship which is tracking an unseen contact by sonar, and presents it with a constantly changing "solution."

"Torpedoes are ready to fire, Cap'n," said the Exec. "Except the tube doors are still closed."

"Keep 'em closed," said the Skipper.

"Contact bears oh double oh, twenty-six thousand yards," came the report from sonar. "The blip is now seven degrees wide. We think it's land."

"If it is, we've made ourselves a great discovery," observed the Navigator, who was bent over his chart board. "Jan Mayen is the nearest land, bearing two two five—two hundred miles."

The Exec walked over to the sonar repeater scope, watched it intently for a few moments, and then said:

"Hah! Well, I'll be damned. The ice floe!"

"Excellent, Dr. Watson, excellent," said the Skipper.

The Exec's face lit up and he said, "I see now how you're going to get rid of him. Nice going, Cap'n."

All hands at their battle stations were watching the Exec and Captain out of the corner of their eyes and had the volume control on their ears turned full up. They began exchanging significant glances, a few muttered words were passed, and pretty soon the tense expression which had been on every face for the past two days was replaced by a broad grin—that is, on every face except the Captain's. His remained stony as he watched the radar scope.

Before long, word came from the sound room: "Range on destroyer is opening slowly—bearing one eight oh, distance twenty-five hundred yards." Then a few moments later word came in: "We are getting a lot of small surface echoes all around us."

"Brash ice," said the Captain. "That's why he slowed down."

"Yes, sir!" agreed the Exec. ". . . If he's going to do anything, he's got to do it now."

The Captain nodded gravely.

The range on the destroyer began opening faster and half an hour later the *Nemo* slipped under the Arctic icecap. She now had a solid roof of thick ice over her head, hundreds of fathoms of water under her keel, and her tormentor was off her back.

"Okay!" said the Captain. "That's that. I want to hold course north for another couple of hours. Then we'll run northeast under the ice until I'm ready to come out again. . . . Secure from battle stations."

There were jubilant whoops all through the boat as the word to secure was passed. Excited groups got together, making glowing appraisals of the Skipper's feat in breaking loose, and obscene and impractical suggestions as to what the Russian skipper could do to himself.

6

Soon after, the Exec, Doctor, and the Captain got together in the cabin.

"I feel a little shaky," confessed the Captain.

"I can prescribe a shot of medical booze for you if you want it, Cap'n," said the Doctor.

"No thanks. I'll wait till we get ashore," said the Captain. "But I don't mind telling you, that last half hour was a rough one. I don't want to go through that again!"

"Yes, I can see what you mean," said the Doctor. "If he was going to do anything he had to do it then."

"Just put yourself in his shoes," said the Captain. "He has done something that's never been done before. For the past sixty hours he has hung onto us despite everything we did trying to get rid of him. He's a big hero. Then all of a sudden he sees us slipping away from him. He can put a torpedo into us and no one but the Russians will ever know what happened to us. He must have been seriously tempted. If I had been in his shoes, I might have done it. In fact, I wonder why he didn't."

"So do I," said the Exec. "In fact, I figured during that last half hour that the odds on us ever getting home again were about six to five and take your choice. It's a hell of a spot to be in."

"Now," said the Captain, "the next item on the agenda is to get off a dispatch to CNO and give him the word. This is going to shake the Pentagon as bad as Pearl Harbor did."

"Why do you say that, Captain?" asked the Doctor.

"Just look what it does to the instant and devastating retaliation idea. Up to now, Polaris has been our persuader. It was much more of a threat to Russia than those Russian missiles in Cuba were to us, because we could blow those missile sites off the map very easily. Up to now, Polaris has been invulnerable. It would survive even a sneak attack that flattened SAC and Minute Man. But any time in the past sixty hours, that Russian could have wiped us out without a trace. This knocks our whole Polaris program into the ashcan until we find out how to cork up that reactor."

"What do you think they'll do?" asked the Exec.

"I think that within forty-eight hours they'll recall all Polaris boats from the northern patrol, or else the boats will start disappearing. The AEC* will have to start a crash project to find out what's getting through our reactor shielding. They'll really hit the panic button on this one. They may even decide to keep half of SAC airborne until they solve it.

"Now," he said, reaching for a dispatch blank, "let's draw up a message with the bad news."

After a few moments he handed the following draft to the Exec:

From: USS *Nemo*

To: CNO

URGENT PRIORITY—TOP SECRET. Destroyer, Russian, has trailed *Nemo* for past sixty hours one to two miles astern.

* Atomic Energy Commission

Unable to shake it off running under layer as deep as 1,000 feet, maneuvering radically at various speeds. Lose him temporarily whenever reactor is shut down. He finds us again as soon as reactor starts at ranges as great as 20 miles. Have eluded him now by going under icecap. Have much vital data for Anti-Sub and atomic experts. Recommend return to base.

"How does that read?" he asked.

The Exec scanned the message carefully and said, "Don't you think we should say something about sonar in it? Otherwise all the experts will say we've gone off half-cocked."

"Yes, of course. Right after 'twenty miles' insert, 'does not, repeat, does not, use sonar.'"

"He has used it a couple of times, Cap'n."

"Yes. But we can't go into long-winded explanations in this dispatch. It's too long already. Get it typed up. I'll release it and you can have it ciphered and waiting in the radio room ready to go as soon as we can get an antenna up."

"How are we going to get one up, Cap'n?" asked the Doctor.

"This icecap isn't solid," said the Captain. "When we came over the Pole in the *Nautilus*, we found quite a few little lakes in it. They call them polynyas, places where the floes have cracked open. We'll have the O.O.D. watch the ice scope and let me know as soon as we get near one. We'll surface in it and get the dispatch off."

"There's one more thing ought to go into that message, Cap'n—our position," said the Executive Officer.

"Okay. Stick that in too—right at the end."

"Of course," observed the Exec, "the Russian will have his direction finders on us as soon as we touch our transmitter key."

"We can't help that. This dispatch is a must. And it won't do him much good to get a bearing on us now, unless he wants to come after us with dog sleds."

"Stranger things than that have happened," said the Doctor.

"What's crazier than that?" demanded the Captain.

"A British sailing frigate was captured by cavalry once."

"Even if that was so, I wouldn't believe it," declared the Captain.

"It's in one of Mahan's books. The frigate got frozen in the ice in the Zuider Zee and had to surrender to a troop of Dutch cavalry."

A few hours later, the phone on the Captain's desk rang, and the O.O.D. reported, "We've got a pretty good-sized polynya coming up ahead, Captain."

"Very well," said the Captain. "Slow down to five knots. I'll be right up."

In the control room the Captain took station behind the ice scope. This is simply a fathometer that looks up instead of down, and bounces echoes down off the ice instead of up off the bottom. The scope showed solid ice overhead, but a clear space half a mile ahead.

"Looks like it's about a thousand feet long and a hundred feet wide," said the Captain. "Plenty of room to surface in. I want to come up to sixty feet, slow down, and stop right under it, and then rise vertically. Do you think you can do it?" he asked the O.O.D.

"Yessir," said the Lieutenant.

The young O.O.D. was as good as his word. Ten minutes later, the *Nemo* heaved itself to the surface in the middle of the polynya, white water pouring off its sides. As the Captain and Exec climbed out of the hatch onto the top of the sail, the Captain said, "Keep a sharp eye open for troops of Dutch cavalry."

It was broad daylight and the sun was about five degrees above the horizon to the south—almost "high noon." The edges of the polynya were only thirty feet on each side of the ship. The level white ice floe extended as far as the eye could see in all directions, with ridges of piled-up, broken ice here and there.

"These things open and close unpredictably," observed the

Captain. "We've got to be careful we don't get pinched in the ice if it happens. Currents, or a puff of wind, can jam the floes together again pretty quick."

"Aye aye, sir," said the Exec. "Don't look now, Cap'n. But we have got company up here."

The Captain trained his glasses out where the Exec was looking and said, "Well, I'll be damned. A polar bear!"

The big white animal was ambling across the ice toward the edge of the polynya. When he got there he sat down, cocked his head to one side, and began a quizzical inspection of the *Nemo* only fifty feet away from the Skipper and Exec.

"By golly, he acts as if he owned this ice floe," said the Exec.

"Do you think we ought to stand at attention?" asked the Skipper.

"It might make a better impression on him if we did," replied the Exec. "He doesn't seem to be overawed by what he has seen so far."

"He's probably trying to figure out how the hell he can make mama bear believe this when he gets home."

In a few moments the bear flopped down on its belly, put its head down on its forepaws, and gazed steadily at the sail.

"I guess he figures it's our move," said the Captain. "Let's let out a blast on our foghorn and see what he thinks of it."

The Exec reached over, pulled a lever, and a loud OOW-OOOH-GAH split the Arctic air.

The bear jumped to its feet and stood erect on its hind legs with its forepaws in the position of a boxer on guard for a few seconds. Then he dropped his guard, sat down, reached up with his hind paw, and scratched his ear in an embarrassed manner. Then he flopped back on his belly, let out a grunt, and resumed his nonchalant inspection.

"Pretty cool customer, isn't he?" observed the Exec.

"You would be, too, if you had your bare belly where he has his," said the Skipper. "Let's see if the galley can produce a piece of fish we can throw him."

A few minutes later, Chief Murphy climbed up into the sail,

lugging a frozen codfish about two feet long. "We got a visitor," said the Captain, pointing to the bear. "I want to see if we can make friends with him."

Murphy clambered out on the fin extending out from the side of the sail, walked carefully out to the end of it, and tossed the fish onto the ice. It landed about five feet from the edge and thirty feet from the bear.

The bear lay on the ice frowning at the sail until Murphy had clambered back into it. Then he got up, lumbered casually over to the fish and sniffed at its tail curiously, and cocked his head up at the sail as if to say, "What the hell?" Then he shuffled around, sniffed disdainfully at the head a couple of times, and looked up at the sail again.

"He seems to me to be making a rude suggestion as to what we can do with our fish," observed the Skipper.

Confirming this opinion, the bear reached out his forepaw, scraped the fish gingerly over to the edge of the ice, and plopped it into the water. Then he flopped back on his belly and stared up at the sail again.

"I've been sawed off by experts in my time," said the Exec, "but that beats them all."

"Boy oh boy!" said Murphy. "Just wait till I tell the commissary steward about this! Not even a hungry polar bear will eat the stuff he tries to feed us."

"Dispatch to CNO has been receipted for by Navy Radio Holy Loch," came a report up the voice tube from O.O.D.

"So that's that," observed the Skipper. "The Pentagon will have it soon, and the JCS will hold a special meeting about it this morning. . . . Before we submerge, Joe, let's give the boys a chance to get a lung full of Arctic air and see what an ice floe looks like. Bring 'em up four or five at a time."

"Aye aye, sir," said the Exec.

For the next half hour the crew came up into the sail in groups of four, looked around for a few minutes, and went below again. A brief glimpse of the outside world was a rare treat for them on one of these patrols.

Halfway through the rubberneck period the polar bear got up, yawned, took a good long stretch, and sauntered off to the north, his stern end waggling from side to side.

That afternoon in the radio room, two operators sat before an array of receivers, headphones clamped over their ears, reading paperback books. One was guarding the hot circuit to the White House. To keep the circuit from getting cold, routine traffic of interest was fed into it by CNO whenever a green light from the White House showed the circuit to be clear.

The other operator was guarding a search receiver that swept back and forth over the range of frequencies known to be used by the Russian Navy. Suddenly he dropped his book, flipped a switch that started a tape recorder, and tuned a receiver to the frequency which had just come alive.

"What's cookin'?" asked the other operator.

The lad held a finger up and listened for a moment. "Nearby station—sending five-letter code groups," he said.

Soon the Communications Officer was peering over his shoulder with a set of phones on his head, too. "It's that Russian tin can," he said. "Are you copying it?"

The operator pointed to the tape recorder.

"We're getting every word of it—including the call up and answer from the receiving station."

Ten minutes later the Communications Officer was reporting to the Captain. "It was a strong transmission, quite loud. The station wasn't more than forty or fifty miles away."

"It has to be the Russian destroyer," said the Skipper. "The nearest land is Spitzbergen, two hundred miles away."

"We've got the whole transmission taped, Captain. He sent three hundred and twenty groups in a five-letter code."

"Good work," said the Captain. "This will give our cryptoanalysts back home something they can really get their teeth into. We know what this message is all about. He is reporting what he has done in the last three days. With a clue like that and a three-hundred-and-twenty-group message, our black-chamber boys may be able to break this code."

"Yessir," said the Lieutenant. "They've done it with much slimmer leads than we've got on this one."

"Be alert for an answer to this," said the Skipper. "This will get top-level action in the Kremlin. I think they will send instructions back within about twenty-four hours. . . . Did you get your direction finders on him when he sent this?"

"Yessir. He bears almost due south—one seven eight degrees."

"Hmmmmm," said the Captain. "He seems to be able to tag right along with us."

7

That evening the bull session in the crew's lounge was a critique of the past few days' operations. Joint Chiefs of Staff procedure was not strictly observed at the meeting, especially in matters of terminology and modifying adjectives. A capability was frequently attributed to inanimate objects which is possessed only by humans of opposite sex. But events of the preceding days were thoroughly hashed over and analyzed. The agreed verdict of all hands on the major matter was: "We sure gave that Russian sonofabitch a good screwing."

Professionals from the Naval War College might challenge this finding as not giving due weight to the fact that, after all, the Russian had stayed on their back for three days. But all sailors, even the smart ones on a Polaris boat, don't worry about bridges they have crossed. They had given the Russian the slip, they had won the battle of wits, and all was well in the world again.

After that matter had been settled, one of the lads at the table said, "I don't mind telling you guys I pretty near peed in my pants a couple of times. I was scared stiff that Russian was going to let us have it before we got under the ice."

Quick grins and nodded heads around the table showed that he had voiced the feeling of all hands.

"What does it feel like when you're really under attack, Chief?" asked one of the lads.

Chief Murphy was the only one aboard who had war experience in subs. As an authority on combat tactics, he therefore outranked John Paul Jones or Admiral Mahan with the crew of the *Nemo*.

"A good depth charge attack makes you wish you had never left the farm," replied the Chief. "It's rough while it lasts. I went through a couple of dozen of them and I never did get to like it."

"Did they ever come real close to you?" asked the lad.

"I'll say they did," replied the Chief with a gleam coming into his eye, the way it always does when Ancient Mariners feel a tale about to unfold. "I'll never forget the first time the Japs caught us in the *Squark*. She was one of the old 'S' boats. You could almost hoist her aboard this one. I never expected to see home and Mother again, that time. It was early in the war, right after we got run out of Manila, and we were based on Freemantle. One day off the north coast of New Guinea, we picked up the masts of a convoy just over the horizon, coming our way, and we ran in on them at periscope depth. There were eight big fat troop ships loaded to the gunwales with Jap soldiers and only three destroyer escorts. We snuck in so close that the Skipper figured we couldn't miss. So instead of firing a spread of four at the middle ship, he fired two at the middle one and two at the ship ahead of her. This was our first attack, and we were all as nervous as old ladies crossing a slippery street. All four shots were perfect—fish running hot, straight, and normal. The Skipper could see the wakes all the way to the target. I was holding the stopwatch for him and the running time for the fish was supposed to be sixty-five seconds. I sang out when the second hand got there and we all held our breath waiting for the four loud booms. But they never came."

"You missed?" asked a listener.

"Missed, hell!" said the Chief indignantly. "I just got through telling you they were four perfect shots. The wake bubbles came up under the stern of the targets, showing the fish either hit 'em amidships or ran under them. The goddam exploders didn't work. We got four duds. Then the three cans jumped us and beat the living hell out of us. They musta dropped a couple of hundred depth charges all around us. Our skipper tried every trick in the book. He twisted and squirmed. He ran silent–ran deep. We squirted out oil and shot a lot of junk and papers out of a torpedo tube to make 'em think they sunk us. We turned loose decoys and noisemakers. We even tried to hide under the convoy. If there had only been two Jap cans, I think we would of shaken them off. But three was too many. Every time we thought we had got away another one of them would stumble across us and the ashcans would start exploding again. This went on for twenty-six hours."

"How deep did you go?"

"Six hundred feet. That was as deep as you *could* go in the old boats. Matter of fact, five hundred was supposed to be our pressure depth."

"Did you stay deep all the time?"

"No. We kept changing depth to confuse the depth setting of their ashcans. Once, we came up to periscope depth and there was a can sitting there dead in the water about a thousand yards from us, picking up some of the junk we had turned loose. He shoulda been a dead duck. But by that time we had been beat up so bad we could only get the door open on one of the bow tubes. But hell . . . at a thousand yards you can't miss–so we fired one at him. I was holding the watch for the Captain again. Fifty seconds was the running time. Right after we fired, the sound room said the torpedo was veering off to the left. Pretty soon the bubbles from the wake began breaking surface and the Skipper could see we were going to miss to the left and he started cussing a blue streak. Then the sound room reported, 'Torpedo noise getting louder.' All of a sudden, the Captain yelled, 'Circular shot! Take her down. TAKE HER DOWN!' "

"What's a circular shot?" asked a yeoman.

"One that turns around and comes back at you," explained a torpedoman. "The beating that jammed the tube doors must of tumbled a gyro. Torpedo gyros are temperamental, and sometimes you get a circular shot even when they haven't been shook up—even with the ones we got today."

"Anyway," said the Chief, resuming the narrative, "we pulled the plug and the Skipper put the rudder hard over and went ahead full speed. But we were almost dead in the water, and that fish came back and hit us smack alongside the control room on the port side."

"Gawd almighty!" said a listener. "Your own fish!"

"Yeah," said the Chief. "Lucky for us it was another dud, or I wouldn't be here telling you about it. It made a boom you could hear all through the boat when it plunked us, like a wallop on a big bass drum. And it put a dent in the port ballast tank as big around as your ass. And of course that got all three cans on our back again and brought down more barrages of depth charges."

"What does it feel like when an ashcan goes off near you, Chief?" asked a listener.

"Depends on how close it is, of course. You can hear them as far as ten miles away. Sometimes more . . . just a sort of a dull WHOOMP in the water. When they're about a mile away, you begin to get the shock wave. At that range it just makes a little tap on the hull. At a quarter of a mile it sounds like somebody hit the hull with a small sledge hammer. Shock waves travel faster than sound waves, so you get the shock wave before you hear the explosion. The closer they are to you, the shorter the time between the shock and the sound waves. You don't feel the shock wave until the ashcans are a couple of hundred yards from you. Then it shakes the boat as if you were backing down full speed. When the shock and sound waves come almost together, it gets pretty rugged. It sounds like the old man with the scythe hammering on the hull. They've got to be within thirty feet of you to crack your pressure hull, and I can't tell you what that feels like. Nobody else can, either. But if they're just outside that distance, it feels like the whole boat has been dropped about ten feet on solid rock. If you're leaning against a bulkhead when it happens, you can get knocked cold. Otherwise you just get knocked flat on your can. A lot of light bulbs and gauge glasses get smashed. The whole boat vibrates like a drum for a few seconds, and big flakes of paint fly off the bulkheads. It damn near jars the filling out of your teeth. It's a hell of a way to make a living. But you'd be surprised what a beating a good boat can take and still come up again. We had twenty-six hours of it that time."

"How come you had five duds?" asked one of the missile technicians. "Somebody goof on the exploder adjustment?"

A look of disgust came across the Chief's face, as if he had just found a cockroach in his mashed potatoes. "Nah," he snorted. "It was defective exploders. We had a hell of a time with duds at the beginning of the war. The ordnance experts loused us up on that one. They came out with a brand-new, top-secret, magnetic exploder that was supposed to be the answer to a maiden's prayer. But the goddam thing didn't work. You get anybody who was in the boats then started on that subject and they'll see red and talk your ear off," said the Chief.

"Well, how did you get away from the Jap destroyers?" asked the first questioner.

"After the cans got on us again they shook us up about a dozen times with charges that were just barely outside lethal range. We didn't have to send up any more junk—they were blasting hunks of it off of us. There's a hundred fathoms of water at that spot off the New Guinea coast, and we weren't supposed to go deeper than five hundred feet. But we finally just settled down on the bottom and played dead for twelve hours. It didn't take much acting on our part to do it, because we damn near were dead. Our battery was just about flat, the air in the boat was so thick you could almost see it, and we were all punch-drunk. We were only supposed to have air for twenty-four hours submerged, but we stuck it out for thirty-six that time. It was midnight when we finally surfaced, and the Japs had gone away. And so . . . kiddies . . . we all lived happily ever after," concluded the Chief.

"Well, anyway, now we know what to expect if *we* ever get caught after the shooting starts," observed an engine man.

"The hell you say," objected a torpedoman. "That's all ancient history. Destroyers have got homing torpedoes now, with atomic warheads. If one of those things ever latches on and catches up with you, you'll never know what hit you. It will just be WHAM-O and that's the end of it. You get vaporized—nothing left of anybody or anything but molecules. Even your teeth get atomized."

"The screws of a high-speed torpedo make a lot of noise," observed a sonar man. "You would probably hear it coming and might be able to goof it—or dodge it."

"I doubt it," objected one of the missile technicians. "And anyway, our destroyers have got rockets now with atomic warheads that they can fire at submarines. You wouldn't hear them till they hit the water right over you. We gotta give the Russians credit for having them, too."

"Actually," said the Chief, "it's much nicer to have it that way. No blood, sweat, and tears about it, next time. Until it happens, we've got it made. Everybody has his own bunk, good chow, four hours on and eight off, and all the beans you can eat for breakfast. Submarine sailors never had it so good before. If it does happen, nobody gets arms and legs blown off, or anything messy like that. If you live through the next war, you come out all in one piece. If you don't . . . you just suddenly disappear off this earth and come to with a halo around your head and a harp in your hand."

At dinner time that evening, the officers stood behind their chairs waiting for the Captain. All wore smug grins like a bunch of cats full of canaries au gratin. A dispatch which had just come in for the Captain had been intercepted by the Exec and was lying on the Skipper's plate. It informed Commander Banks that he had just been selected for Captain.

When the Skipper came in he said, "Good evening, gentlemen," pulled back his chair, sat down, and picked up the dispatch. The others remained standing.

As he read the message the Skipper's eyes popped, his jaw dropped open, and then he broke into a broad grin. He looked up at his officers and said, "Well, boys–I guess this proves there's hope for all of you."

"Congratulations, Captain," said the Exec, and stuck out his hand. All the others crowded around to shake with the Skipper too, including the mess boys.

When they finally sat down, the Exec said, "I thought your class didn't come under the guns for selection until next year, sir."

"That's right–we don't," said the Captain.

"Well, this renews my faith in the early selection policy," said the Exec.

"Thank you, Joe," said the Skipper. "It's an example of what old Abe Lincoln meant when he said you can fool some of the people all of the time."

After dinner, when the Captain left the wardroom, one of the Lieutenants said, "What's the selection rate for captain, now?"

"One out of four," said the Navigator.

"One out of four! That means a lot of good men get passed over in the regular zone. . . . They went way beyond the zone to select the Skipper. It looks like he's got it made for admiral, some day."

"He's a sure bet for it in my book," said the Exec. "He's a winner. Could go right on up to CNO. Some day you'll brag to your grandchildren about having served under him."

The CNO Ops Room on the third deck of the Pentagon is the command post for the Navy Department. It is set up to tell the CNO anything he wants to know about his fleets and ships—where they are, what they are doing, and what's going on around them. To get in there, you need background checks by the FBI and CIA, plus a Q clearance from the Atomic Energy Commission and a few barnacles on your bottom. No rubbernecks who don't know port from starboard can get in, except for assistant secretaries of Defense, and the Navy would bar them, if it could.

When things get really hot in some far corner of the world, this is the best vantage point in Washington to watch them from. There are more elaborate ops rooms in town, with bigger display boards, fancier gimmickery, and plushier VIP accommodations, notably those of the Joint Chiefs of Staff, Air Force, and the White House. But when you want the very latest news from some remote hot spot, the CNO Ops Room is where you get it.

This results from several facts of life. Three quarters of the earth's surface is water. The Navy has ships scattered all over it, and these ships all have fine radio equipment. The Navy spent years building a network of high-power radio stations that covers the globe, and is independent of cables and land lines that can be cut in wartime. By World War II, CNO had instant dot-dash communication with any ship anywhere. As radiophones, side band, TV, and satellites came along, the Navy latched onto them. Now it not only has a shore-based network with all the latest electronic marvels—it has ships with similar equipment at the far end of the line.

In the Ops Room there are the usual vertical display boards, showing all the oceans of the world, with movable magnetic symbols stuck on them to show what the Navy is currently doing in them. There are status boards showing the various fleets, ships assigned to them, the task forces within the fleets, and the present combat readiness of these ships. There are teleprinters to mechanical brains with memories storing the vital statistics for every ship in the Navy, from name of skipper to cruising radius at maximum speed.

Scrambler phones and teletypes to Naval Communication Headquarters up on Nebraska Avenue practically put the radio operators, decoding officers, and supervisors at desks in the Ops Room. There are hot lines to all major naval commands and, in short order, special circuits can be set up direct to any ship as big as a destroyer, or hookups can be arranged to let you kibitz on the voice traffic between a carrier and its planes on the other side of the world. This often involves satellite relays, and sometimes, bouncing waves off the moon. The room is fully manned around the clock by a crew of alert junior officers, sailors, and Waves who keep the display boards corrected up to the minute. Each watch is headed by a smart young captain, who will probably make admiral on the next selection.

Originally, the direct ship circuits were devised to enable CNO to get accurate, first-hand info from the scene of action. When CNO actually commanded the fleets at sea, as "Uncle Ernie" King did during the war, CNO never used them to issue direct orders to ships, bypassing the normal chain of command. But CNO isn't even in the operational chain of command any more, except indirectly as one of the JCS. Even so, no skipper of a ship at sea would question an order from CNO, unless he was figuring on retiring pretty soon anyway.

But after Unification, when the Secretary of Defense's whiz kids found out about the Ops Room, they moved in on it whenever a crisis came up. For a while, they were content to just listen to the hot dope in wide-eyed amazement. But soon they couldn't resist the temptation to tell the ships at sea what to do. This led to several confrontations between CNO and SecDef when whiz kids ignored regular command channels, and butted in on operations thousands of miles away. It also led to setting up a "CNO-eyes-only" top-secret cubbyhole adjacent to the Ops Room for dope deemed too secret for the whiz kids—who are notoriously leaky with friendly reporters.

There is a special circuit to Polaris boats on patrol. The President can talk to them direct from the White House. And if he ever releases the order to "shoot," the Polaris skippers will have it in their hands within minutes.

When the *Nemo*'s message to CNO came in over this circuit, the URGENT PRIORITY on it was really unnecessary. Polaris boats on patrol don't send anything unless it is urgent.

The receiving operator tore off the tape with the coded message, stuck it in a cylinder and shot it through a tube to the code room. Here the five-letter code groups were fed into a machine which filtered them through an intricate maze of analyzers, rearranging, permuting, and unscrambling groups, and producing the plain English of the dispatch on a tape at the other end.

A minute later the Communication Watch Officer handed a sealed envelope containing two copies of the dispatch to the CNO Duty Officer in the Ops Room. "Sign here, Captain," he said, handing his clipboard to a sharp-looking young four-striper. The Captain signed for the message at 0732, five minutes after it had gone on the air from the *Nemo* up above the Arctic Circle near Spitzbergen.

One quick glance at the dispatch and the Captain picked up his direct phone to CNO's quarters at the Navy Observatory. "CNO Duty Officer," he said to the Admiral's mess boy who answered the phone. "Let me speak to the Admiral."

When the Admiral came on, he said, "I have an urgent message from the *Nemo*. Do you want it now on the scrambler? Or shall I hold it till you get to the office?"

"I'll take it on the scrambler," said the Admiral, reaching for a red phone on the table.

The Duty Officer shifted to a similar red phone and read the dispatch.

Nearly all phones in Washington these days are, or can be, tapped and bugged. But it would be useless to bug CNO's red line. Nothing but squeaks and gibberish would come out of it anywhere except through the unscrambling receiver.

Admiral Baker said, "Get that to the Vice Chief right away. Tell him I'll be in the office in half an hour and I'll want to see him, OP-03, OP-57, and Admiral Vickory."

OP-03 is Navy parlance for the Deputy CNO for Operations, Vice Admiral Foster. OP-57, Vice Admiral Radbury, was the Deputy for Research and Development. Vice Admiral Vickory was the Navy's top expert on atomic physics.

CNO's office is on the outside ring of the third deck in the Pentagon. This ring houses all the big wheels, including the Secretary of the Navy, half a dozen assistant secretaries and special assistants, and the five Deputy CNOs. All the Deputies are vice admirals with staffs including several two-star admirals. Their waiting rooms are manned by eagle-eyed aides and flag secretaries, mostly at least lieutenant commanders.

CNO's office is a king-sized one, big enough to hold a conference of all the Deputies plus their expert advisers. The windows look north over the mall, up the Potomac. The inner wall has a big picture of the President with a large American flag on one side and the Navy's official flag on the other. CNO's special four-star flag is in one corner, with John Paul Jones squinting out from behind it. In front of the President's picture is a large globe of the world with a plotting table alongside it for laying out navigational charts. The CNO's mahogany desk is always clear except for whatever item of business he is working on at the moment. His incoming, outgoing, and hold baskets are on the desks of his aides and the Vice Chief in the adjoining offices.

The Vice Chief—also a four-star admiral—has a similar office, separated from the Chief's by the common waiting room in between the two. In the reception room are the desks of the aides, secretaries, yeomen, and orderlies.

The Chief's office has an adjoining bedroom where the CNO can spend the night when things get hot in far corners of the globe. There is a door from the bedroom to the side corridor. By going out that way, the Admiral can elude visitors who are waiting to waylay him in the reception room. Admiral Baker called this his emergency escape hatch.

The Admiral came in through the escape hatch this morning. As he seated himself in his leather swivel chair, the Filipino steward who had served him for many years brought him black coffee in a cup with a four-star blue flag on it.

"Pine day, Admiral," said the steward. "How do you peel this morning, sir?"

"I feel fine, Orlando," said the Admiral. "Get some more cups and coffee. I'm going to have some of the Deputies in."

His aide came in from the anteroom, handed him the *Nemo*'s dispatch, and said, "Admiral Homer has the others in his office now."

"Wait a minute," said the Admiral. "Let me read this dispatch.

"Okay," said the Admiral as he finished reading. "Tell the others to come in . . . and don't interrupt us except for SecDef or the White House."

As Admiral Homer and the three Vice Admirals entered, the CNO said, "Good morning, gentlemen. It looks like we've got a can of worms first thing this morning."

"This fellow has gone off half-cocked," blurted Admiral Vickory.

"Why do you say that?" asked the CNO.

"He as much as says that they are tracking him by means of the reactor. That's ridiculous. That reactor is so heavily shielded, absolutely nothing can get out of it."

"You sound mighty sure of yourself, Vick."

"I am sure."

"Are you sure you know everything that goes on in there? Some very powerful forces are turned loose inside that thing."

"And they stay inside. Nothing can get through that shielding."

"Don't you believe he has had somebody tracking him for three days?"

"Sure. I believe that. But when he implies that they are doing it by the reactor, that's just—just stupid."

"Now don't get your tits in a flutter, Vick. You know this skipper. He's Commander Banks—Admiral Banks' son. You must have thought he was a reliable, intelligent man when you okayed him for this job."

"We all slip up some time, and I'll admit I must have done it in this case."

"Well . . . thanks for your opinion, Vick. I'll give it due weight. . . . What do you think, Mike?" he asked of Vice Admiral Radbury, Deputy for Research and Development.

"I hardly know what to say," said Radbury. "The first thing that comes to mind is that they've made a breakthrough with some new sonar technique that we don't know anything about. But we have the best sonar experts in the world. We have spent millions exploring every avenue that any of them thought had the slightest promise. It is possible we missed something. But it's highly improbable . . ."

"How can you say that?" interrupted Vickory. "When you've got the evidence right here that you missed the boat. Just because you couldn't find it doesn't mean that it was impossible."

"I can say the same thing about you and your reactor."

"By God, I'll . . ."

"All right now," said Admiral Baker sharply. "Knock off the bickering, gentlemen. This isn't a waterfront barroom. This is supposed to be CNO's office, remember?"

"I beg your pardon, sir," said Vickory.

"It seems obvious," said Baker, "that neither of you technicians can offer any clue as to how our boy is being tracked."

"Maybe he's got an oil leak," said Vickory.

"All right," said CNO. "Thank you, gentlemen. That's all the technical advice we need. . . . Hank, I want you and OP-03 to stay."

Radbury and Vickory left.

"An oil leak!" said CNO, making a wry face. "Can you imagine how he would ridicule anyone else who made such a suggestion about a Polaris boat?"

OP-03 was a submariner himself, of older vintage. "Even if she had an oil leak," he said, "she runs so deep, goes so fast, and oil rises so slowly that nobody could stay that close to them following oil that was coming up from a thousand feet."

"I agree," said CNO. "Now what we've got to decide is: how do we handle this message?"

"I think there's no room for doubt about how we have to answer it," said the Vice Chief. "He's run into something brand new which he can't explain and neither can we. He thinks he has important information about it. We've got to get him back here as soon as possible and let the back-room experts analyze whatever dope he has."

"I agree," said Vice Admiral Foster.

"That makes it unanimous," said Baker. "Answer this: 'Affirmative. Return to Holy Loch.' Then get a crew of experts on their way up there to meet them."

"Aye aye, sir," said Homer. "It will be ready for your release in a few minutes. I'll have Radbury and Vickory and their people flown up to Holy Loch."

"I'll have to tell SecDef and the President about this," said CNO. "This only reduces our retaliation force by one boat—but it has far-reaching implications."

"I was just coming to that, Admiral," said the Vice Chief. "OP-03 and I think you should consider recalling all boats from the Norwegian Sea."

"Now wa-a-a-it a minute," said Admiral Baker. "Why should we do that?"

"We're not saying you should recall them *yet*. We do think we ought to take a hard look at the situation."

"All right. Let's take it."

"On the face of things, this upsets the whole balance. Up to now, we have operated on the theory that Polaris was invulnerable . . . that they couldn't find our ships in the first place and couldn't stay with them if they did happen to stumble across one. This message casts serious doubt on this."

"It sure does. But I don't see why this means we have to call off the whole northern patrol. Suppose all this is true, and they can find and track us now. So what? Why recall anybody except the *Nemo*, who may be able to tell us how they're doing it?"

"Admiral," said Homer, "we think there is a good chance the Russians may destroy one or more of our boats."

"The sons-of-bitches had better not!" said Baker. "We have a perfect right to do what we are doing."

"Quite true," said Homer, "but–"

"And the Russians," interrupted Baker, "have had their subs prowling around off our coasts. We've ridden herd on five of them in the last six months, and forced them to surface. In fact, we're sitting on top of one off Cape Kennedy right now."

"Right, Admiral," said OP-03. "But they were diesel boats. Otherwise, we never could have forced them to come up. And the missiles they can carry are primitive compared to Polaris. As you know very well, the only reason we haven't protested about this is that we're posing them a much bigger threat with Polaris."

"Well–that's right, too," conceded Baker. "So let them protest if they don't like Polaris and then we can consider whether we should withdraw."

"But suppose, Admiral, that Polaris boats start disappearing?"

"You mean that they start sinking them?"

"Yessir. How would we know what's happening? A boat simply disappears. We never hear from it again. How will we know what happened to it?"

"We'll know goddam well what happened to it!"

"Sure, the three of us will know. But how will we prove it to the rest of the world? We'll have to announce it if a boat is lost. The public will want to know why. What are we going to tell them? Are we going to accuse the Russians, when we would have no proof and they could simply point to the *Scorpion?* Just imagine trying to sell that to the UN!"

"Hmmmmm," said Admiral Baker. "I see what you mean. This is something to think about."

"They'd have us over a barrel, Admiral. They wouldn't have to say a word. We would be the ones who would have to protest, and we would have no proof to back it up."

"Yes. You're right," said CNO. "They might point out that we have been threatening them for years, and they never have protested. They might even say they have no objection at all to our northern patrol—but meantime, our subs would keep on disappearing."

"That's it exactly, Admiral. This break could give them the whip hand—and if it does, I think they'll use it."

"I think you're right," said CNO. "We should recall all our boats—at least until we know more about this."

"That's what Foster and I recommend, Admiral."

"Of course, this will have to be settled in the White House. I'll recall the *Nemo* on my own hook—and tell them what I'm doing. But if we recall them all, the President will have to do it."

"This could be pretty urgent, Admiral."

"Why? They had three days to sink the *Nemo* if they wanted to, but they didn't."

"Yessir. But this was the first time they were ever able to track a Polaris boat. They probably surprised themselves. The destroyer that did this may not have had authority to go any further. But now that *Nemo* has given them the slip and the news has got back to the Kremlin, they've had time to make up their minds and issue orders to their destroyer skippers. Next time they make contact, they may shoot."

"All right. I'm convinced. We've got to set up an emergency meeting of the JCS this morning. I'll see SecDef right after that, and we'll get this to the White House this afternoon!"

"Are you sure you can swing it with the JCS?"

"No trouble at all. This is a Naval operational matter, on which they would all go along with me in any event. In this case, the Air Force will be enthusiastic—Polaris always has been a bone in their throat!"

The JCS meeting went just as CNO had predicted. The Chairman and the Army deferred to CNO on this operational matter without question. The Chief of the Air Force put on a great show of being "sorry about that." He pointed out that if we were to keep the level of deterrence undiminished, SAC would have to take over an additional load and supplemental appropriations would be necessary. "This would seem to indicate that Polaris is no longer an effective weapons system," he said.

"I wouldn't say that," said CNO. "This is simply an interim measure until we can find out more about this thing. For the time being, we will have to redeploy a little further back from the Russian shoreline. But Polaris has a range of twenty-five hundred miles. Even if we pull back to the Atlantic west of Scotland, we can still cover all of European Russia and reach way beyond the Urals. All it means is we may have to reshuffle some of the strategic target assignments."

"SAC will be glad to help the Navy out by taking over any of your presently assigned targets which you can no longer reach," said the Air Force Chief of Staff, smugly.

8

It wasn't quite so easy with SecDef. Secretary Wood was busy, and CNO had trouble even getting in to see him.

The Secretary had built up quite a public image as a smart, tough boss, with a brain like an electronic computer, who took no nonsense from the generals and admirals. One of his predecessors, Mr. McNamara, had brought in a bevy of eager, bright-eyed young civilians to help him straighten out the Pentagon. They had banished history books to the dead files, and had put in a system of cost accounting to replace the old-fashioned ways of defending the country. They took over complete control of the defense budget, put in scientific cost analysis methods, and installed batteries of mechanical brains to check up on what the brass told them.

By the time McNamara resigned from the Defense Department, the fears expressed by President Eisenhower in his farewell address had come true. Ironclad control of the huge defense budget had made SecDef nearly an absolute czar. In fact, he was now more powerful than the President, except that the President could—if he had to—fire him.

Secretary Wood forced combat-seasoned generals, accustomed to figuring that national security was worth whatever it cost, to think first of dollars and cents. In the process, he rode roughshod over service traditions and fired a number of generals and admirals who tried to drag their feet. For this, the press hailed him as a fearless genius who had brought the brass to heel and had finally enforced civilian control of the military.

So long as his crusade was aimed only at the moneybags and business methods, the Secretary had done pretty well. His young experts could produce figures which, they claimed, showed billions of dollars being saved for the taxpayers, even though the total military budget was swelling up like a balloon.

After they got the Pentagon on a business-like basis, they moved in on military and naval operations overseas. Field commanders, at grips with the enemy in Vietnam, began getting orders about how to fight the war from cost effectiveness experts in the Pentagon. Often these orders aimed at killing the last enemy with the last bullet produced under current contracts. The Joint Chiefs of Staff interfered for a while, but were finally kicked upstairs, like the Chairman of the Board in big corporations. Questions of global strategy, which used to be handled by them, were farmed out to "think factories," and Joint Chiefs often cooled their heels in the waiting rooms of assistant secretaries of Defense.

For a while, the Secretary had a good press on this, too. But now, the war in Vietnam was dragging out way beyond the date predicted by his computers. Casualty figures and draft calls were mounting, and the Secretary could no longer shift the blame to the downgraded Joint Chiefs.

This was all bad enough for the Secretary's image and peace of mind. But now one of SecDef's early triumphs over the brass, a landmark in his rise to power, was turning sour, too—the XFQ Contract.

The Secretary was closeted this morning with his cost effectiveness experts, getting a special briefing on the XFQ. This multi-billion-dollar contract for new combat airplanes had been awarded five years back by SecDef over the protests of the Air Force and Navy flyers. There had been a great splurge of publicity at the time about new methods of cost analysis used in making the award, and the huge savings to the taxpayers that would result. At first, the XFQ was hailed as a victory for scientific management over the generals and admirals. But the victory was coming apart at the seams.

The new plane was still not operational and costs had skyrocketed way beyond the original rosy estimates. Experimental models had been plagued with bugs requiring costly fixes that didn't really fix. Now the Navy had finally turned it down for operation from carriers because it was too heavy.

Despite glowing press releases on every item of good news during the trials, and top-secret classification of all bad news, word was beginning to leak out that the XFQ was a flop. SecDef's public image as a shrewd analyst and tough administrator who had made the brass knuckle under was in danger. At the briefing this morning, the Secretary and his bright-eyed young experts were trying to find loopholes in the Navy's report that would get them off the hook.

Admiral Baker had to throw his weight around with the Secretary's aides, who didn't want to interrupt the briefing. The Secretary sent word out from the briefing room that the Admiral should see one of the assistant SecDefs about whatever he had on his mind, and the CNO had to insist rather bluntly that his business required action by SecDef himself.

When SecDef finally came to his office from the briefing room, he was not in a genial mood.

"What's the trouble now, Admiral?" he asked.

The Admiral handed him the *Nemo*'s message.

The Secretary scanned through it twice. "This is rather disconcerting news," he said. "We've got to get a lot more information on this. But just what do you want me to do about it?"

"So far as the *Nemo* is concerned—nothing. I've already taken care of that myself, and ordered her back to Holy Loch. Our best technical experts will meet her there."

"Well . . ." said the Secretary, "that takes care of it. Doesn't it?"

"No, sir. This affects the security of all our other subs on the northern patrol. We think that until we know more about this, it is advisable to redeploy the Polaris boats we've got on patrol in the Arctic Ocean and put them in the Atlantic west of Scotland."

"It also affects our readiness to retaliate. I'd want the JCS to study this before I consider it," said the Secretary.

"We just had a special meeting, sir. This requires a small reassignment of strategic targets, which SAC can take over for the time being. The JCS have unanimously approved this."

"I would also want to consult with my scientific advisers."

"When the *Nemo* gets in, we will be glad to have all the scientific and technical advice anyone can give us," said the CNO. "But meantime, redeployment of the other boats is an operational rather than a scientific or technical matter."

"So it is. But what's so urgent about it? Why can't we wait till we can evaluate the data that *Nemo* is bringing in?"

"We are afraid the Russians will be tempted to destroy one of our ships if we leave them in the Arctic."

"Destroy one of our ships!?" said the Secretary. "I think you're hitting the panic button. We have been patrolling the Arctic for years. We have a perfect right to do it. They have never protested about it."

"They have never been in a position to do anything about it before. They have never even found one of our ships before. But they have tracked *Nemo* for three days. They could have destroyed her without trace, and we would never have known what happened."

"But they didn't."

"We think they surprised themselves, and their destroyer skipper couldn't take such drastic action on his own hook. Now that he has had time to report what he has found out and to get instructions from Moscow, we think he may shoot next time."

"But that would be an act of war!"

"So it would—except that we would never know what happened."

"Can't our ships defend themselves? Can't they send us a radio if they are in trouble?"

"The only way they could defend themselves is to shoot first . . . on suspicion. Against a sneak attack, radio would be no use."

"I just don't believe the Russians are that desperate. They would be risking atomic retaliation."

"I don't think so, sir. Not if one of our subs just disappeared, like the *Scorpion* did. We didn't think the Japs were desperate enough to attack us at Pearl Harbor."

"Admiral," said the SecDef, "it seems to me you haven't thought this thing through to its logical conclusion. If the Russians have decided to do anything that drastic, they can do it in the North Atlantic just as well as in the Arctic. If one of our ships disappears in the Arctic they know damn well we will blame them for it, and probably the rest of the world would, too. But if a boat disappears in the North Atlantic, it would be much more difficult to persuade others the Russians had done it. It seems to me that if we decide to pull back at all, we should logically pull back all the way to our own coast."

"I don't think so, sir. In the Arctic, we're right in their backyard, and it's an empty ocean. Nobody knows what goes on up there. Off Scotland, we are a thousand miles further west and in busy air and sea traffic lanes, where Russian destroyers would be conspicuous. Sinking one of our ships out there would be quite a different matter from doing it right off their own shores."

"Well, I must say," said the Secretary, "this is a different tune from any you admirals have ever sung before."

"This is a different situation, sir."

"Up to now, in arguments about territorial waters at the UN, you people have insisted on the three-mile limit. You claimed that outside the three-mile limits the oceans should be free to everybody. Now you are proposing that we back off a thousand miles."

"I'm not talking about rights under international law. I'm talking about what is prudent and in the national interest while we are making up our minds how to deal with a new situation. . . . I'd like to do this today—unless you object, sir."

"Sit down, Admiral," said the Secretary to the CNO, who had been standing up to this time.

The Secretary drew a square on a piece of paper, divided it into four equal sections, and put small circles, diamonds, and xs into each section. Finally he said, "I think this should go to the White House for decision. The President will probably want the National Security Council to advise him on it."

"I'm ready to go to the White House this afternoon, sir."

"I don't think the matter is that urgent," said the Secretary. "I'll have it put on the agenda for the Council's meeting next week."

"Mr. Secretary," said CNO, "this thing is either very urgent or there is no reason for doing it at all. I think it is urgent. In fact, I feel it is an operational matter which CNO should handle on his own responsibility. I took it to the JCS because we had to make a small change in strategic target assignments. The JCS have approved this. This is an important matter on which I have to keep you and the President informed. But I think I should decide it."

The Secretary began blacking out the neat doodles he had made. He thought to himself, civilian control of the military rears its ugly head again! I thought we had slain that dragon.

After a moment, he said, "No. This has to go to the White House. It has far-reaching political implications."

"Yessir, it does. It upsets the balance of power for the time being. It raises some sticky international questions . . ."

"I mean right here at home, too," said the Secretary. "The Navy has already put the Administration in a bad light on the XFQ. Now you're telling me that Polaris, on which we have spent billions, isn't as good as we thought it was. Some of our newspapers would just love to get hold of that news."

"Well, I'm certainly not going to give it to them. And after all, this is a military decision, not a political one."

"Every decision would be a military one if you had your way, Admiral. There are other things that have to be considered, too."

"The things I'm thinking about are that the Russians now have a chance to take advantage of us, and second, that the safety of my ships and lives of my men could be in danger."

The Secretary leveled a cold stare at CNO and said, "Admiral, I will speak to the President about this this afternoon. My recommendation will be that we refer it to the Security Council at their meeting next week."

The Admiral made a quick mental estimate of the situation. Was it worthwhile to have a showdown with the Secretary about this? After all, the whole thing hinged on what we think the Russians might do. So far, there was no indication that they intended to do it. If he insisted on taking this to the White House immediately, either he or SecDef would get badly hurt. CNO didn't mind sticking his neck out when it might accomplish something. But in this case, where it all depended on trying to read the Russians' minds, it seemed unlikely that he could accomplish anything.

"Aye aye, sir," he said.

As Baker started to leave, SecDef said, "Just a minute, Admiral. I've got something else to discuss with you."

"Yessir," said Baker.

"I've just come from a briefing on the present status of the XFQ project. It has turned out very well in most respects.

The flight tests so far have equaled, or exceeded, the performance we predicted for it. The Air Force is well pleased with it. And I believe that in most respects, the Navy is too."

"Yessir. It's a good airplane for operations from shore bases."

"Now, as you well know, we are heavily committed to this project. There was much ill-informed criticism of the way we made the contract awards, and there were predictions of failure right from the beginning. But so far we have proved the critics were all wrong, and have got ourselves a fine airplane. The only black mark against it is your rejection of it for carrier use."

"Yessir."

"What I'm leading up to is this. Performance figures such as speed, rate of climb, operating radius, and so forth are matters of fact which have been determined by flight test. And on all these things, the plane meets specifications. Now . . . the question of whether this plane is suitable for use from carriers or not is a question of judgment—isn't it?"

"I suppose you could put it that way, sir."

"But in your report, you make the flat statement that the plane is not suitable for use from carriers."

"Yessir."

"Since this is a matter of judgment, don't you think it's premature to make such a statement before the plane has been tested on your carrier decks?"

"Well, sir—the weight of the plane is a matter of fact, and the weight exceeds the specifications by twenty thousand pounds. In my judgment, and in that of the engineers who designed our carrier decks, and of our test pilots, this is too much for safe operation from those decks. This is what I say in my report."

"As you know, Admiral, there were many new concepts involved in this project—commonality, cost effectiveness, competence of contractors, effect on the national budget and economy. These are matters which are in no sense operational, and in which military background is not needed to form a judgment."

"Yessir. I realize that a great deal of scientific analysis went into the making of this award, and that it was done by competent experts. The test vehicles which we have seen so far are fine, modern airplanes, and in most respects they perform just about as well as your experts predicted they would. But somewhere along the line, some bad data on weight must have been fed into their computers, because the plane has come out twenty thousand pounds heavier than it should be."

"Well, after all, isn't that a small price to pay for all the other advantages we are getting?"

"Except that it exceeds the weight limit that we can safely handle on our carrier decks."

"How can you say that before you've tried it? It's a matter of judgment, isn't it?"

"Mr. Secretary, I'm sure your analysts can set the problem up on their computers and find out that the decks just won't handle that weight."

"All right, Admiral. That's all."

Back in his office, the CNO buzzed for the Vice Chief.

"How did you make out, sir?" asked Admiral Homer.

"Just as I expected with the Joint Chiefs. They approve. The Air Force will take over any targets we can't reach. But SecDef can't see any urgency about it, and wants to refer it to the Security Council. He is also burned up about the XFQ report."

"That means a delay of two days," said the Vice Chief. "It seems to me that if we are going to do it at all, we should do it right now."

"The more I think about it, the more I feel the same way, too. But the trouble is we have nothing but a hunch to base this on. Before Pearl Harbor, we were reading the Jap codes, but we still couldn't believe they would attack us. Here, we are trying to read the Russians' minds."

"But this is an operational question," said the Vice Chief, "on which you should have the final say. Do you think he would fight you on a real showdown?"

"I'm sure he would. We have been close to a showdown

several times lately, and he's madder than hell now because I said the XFQ is no good for carrier operations. He talked more about this than he did about Polaris this morning. He would welcome an excuse to get rid of me. And he's going to have his chance soon. Before long, I've got to go to bat with him and settle who runs the ships at sea. But I'm afraid it would be premature to do it on this question."

"You really think he would try to fire you, if he could?"

"I sure do."

9

On the USS *Nemo*, the Communications Officer came up to the cabin and handed the Captain a dispatch which had just come in over the hot line from CNO. It read:

URGENT PRIORITY–TOP SECRET. Return to Holy Loch.

"Well! We got fast action on that," observed the Skipper.

"I think the Russian has got his orders too, sir," said the Lieutenant. "We just heard a ten-group dispatch in five-letter code on the Russian Navy frequency. It was followed immediately by a short transmission from a nearby station—probably the destroyer receipting for the dispatch."

"That's what it was, all right," said the Captain. "They've given him his orders. And they're not beating around the bush about it in a ten-group dispatch. I'd sure like to know what it says."

"We got a bearing on him when he receipted for it," said the Lieutenant. "He's still due south of us."

"Hmmmmm," said the Skipper. "We've moved east about a hundred and fifty miles since we went under the ice. He seems to know it!"

A few minutes later, the Captain, Exec, and Navigator gathered around the chart desk in the main control room.

The Captain said, "We got a bearing a few minutes ago on our Russian friend, talking to Moscow . . . at least I think it was him. He's still due south of us. I want to reverse course now, and run west all day tomorrow. Then we'll come out from under the floe, and see what happens."

Next morning, the Captain sent for the Exec and Doctor to come to his cabin.

"Gentlemen," he said, "I'm trying to figure out what I'm going to do when we come out from under the ice."

"Do you think he'll be on our back again when we come out?" asked the Doctor.

"I don't know," said the Captain. "I hope not. But I've got to figure out what to do in case he is there again."

"Until we got that bearing on him last night," said the Exec, "I would have bet we had shaken him. And the bearing doesn't prove he's following us. He had to turn either east or west when he got to the icecap and his base is to the east. It may be just a lucky chance that he is staying south of us."

"I hope you're right," said the Captain. "Before I come out from under the cap I'm going to reverse course and run west till we're directly north of Scotland."

"My guess is, that will lose him," said the Exec. "He first picked us up at twenty miles the other day. We're thirty miles from the edge of the brash ice now. I don't think he can track us here."

"Maybe you're right," said the Captain. "But we don't know how far he picked us up in the first place. All we know is that he was twenty miles away when we first heard him. He may have been tracking us long before we heard him."

"Maybe so," said the Exec. "But I'm betting he can't follow us this far and that he has lost us."

"If he has, we've got no problem," said the Captain. "We just proceed to Holy Loch. If he hasn't, and gets on our back again, we may have a real big problem. That's what I want to discuss with you gentlemen now."

"Will the situation be any different than it was for the three days before we went under the ice?" asked the Doctor.

"I'm afraid it could be very different," said the Captain. "I think that during those three days, he was on his own. So far as we know, he sent no radio messages and didn't get any. But he sent a long dispatch last night and got a short answer a little while ago. A lot depends on what that answer was."

"You think they've given him his orders?" asked the Exec.

"I do. But it really doesn't help much to know that. If they simply told him 'continue as before,' we've got nothing to worry about. If they told him something else, we could have plenty to worry about. This is the angle we've got to explore."

"What do you think they might have told him?" asked the Doctor.

"There's no use in mincing words about it," said the Captain. "They may have told him to destroy us."

"This is possible, all right," said the Exec. "But it isn't necessarily all bad from their point of view to let us get home. When we get back and make our report there won't be any doubt about the fact that they can track us. If we just disappear, our people can't be sure of what happened—like you said, maybe another *Scorpion*. It's quite a bit similar to this Polaris business. If we had kept Polaris under wraps so that nobody knew anything about it—it wouldn't have had any deterrent effect. But we publicized it, the Russians believed it, and it has helped to keep the peace for a while. Suppose that right after we announced the Polaris program, the Russians had said, 'We're not afraid of Polaris. We track your boats whenever they come into the Arctic Ocean and we can blow them out of the water any time we want to.' We wouldn't have believed them—would we?"

"No, we wouldn't."

"But after we get home, our people will believe it. They might figure it's worthwhile to let us get home."

"You've got something there, Joe," said the Captain. "One way of getting the news to Washington is to let us deliver it. On the other hand, they know that if a couple of Polaris boats should just disappear, that would make it pretty official too."

"You said the other night," observed the Doctor, "that if you were in his shoes you would let us have it."

"Yes, I did say that. But I'm afraid I was just popping off to hear myself talk. I doubt if any military man would do a thing like that, in peacetime, on his own responsibility . . . especially a naval officer. . . . Seafaring men just don't do things like that to each other."

"How about Pearl Harbor?" asked the Doctor. "That was done by military men—Jap naval officers, in fact."

"Right you are, Doctor. But it wasn't a boatswain's mate or a destroyer skipper who made that decision. It was the Jap CNO. Everybody down the line had official orders when they made the attack. It just isn't in the cards for some young lieutenant commander to do something on his own hook that might start a war. But now he has had time to talk to Moscow, and he may have orders to do it. But if we go off half-cocked, we could start the war that will really end wars—the war that we're out here to prevent. We can't take any action against him until we are certain that he is trying to kill us. How the hell can we be certain before it is too late?"

Nobody had a ready answer to that question.

The Doctor spoke up first. "If he fires a torpedo at us, we'll hear it coming, won't we? At least a minute or so before it hits us?"

"Yes. We will," said the Captain.

"Can't we dodge it, or run away from it, or turn loose a noisemaker or decoy to confuse it?"

"Not if his torpedoes are as good as ours—and we've got to assume they are. We have torpedoes that can go twice as fast as this ship. They have 'homers' that will follow any squirming we do. We've got sonar sets in the warheads that won't be fooled by noisemakers or decoys. He might not even use a torpedo. They've probably got depth charges with atom warheads the same as we have. They've got rockets that drop them in the water right over a sub a couple of miles away. We wouldn't hear one of them till it hit the water right over us."

"By the same token, Cap'n," said the Exec, "we've got a homing torpedo he can't dodge. It's got an atomic warhead that can blast him to atoms without trace."

"That's right, Joe. The thing I've got to decide now is how sure do I want to be that he is trying to kill us—before I fire it."

"Well . . . how sure do you want to be?" asked the Doctor.

"I'm afraid much more so than I ever can be. Suppose I let him have it, and it turns out later that I went off half-cocked. If that's all there was to it, I'd have trouble sleeping for a while, but I might learn to live with it. But it couldn't stop there. The Russians would know damned well that we did it. There would be an eyeball-to-eyeball showdown, and we would be the ones that had to blink. God knows what they would demand. They might make us pull our armies out of Europe."

"How could they be sure we did it?" asked the Doctor. "We could deny any knowledge of it."

"I don't think we could," said the Captain. "We just haven't got the guts to lie with a straight face when the chips are down. Look what happened on the U-2 flights. We tried to do it, but got booby-trapped so bad we'll never forget it . . . and in that case what we were doing wasn't a bit worse than what they had done with Sputnik. But they not only shot our plane down, they made us eat crow over it. I'm afraid we'd tell the truth now even if we knew it was going to blow the world apart."

"A grave flaw in our national character," observed the Doctor. "Any great nation that isn't willing to lie when necessary to preserve the peace doesn't deserve to be great."

"All right," said the Exec. "Suppose we both disappear off the face of the earth. What then?"

"You mean we destroy each other?"

"Yes. I think we'll have at least a minute or so warning before any weapon he fires at us hits us. By that time we will be sure. It only takes a few seconds to fire a torpedo, and we could have one well on its way before we get hit."

"Yes. That's possible, all right. Like the calico cat and the gingham dog—we eat each other up. In a few days, we and the Russians would both know that one of our ships was missing. We would both think we knew what had happened, but neither would be sure. The Russians would have the advantage of us because we would have to announce the loss of the Polaris boat. We wouldn't know their destroyer was lost unless they announced it. They could set a bad booby trap for us. We would be so full of righteous indignation over the sinking of our sub that we would try to take them to the brink again—like in Cuba. This would be a very dangerous situation, because although we can eat crow when we know we're wrong, we're apt to gag on it if we think we're right!"

"So where does that leave us?" asked the Doctor.

"Back where we started, I guess," said the Captain. "Actually, I don't think that anything we can do will have much effect on world history one way or the other. Now that the Russians have learned how to track us, we have the Cuban missile situation in reverse, except it's a much better setup for them. In the Cuban case, if we had wiped out their missile bases, the whole world would have known it. All the banana republics and cannibal nations would have screamed about attacking Cuba. But in this case, they can knock us off and nobody else will know what happened. I doubt if they fully understand this back home yet, although our message to CNO should tell them—if they believe us. We humiliated the Russians in Cuba, so they're going to rub our nose in this. And we'll have to either back down or—shoot the works."

"That's the problem for the statesmen back home," said the Exec. "What are we going to do up here in the Arctic Ocean?"

"Why not surface, Cap'n, and send him a signal?" asked the Doctor. "What would you have to lose?"

"Nothing to lose. But I can't see that we could gain anything, either. . . . There's no problem unless he has orders to destroy us. If he has, he will try to do it whether we are submerged, surfaced, or airborne . . . unless we come out on deck holding our hands up and surrender. I'm afraid CNO might say we hadn't ought to do that. But I am going to come out from under the cap during daylight . . . just in case. . . . Well, maybe we might want to come up and take a look at something."

The Doctor said finally, "What do you think his orders are, Captain?"

"I don't want to put this in the Plan of the Day," replied the Captain. "In fact I don't want either of you to mention it beyond the door of this cabin. But I think he has been told to get us."

The Doctor said, "If you think he is trying to destroy us, you should hit first."

"What do you think, Joe?"

"Captain, I will go along with what you decide when the time comes . . . whatever it is."

"Frankly, I don't know what I'm going to do," said the Captain, "and I won't know until the last minute. I've got to play it by ear. That's one of the big difficulties, because I mean 'by ear' literally. The only way either of us can guess what the other is up to is by interpreting noises that come out of the water. We're both pretty good at that trade. But it's a pretty slim thread for the future of our civilization to hang on."

"But there must be some rational solution to this," protested the Doctor.

"That's the big trouble, Doctor. I don't think there is any

rational solution, because when you come down to bedrock, the problem isn't a rational one. We claim to be civilized, and yet the two biggest countries in the world devote perhaps half of their time, brains, and resources to developing systems of mutual terror. We now have weapons systems, bore-sighted on each other and balanced on knife edges, with which we can knock each other back into the Dark Ages. The problem is, how long can we live this way before somebody or something jars the knife edge? If cannibal tribes tried to live in peace with their neighbors that way, we would laugh at them. The *Nemo* and that destroyer are just little caps in the big international game of Russian roulette."

"At any rate," said the Doctor, "we haven't been a dog in the manger about the atom bomb. We've let the Chinese, French, Israelis, and Arabs develop it too. Maybe pretty soon some of the cannibal republics in Africa will get civilized enough to quit eating each other and start making atom bombs too!"

"I'm afraid civilization has just dealt this generation a lousy hand, and there's no chance of declaring a misdeal and starting over," said the Captain. "We're going to play the hand out and blow ourselves up. But life will go on, in a primitive sort of way, after the big blow-up and maybe a couple of thousand years from now a more sensible civilization will evolve."

"You make things sound pretty hopeless, Cap'n," said the Doctor.

"I'm not saying they're hopeless for us when we come out from under the ice," said the Captain. "This may not be the showdown. The Russian may be very polite to us and just let us go. But the very fact that such an absurd situation as this can develop shows that this crazy world can't last much longer."

"What other way is there to keep peace in the world, Captain, except by a balance of terror?" asked the Exec. "After all, it has worked for over twenty years."

"That's the sad part of it," said the Captain. "I'm afraid there isn't any—at least none that the world is ready for yet. The UN was the best answer that all the starry-eyed idealists in this world could come up with toward the end of the last world war. Look what a sad sack it has turned out to be. The UN can't work until men learn to trust each other. And if we trusted any other nation today, we'd be fools."

"What is the answer, then?" persisted the Doctor. "You're a religious man. You have a brother, a priest, and I suppose you believe in God. Does our hope lie in that direction?"

"Frankly, I doubt it," said the Captain. "I do believe in God. How any thinking man can believe that this whole universe just happened by chance is beyond me. But I think the God who created the universe and gave man a brain to think with takes little hand now in the affairs of this puny flyspeck of a planet we live on. He has given us all we need for a pretty good life down here. If we mess it up, it doesn't upset the rest of His universe very much."

"All the churches are opposed to war," said the Doctor. "Maybe if we took religion seriously enough, we could live in peace."

"Perhaps. But some of the most barbarous wars in history have been holy wars. And I can't see much hope for peace on earth from churches that consign you to hell for an offhand roll in the hay, and bless opposing armies that are going out to slaughter each other. Most religions say this world will come to an end some day. Maybe God's way of winding it up is to let man destroy himself."

"How do you feel about the rather-red-than-dead bit, Captain?"

"That's one way of solving the problem—if all you want is that kind of peace. But I don't want any part of it. I'd rather be dead than red, myself. . . . Personally, I'm glad I wasn't born thirty years later than I was. I don't want to be around after the big blast. Now . . . let's get back to our immediate problem—coming out from under here the day after tomorrow."

The Exec had been doodling on the scratch pad while this discussion was going on. He slapped down his pencil, looked up, and said, "Captain, I've got an idea for getting away from that guy and getting our information home even if he is still tracking us and has orders to destroy us."

"Sounds too good to be true," said the Captain. "Let's have it."

"Go home to the West Coast over the Pole."

The Captain's eyes lit up and a pleased grin spread over his face. "Joe, you're a genius. . . . We just follow the *Nautilus*' route in reverse! No showdown is possible! . . . For us, anyway. Too bad we didn't put that in our first dispatch. Let's frame another dispatch to CNO right now."

A few minutes later the two of them had worked out the following:

> To: CNO
>
> URGENT PRIORITY–TOP SECRET
>
> Due to possibility that Russian may attack when we come out from under icecap recommend we return to West Coast via North Pole route.

"How do you think CNO will react to that?" asked the Doctor.

"I know Admiral Baker well, and I know he'll go for this. But he won't make the decision on it. SecDef and his whiz kids will have to feed it into their computers. CIA, the JCS, and the State Department will have to be cut in on it. It will wind up in the White House."

"I should think on an operational matter like this, they ought to let CNO decide it."

"That's what they should do. But they won't. I'd like to lay a bet right now that Admiral Baker goes to bat for this and gets smacked down by the ivory-tower strategists. They vote 'no' on any smart schemes they don't think of first. But I'm going to send it anyway—just for the history books, in case any more are written."

10

Next morning the Vice Chief and OP-03 came into CNO's office with the dispatch about returning via the North Pole. As Admiral Homer handed it to the Chief, he said, "The *Nemo* feels the same way we do about the danger of an attack."

"Indeed they do!" said CNO after reading the dispatch. "The Skipper seems to think the Russians are looking down his throat. . . . If they are, this is a smart way of avoiding them—in fact, maybe the only way."

"Do you want to get Radbury and Vickory in to discuss this?" asked the Vice Chief.

"No. There's nothing technical about this. It's a purely operational matter. We've got all the talent we need right here to settle it. Let's have a look at the globe."

The three officers gathered around the big globe under the President's picture and marked off the *Nemo*'s position on it.

"About nine hundred miles to Holy Loch," observed CNO. "Less than two days' run. . . . Where would we send him in Alaska?"

"Naval Air Station, Kodiak would be the best place," said OP-03. "Here it is, just south of the mainland."

They stepped off the distance over the Pole to the Bering Strait, south through the Bering Sea to Unimak Pass, and then northeast to Kodiak.

"Close to four thousand miles," announced CNO.

"A little more than that," said OP-03. "You can't run direct from the Pole to Bering Strait—too much shallow water. You've got to head for Point Barrow, following the Barrow Sea Valley along the ocean floor. And you can't run at high speed on any route under the icecap. You've got to feel your way, or you could get jammed between the ice and the bottom. It would take him at least eight days longer to go over the Pole than it would to Holy Loch."

"Eight days is a long time to wait for his data," said CNO. "But, of course, if his fears are well founded, we would never get it the other way."

"Another thing," said OP-03. "The *Nautilus* went over the Pole in August. The icecap will be much closer to the north coast of Alaska now. It may even extend all the way to Point Barrow. We have to fly an ice recco up there to be sure she could get out from under the icecap at this time of year. I've already told Kodiak to do this."

"Hmmmm," said CNO. "That's something to think about. But Banks went over the Pole in the *Nautilus*. He knows what the problems are. I'm sure he wouldn't just barge on ahead until he got pinched between the ice and the bottom. He could always turn around and go back to Holy Loch."

"This is a sticky business," said the Vice Chief. "We told SecDef we wanted to redeploy the other boats because we were afraid they would be attacked. He didn't take any stock in that. Now, *Nemo* expresses the same concern. If we tell her 'no,' we are more or less admitting we were not really serious about the danger of attack. If we tell her 'yes,' we've got to wait eight days or more for vitally important information."

"It's sticky, all right," agreed CNO. "The only hard fact we have to go on is that the Russians have found some way to track us. All the rest is speculation about what this might lead them to do. We really have nothing to base this on except that we don't trust the sons-of-bitches as far as I could sling an anchor."

"And they don't trust us half that much," said Admiral Homer.

"We could hem and haw about this thing for days," said CNO, "and get no closer to the answer than we are right now. The trouble is that we are trying to find a sensible answer to a small piece of a big problem that doesn't make any sense and will finally be solved by blowing the world apart. We say to the Russians, 'Don't get nervous just because we've got our subs lying offshore with all those rockets aimed at your big cities—after all, they've been there for some years and we haven't fired them, so just relax and take it easy. But we're getting nervous about your blowing up our ships.' . . . How the hell can rational human beings try to run the world that way? Anybody in the nonviolent ward over at St. Elizabeth's could answer this just as well as we can."

"Don't you think we've got a right to do what we're doing?" asked the Vice Chief.

"You're damned right we have," said the CNO. "The right of self-preservation, freedom of the seas, and all that sort of thing. But it's like an airline pilot insisting that he's got the right of way when another plane looms up in front of him. It's a dangerous way to live."

Turning to OP-03, he asked, "Are we still sitting on top of that sub off Cape Kennedy?"

"Yessir," said OP-03. "We had a report on it only two hours ago. He comes up and schnorkels for a couple of hours each night—so he may hang around there for a couple of more weeks."

"Well, Admiral," said the Vice Chief, "what we've got to decide now is how to answer the *Nemo*. The only reason to bring her back over the Pole is that we think she may be attacked. If we believe this, we should recall all the other boats, too. Since SecDef doesn't want to do that, why not buck this question up to him for decision?"

"You mean just dump it in his lap and say, 'You decide it'? I'll be damned if I'll do that. This is a straight operational question involving the safety of one of our ships at sea. He is muscling in on our proper business more and more all the time. I've got to cut him in on this, of course. But this time I'm going to hand him our answer and say, 'Here's what I'm telling the *Nemo.*'"

"So . . . what will the answer be?" asked the Vice Chief.

"I want to give them an AFFIRMATIVE on this. We should have an answer from Kodiak within twenty-four hours on ice conditions off Point Barrow. If they are okay, I'll bring the *Nemo* back over the Pole."

"Do you think SecDef will go along with this?" asked the Vice Chief.

"I can see no reason why he shouldn't. It's a purely naval matter. The only possible objection is that it will delay getting the news to our technical people by eight to ten days. That means a lot of us, including me, will be chewing our fingernails down to the bone while we're waiting. But they will grow back. . . . If we tell *Nemo* to return to Holy Loch and she doesn't get back, we'll be in a hell of a mess. I'll go to bat with SecDef on this, if necessary. It doesn't concern the other services, or the State Department. I'm going over right now and tell him what I'm going to do. In fact, I'm going to tell him I've done it. That will make a real issue of it."

Soon CNO was in SecDef's office with the *Nemo*'s dispatch and his answer.

"What did the President say yesterday about the news from the *Nemo?*" asked the CNO.

"He was concerned about it, and wants to be informed as soon as we find out how the Russians are doing it."

"Did he make any comment on redeployment?"

"I told him what you want to do. But I didn't press him on that. I didn't want to burden him with details about possible trouble in the Arctic when he has plenty of real troubles, such as a shooting war in Vietnam, to worry about. The Security Council will take that up at their next meeting."

The Admiral handed him the latest message and the answer which he had drafted. "Here's some more on the *Nemo*," he said.

The Secretary studied the two dispatches. "How long a delay would this involve?" he asked.

"Eight to ten days, sir."

The Secretary considered for a moment and said, "This seems inconsistent with your recommendation to redeploy."

"I think it's the other way, sir," said CNO. "Both are based on the assumption that the Russians may be tempted to attack one or more of our ships."

"If there is reason for such a fear, then isn't it important to get *Nemo* home as soon as we can and find out what she can tell us?"

"It is important to get her home, sir. But if we take the threat seriously—and I do—it's more important to make sure she gets home. I'm willing to accept the delay."

"Admiral," said SecDef, "we have a great deal of information back here that your man on the *Nemo* does not have. There has been nothing in recent intelligence briefings to indicate the Russians might contemplate taking such a step as this. In fact, they seem to be thawing out a bit toward us."

"You're putting this in terms of global strategy now, sir," said the Admiral. "But our Skipper is confronted with a tactical situation involving the safety of his ship. The man on the spot is better able to judge such things than we are down here. Sometimes he can feel things in his bones that he can't put into a dispatch. Our Skipper has given us his best judgment on this matter, and I think we should back him up."

"Have you consulted the Joint Chiefs on this?" asked the Secretary.

"No, sir. There is no reason to do that. This is a purely naval operational matter."

"It's a matter that affects our whole defense posture," said the Secretary. "You have recommended redeployment on account of it. And it seems to me your proposed answer is based on an assumption which is not realistic. Going to Holy Loch, our ship will be on the high seas, where she has a perfect right to be. The Russians have ridden herd on her for three days and haven't molested her. Now you are assuming that they are willing to commit a flagrant act of war, right out of a clear sky."

"Of course, Mr. Secretary," said CNO, "I can't prove that the Russians intend to attack our ship. But now, for the first time since we deployed Polaris, they can do it. They can do it in such a way that we'll never know what happened. The stakes involved are so high that I feel we must take all possible precautions."

"I'm certainly in favor of all reasonable precautions," said the Secretary. "But we are urgently in need of more information. And now you are proposing something, for rather dubious reasons, which will delay getting that information by eight to ten days. I just can't see having our ship slink home with her tail between her legs as if she were doing something wrong. I want to be able to tell the Security Council what she has found out when they consider redeployment."

"Mr. Secretary, obviously I'm trying to read the Russians' minds, and that's a very difficult thing to do. But I think if I were in their shoes now, I would order my ship to destroy the American submarine."

The Secretary looked at the Admiral incredulously. "I'm astounded to hear a responsible officer make such an irresponsible statement," he said.

"I say, *IF* I were a Russian, sir. I'm not. And for that very reason, I can't tell our Captain to protect himself against such an attack. The only way he can protect himself is to shoot first, which we can't do. Events beyond his control and ours have put him in an impossible situation. The only way to get him out of it is to bring him home over the Pole. Then he gets in free, no matter what the Russian intentions may be. If we bring him back to Scotland, we should have destroyers meet him at the edge of the icecap and escort him."

"I think you are unduly alarmed, Admiral," said the Secretary. "I don't want this answer to go out. I take it that you brought it here for my approval?"

"No, sir. I have already released it. I think as a matter of courtesy I must inform you of what I am doing."

The Secretary considered this impasse for a few moments and then he said, "Admiral, I don't think you should send any message in a matter of this kind without my prior approval. In this case, I'm willing to compromise with you, against my better judgment. Change your answer to say, quote, unless you have solid reason to believe you are in danger, return to Holy Loch, unquote. I will reluctantly approve that."

"Mr. Secretary," said the CNO, "I will not be a party to any such . . . er . . . message. Our Captain has told us what he thinks, has made a recommendation, and asked us for a decision. I want to give it to him. It's wrong to throw it back in his lap. We have to give him a clear-cut answer one way or the other and accept responsibility for what comes of it. This is what my answer does."

"I want you to change it," said the Secretary, "and word the reply the way I have indicated."

"Mr. Secretary. I respectfully decline to do it unless specifically ordered to do so by the Commander in Chief."

"Would you mind repeating that?" asked the Secretary, reaching under his desk and switching on a tape recorder. "I didn't quite get it."

The Admiral repeated.

The Secretary got up from his desk, strode over to a window, and stood gazing out for a moment with his hands behind his back and his jaw set. Finally he turned and said, "John—what would you do if one of your subordinates refused to obey an order?"

"I would court-martial him, sir."

"Don't you think you are bound to obey orders, too?"

"Yes, sir. But in this case, the order will have to come from the President."

"Why?"

"Mr. Secretary, I see no point in trying to cite chapter and verse of the statutes in a case of this kind. Obviously, I think I'm within my legal rights, and consider that a grave matter of national security is involved. I have decided as I think best for the national interests of the United States. I will stick to that decision unless overruled by the President."

"It's going to the President. And I think you'll be overruled."

"Shall I go to the White House with you, sir?"

"No. If the President wants to see you he will send for you."

"The *Nemo*'s dispatch should be answered promptly, sir," said the CNO.

"It will be," said the Secretary, buzzing for an aide. "I want a car to the White House right away," he said. "Phone the White House and tell them I must see the President right away on an urgent matter."

As the aide bustled off, he added, "John—I want you to go back to your office and stand by for a call from the White House."

"Aye aye, sir," said the CNO.

"Just one more thing, Mr. Secretary," said Baker. "If you're going to pass the buck back to our Skipper this way I want to send destroyers up to the edge of the icecap to meet him and escort him to Scotland."

"I don't like your statement about passing the buck, Admiral," said the Secretary. "And I see no need for an escort. This would just be waving a red flag at the Russians."

Back in his office, the Admiral buzzed for the Vice Chief. "Get ready to take over this job, Hank," he said. "Temporarily, at least–maybe permanently."

"What happened?" asked the astonished Vice Chief.

"This is IT–the showdown. He says I can't send that answer to the *Nemo* without his approval. He wants me to change it and put in weasel words and dump the decision back in the Skipper's lap. I have declined to do it except on order by the President. He's on his way to the White House now to get the order."

"Do you think he will?"

"I'm almost sure of it. In a showdown of this kind between his SecDef and CNO, the President just about has to fire the one he overrules. It won't be SecDef."

"You've disagreed with SecDef before and gone to the White House about it without getting fired."

"Only on matters like the budget and the XFQ contract where he has the legal right to the final say. And those were things that he could feed into one of his goddam computers. This is different, and he knows it. He also knows the President will back him up, or he would never have taken it to the White House. He was even calling me John before I left him, and you know what that means around this town–when they start first-naming you, they're getting ready to stick a knife in your back!"

"So what happens now?"

"We'll get a call from the White House within the hour, and I think you'll be sitting in this chair before the day is over."

"I don't want the job. I won't take it," said the Vice Chief.

"Oh yes you will. You've got to take it. We can't afford to have another so-called admirals' revolt. All of us have to take jobs at one time or another in our career that we don't want. It's your duty to the country to take over if I get fired. After you've taken it, if something comes up that is too rich for your blood, you can do what I've just done. But if they ask you to, you've got to take over."

"I guess you're right, John," said the Vice Chief.

"I've got to get in and see the Secretary of the Navy, now, and tell him he had better start looking around for a new CNO. While I'm doing that, you hold the fort here in case a call from the White House comes in."

Ten minutes later, CNO was back in his office with the Vice Chief.

"How did the Secretary take the news?" asked Admiral Homer.

"It sort of shook him a little bit. I think he likes me and will be sorry to see me go. He even offered to go to bat for me with SecDef."

"What did you say to that?"

"I asked him not to. I told him his allegiance belonged on the political side and I didn't expect him to go to bat for me."

The squawk box on the Admiral's desk said: "White House on the green scrambler phone, sir."

The Vice Chief started to leave, but CNO motioned him to stay, and said, "Admiral Baker speaking."

After a moment's delay, he said, "Yes, Mr. President . . . yessir—a difference of opinion has come up on an operational matter. . . . Yessir, I feel the matter involved is of vital importance to the national defense. . . . Of course we have a right to be there, sir, but it will give the Russians a chance to sink our ship without warning, and the only way we can prevent it is to shoot first. . . . Yessir, I told him I would not change it unless the order came from you. . . . Aye aye, sir. It will be done as you say.

"I guess you heard enough of it to know what the answer is," said CNO as he hung up the phone.

"Yes," said Admiral Homer. "He's backing SecDef. Did he seem upset about your hassle?"

"No indeed. He just said he wants it done the way SecDef

says. He was quite calm and friendly about it—even called me John, so I figure I'm on my way back to the farm right now."

"We've got some good friends in Congress," said the Vice Chief. "Is it okay for me to alert them on what's cooking?"

"No. I want an airtight lid on this thing so far as anyone in a blue uniform is concerned. It will be leaked to the morning papers either by the White House or SecDef. The papers will be after us for our side of this, but I don't want a word out of anybody in the regular Navy on this except 'no comment.' Let SecNav handle it. . . . Now, who knows about the *Nemo*'s dispatch?"

"Just you and I and OP-03—except for the decoder and the Watch Officer . . . and while you were out, we got a message from Kodiak. They had made an ice recco yesterday, and the icecap is thirty miles from Point Barrow."

"Good. Here's the answer to *Nemo*."

CNO wrote on a dispatch form:

"To *Nemo:* Unless you have solid reason to believe you are in danger, return to Holy Loch."

"That's a hell of an answer, sir," said the Vice Chief.

"You're telling me! That's one reason why I squawked about it. From a military point of view, it's no answer at all. It throws the decision right back in the Skipper's lap. If anything goes wrong now, they can blame him. It stinks. But that's the way top-level decisions are being made in this country today. . . . Get this typed up and I'll take it to SecDef as soon as he gets back to his office."

Soon after SecDef returned, CNO was back in his office handing him the answer to the *Nemo*.

SecDef read it carefully and said, "This looks all right to me."

"I'd like to have you initial it, sir," said the CNO.

"I see no need for that. You have your orders from the President. That should be enough."

"He told me to send it the way you want it, sir. I want to be sure it is that way."

"I have told you it is."

"Then how about sending destroyers up there to escort him?" said the Admiral.

"No. I see no need for that."

"Aye aye, sir," said the CNO. "I've told you what I think," and started to leave.

The Secretary said, "Wait a minute, John. . . . I would like to have you take two weeks' leave, beginning now."

"Aye aye, sir. I'll be at my quarters beginning an hour from now. . . . Would you care to have my list of recommended candidates for the job of CNO?"

"Yes. Let me have your list, John," said SecDef, "and for the time being, I don't want the press to know about this."

"Mr. Secretary," said the Admiral, "the matter on which this hinges is top-secret and involves the safety of our ships. It could involve the peace of the world. You should know me well enough by now to know that I understand what TOP SECRET means and that I don't leak military information to the press."

"I'm not referring to the *Nemo* business," said the Secretary. "I mean the possibility of a change in CNO's."

"The two are so closely related you can't possibly separate them. If one gets out, the other will. I'll say nothing about either one, and I have directed my people to keep their mouths shut. But I'm sure you know as well as I do that this thing will be leaked–probably today. I think the leak will be either in your office or the White House."

"All right, John. That's all."

11

An hour later, up in the Arctic, the Exec came up to the cabin with a top-secret dispatch in his hand and a puzzled look on his face. "Here's our answer, Cap'n," he said. "They pass the buck right back to us."

"Well, I'll be a son-of-a-bitch," breathed the Captain, scanning the dispatch. "CNO never sent this. I know Admiral Baker well. I heard him cut his Chief of Staff off right at the ankles, one time out in the Pacific, for trying to give a destroyer an evasive answer and toss the buck back to them."

"I was surprised at this answer too," said the Exec.

"So now it's up to us. And the one thing we can be sure of is that whatever we do will be wrong. If we try to go back to Holy Loch and the Russians nail us, I'll feel bad about it. The rest of you guys will probably never speak to me again! But whoever sent this dispatch will be able to say, 'Hell, we gave him his choice. He just made a bad decision.' If we go back over the Pole, we'll never be able to prove we couldn't have made it the other way."

"That's right, Cap'n. Which way do we go?"

"This thing is worded so that I've got to have 'solid reason' for thinking we are in danger if I go back via the Pole. I told them quite plainly I think the Russian may attack us if we give him another chance. They obviously are not alarmed about it, and I have nothing more to base my fears on now than I had before. How nervous do you have to be to make a reason 'solid'? Hell, he sat on top of us for three days and didn't bother us–much. I'll be damned if I'm going to spend the rest of my life trying to explain why I dreamed up a hobgoblin that scared me so bad the U. S. Navy had to run from it."

"Well, we gave it a good try, anyway," said the Exec.

The Captain reached for a dispatch blank and a pencil, and wrote the following to CNO.

TOP SECRET
LAT. ________LONG. ________ Departing icecap for Holy Loch full speed at ________.

The Captain handed the Exec the dispatch, and said, "Here's our answer. As soon as we come out from under the icecap, put in the position and time and bat it out."

The Exec read the dispatch, nodded gravely, and said, "I'd do the same if I were in your shoes. But it's a hell of a way to run a Navy."

As he started to leave, the Captain said, "Wait a minute. Give me back that dispatch."

The Exec handed the paper back, and the Captain took up his pen and scratched out the words TOP SECRET. "Why do we have to be so cozy about this?" he asked. "We've got nothing to lose by sending it in plain English. It does give him our exact position, but he probably knows that now, anyway. And this way we let him know that this is a matter of public record."

"Aye aye, sir. Radio will be standing by to send this whenever you say."

"When we make our move, I want you up in the torpedo room, and I want tubes one and two reloaded with atomic warheads," said the Captain. "I want to keep the problem set up on the attack director, ready to shoot if I say so. But keep the outer tube doors closed until I tell you otherwise. We'll come out tomorrow morning."

"Aye aye, sir."

Next morning, all hands not on watch drifted into the crew's lounge. Normally half of them would be in their bunks at this time. But not today.

Everybody felt that a showdown might be coming up soon. Nobody was really worried about it. Smart lads like those in a Polaris crew don't worry about things that are beyond their control. Like the people who live on the slopes of Vesuvius, they live one day at a time. Maybe there will be an eruption someday, but worrying about it won't stop it. And they never expect it to be today. But there's no use trying to sleep when the mountain is rumbling.

The lounge room was unusually quiet today because nobody could think of anything he wanted to say right out loud.

Finally one of the new lads in the crew broke the silence. "Chief," he said. "We reloaded our torpedo tubes last night. . . . Why?"

"Well, son," said Murphy, "usually you do that so they'll be ready in case you want to shoot them at somebody."

"Hunh," said the lad. "I hope we haven't got any of those Yo-Yos that circle back, like you told us about the other night."

"Now you just let the torpedomen worry about that," said the Chief. "You do your job and let the other guy do his. I'll lay anybody a hundred to one odds that we don't blow ourselves up."

"Where will you pay off the winners, Chief?" asked an old hand in the crew.

"You're entitled to your own opinion about that, Mac," said the Chief. "But if you're not up there when I'm paying off, I'll send the money down to you."

Later that morning, in the control room, the Captain and Exec were studying the ice scope. The edge of the cap was just showing up across the front of the scope. Beyond the edge was open water cluttered with many patches of brash ice.

"There's the edge of the cap," observed the Exec. "We'll be up to it in another half hour."

"I want to surface when we get there," said the Captain. "But we'll have to be careful. Some of those blocks of brash weigh a couple of hundred tons. I don't want to nudge one too hard. Let's slow to five knots."

The Exec passed the word to the O.O.D. to slow down. "The sound room still has no sign of our Russian friend, Cap'n," he said.

"We've never been more than fifty miles from the edge of the cap," said the Skipper. "So if we've shaken him off, it gives us a good reading on how far he can track us—he picks us up somewhere beyond twenty miles, but not as far as fifty. Let's come out from under here at sunrise and stick a periscope up."

An hour later the *Nemo* eased gently up near the surface, just beyond the edge of the cap. As the top of the periscope broke surface, the Captain made a quick sweep around the horizon.

"Ice all around us," he announced. "Lots of good-sized chunks that will return solid echoes on either sonar or radar. Even if he's waiting out there somewhere, he'll never be able to sort us out from all the other echoes he'll be getting. Take her up."

As they broke surface, the Captain and Exec climbed out of the hatch into the top of the sail and surveyed the scene. The sun was still a few diameters below the horizon, but the light to the south was good. There was a fresh breeze from the north, a cloudless sky, and the air was clear and cold.

A few hundred yards astern of them the icecap stretched as far as the eye could see, the edge only a few feet above water. The cap itself was low and level, except where wind and wave had jammed the floes together here and there, and piled up debris along the seams. South of the cap, all around them, were hundreds of chunks of brash which had broken off the edge of the main floe. Some were no bigger than a tennis court. Others were the size of a football field.

"I think I'll slide our bow under that big slab dead ahead of us," said the Captain. "Then we can sit here and take it easy for a while with our sail just barely out of water."

"Aye aye, sir," said the Exec. "Do you want me to do it?"

"Yes. Take over—and remember that ice is like concrete."

As the Exec was easing up to the floe, word came up from the sound room: "Propeller noises—twin screws—three-bladed props, two hundred rpm. Sounds like the Russian again."

The two officers looked at each other gravely for a moment without speaking. Then the Exec said, "We didn't shake him after all. Do you still want to squirm under that floe?"

The Captain shrugged his shoulders, and said, "We might as well. Let's just sit there for a while. He won't see us."

Five minutes later the *Nemo* was snugly berthed with its nose tucked under the floe and the hatch leading down from the sail only a foot or so above water.

"He'll never spot us visually here," observed the Exec. "The sail only sticks up a couple of feet above the ice, and he'll stay a few miles south of the brash. He'll have sonar and radar echoes all over the place."

"Right," said the Captain. "I imagine he will patrol back and forth about ten miles south of the icecap waiting for us to start the reactor again."

"Screw noise getting louder," reported the sound room. "Bearing one two five, distance thirty thousand yards."

"Very well," said the Captain. "Fifteen miles to the southeast. How far away do you figure we can see him, Joe?"

"Ummmm. Let's see. We're nearly at sea level here. His mast isn't more than a hundred feet high. By the old thumb rule we should be able to see him at ten miles plus fifteen percent—eleven and a half miles, Cap'n."

"Check," said the Captain. "Judging from that last range and bearing, I'd say we ought to pick him up in about half an hour."

The Skipper and Exec both trained their binoculars on the horizon to the southeast. Very soon the Exec sang out, "I've got him! I can see his mast with a radar antenna on top of it."

The Captain took a quick squint at the Exec's glasses and aimed his own at the same spot. "Yep. There he is," he said.

"Those guys in the sound room must be way off on the range," said the Exec.

"Not necessarily, Joe," said the Skipper. "You often have freak refraction in this Arctic air. Sometimes you can see twenty or thirty miles beyond the horizon. You get strange mirages. I've even seen ships appear upside down beyond the horizon."

"Well, anyway. There he is again," said the Exec. "What do we do now?"

"He's got his search radar going," reported the O.O.D. from below.

"That won't help him much," observed the Captain. "I'll bet he runs right past us."

Pretty soon the sound room reported: "He has just started pinging."

"You see," said the Skipper, "just like we figured. He can't sort us out among all the radar blips he's getting. It'll be the same way with sonar, too. I'll bet he'll go on another ten miles or so."

Soon the destroyer's upper works came over the horizon and her masts and the top of her stacks were clearly visible to the southeast.

"You know, Captain," observed the Exec, "I've never really

doubted that the world is round. But until you've watched a show like this, you can't really be sure, either."

"Yep. I see what you mean, Joe. Let's get some more pictures when he gets a little closer. We'll have a fine silhouette of him against the southern sky."

Twenty minutes later the Russian cruised past them five miles to the south, keeping outside the brash ice and heading west at ten knots. A photographer got pictures with a telephoto lens and the two officers scanned his upper works with their glasses as he went by. "Look at that big radar dish just aft of the bridge," said the Exec. "We've got nothing like that on any of our cans. I'll bet that's what he picks up our reactor with."

"Could be," said the Captain. "He's got several things topside that I don't recognize. Our intelligence people will have a ball with these pictures."

As the destroyer began dropping below the horizon again, the Captain said, "Of course, we're just burying our head in the sand, lying here this way."

"Pretty cold sand, Cap'n," observed the Exec. "Why do you say that?"

"The only way we can get away from him is under the ice. We've been under it for two days. We moved east a hundred and fifty miles and came back west two hundred. But there he is, nearly on top of us again. So he has been tracking our reactor all the time and knows where we are within ten miles or so. We've already found out he's a real smart cookie. So as long as he gets nothing from our reactor, he knows we're not running submerged. He gets nothing on radar, so he knows we're either hiding among the brash here, or up against the bottom of the cap."

"He's a smart cookie, all right," agreed the Exec. "Smarter than many of our tin-can skippers."

"By now he knows that all he has to do is to patrol back and forth out there and wait. We've got to start our reactor again sometime, and when we do, he'll be right back on us again."

The Exec, watching with his glasses, could still see the top of the destroyer's masts. "He's reversing course now, Cap'n," he said.

"So there you are," said the Skipper. "He can't pinpoint us. But he knows we're not far away. Let's have the O.O.D. stand his watch up here till the sun gets up. Then I want to send that message to CNO, and we'll make our move."

"Aye aye, sir," said the Exec.

"What kind of warheads have you got on the fish now?" asked the Captain.

"Atomic."

"Okay. I'll be in the cabin," said the Skipper.

12

An hour later the Captain came to the bridge, and said, "I want to go down to four hundred feet and run south at full speed."

Soon the *Nemo* was at four hundred feet and working up to full speed. "Bearing oh nine five, range twenty-seven thousand yards," said the sound room. "He is increasing speed . . . rpm three-fifty."

The Captain stood looking over the Navigator's shoulder as he plotted the dope coming in from the sound room.

"I suppose he'll take up his regular station astern of us again," said the Navigator.

"Maybe," said the Captain.

Five minutes later the sound room reported: "He's speeding up. Rpm four hundred. Bearing one double oh, drawing ahead. Range twenty-five thousand yards."

Soon after that came the report: "Increasing speed some more. Rpm four-fifty. Still drawing ahead."

"He seems to have changed his tactics, Cap'n," observed the Exec. "I think he's going to pull up ahead of us this time."

"Looks that way," said the Captain. "What speed will four-fifty rpm give him?"

"Over thirty knots."

"Sound General Quarters," said the Captain. "Joe, I want you up forward in the torpedo room."

All stations were quickly manned and reported ready. The Exec went forward.

"Range twenty thousand yards, bearing one oh five. Still drawing ahead and closing."

"Start weaving," said the Captain to the helmsman. "Twenty degrees on each side of south."

From here on, the *Nemo* swung ponderously through arcs of forty degrees right and left, never steadying down on any one course.

The Captain pulled a cork-tip cigarette out of a pack, stuck the wrong end in his mouth, and lit it.

The Navigator debated for a moment and then said, "Wrong end, Captain."

The Skipper snatched the cigarette from his mouth, looked at it in disgust, and ground it out.

The Russian kept drawing ahead. The range was decreasing fast. In half an hour he was broad off the port bow and only three miles away. This is a position from which any torpedo-man figures he is looking down your throat.

The Exec called from the torpedo room over the battle phone and said, "I don't like the looks of what he's doing, Captain."

"Keep your shirt on, Joe," said the Captain, twisting a paper clip in two and dropping it in the trash can.

By this time all hands knew that there was something to be concerned about. Chief Murphy stood gripping the railing near the periscopes, eyeing the Captain, with his jaw set. A flake of dandruff hitting the deck in the control room would have made an audible thud.

"Start weaving in depth," said the Captain. "One hundred feet up and down from four hundred."

"NEW SCREW NOISES! SMALL HIGH-SPEED PROPS!" said the loudspeaker.

All eyes locked on the Captain. Everyone knew what that probably meant—TORPEDO.

"Very well," said the Captain coolly. "Ping on it. Keep the dope coming."

"Number one armed and ready, Captain," said the Exec over the battle circuit. "Shall I fire?"

"Negative," snapped the Captain. "Just stand by."

"Torpedo room, aye aye."

The Captain did a rapid mental calculation. "Six thousand yards—forty knots—I've got about two minutes to decide."

"Screw noises getting louder," said the sound room.

"OPEN THE TORPEDO TUBE DOORS," said the Captain over the battle circuit.

"Aye aye—opening doors," came the reply.

"DO NOT—REPEAT, NOT—FIRE UNLESS I TELL YOU."

"Aye aye, sir."

Then the sound room said, "Screw noise is decreasing—bearing is changing rapidly."

Chief Murphy's hands relaxed on the handrail. At this moment he happened to catch the Captain's eye. The two read each other's minds as old-timers can often do. . . . That torpedo was not on a collision course. Their number wasn't on it.

Suddenly a shattering blow hit the *Nemo*. It smashed light bulbs, staggered the ship as if she had hit a seamount, and threw all hands to the deck in the darkness. Some men were knocked cold. Others were stunned as a fighter is by a blow on the jaw. Broken glass showered down everywhere.

While the whole ship trembled like a bass drum from the first blow, deep rumblings like the crash of nearby thunder came in through the hull and more heavy blows smashed against it. The ocean jiggled like a bowl of jello. The ship was shaken as if by a violent earthquake.

As men scrambled back to their feet and shook their heads to unscramble their wits and see if they were still alive, the Captain's voice cracked out in the darkness: "BLOW MAIN BALLAST! TAKE HER UP!"

Chief Murphy and the Captain were the first ones back on their feet. The Chief flipped on his flashlight, shoved it into the Captain's hand and leaped to the steering station. The helmsman was lying unconscious across the top of the control column, thus throwing the after fins to the full nose-down position. Murphy dragged the limp figure off the control column, dropped it on the deck, and hauled back on the control column. Nothing happened.

"Planes are jammed, Captain," he yelled. "We have no control."

"Engines back full speed," said the Captain.

Murphy slapped the engine-room telegraph to full speed astern. After a couple of long seconds, the answering pointer from the engine room swung over to "full astern."

Back in the engine room, tense hands spun the ahead throttle closed and the astern throttle wide open. High-pressure steam smashed against turbine blades moving in the wrong direction. Rotors, gears, and shafts spinning at high speed tried to tear loose from their moorings as thousands of horsepower struggled to spin them the other way against their momentum and the windmill action of the propeller. The ship shook like a flag in the wind. The rotating machinery groaned to a stop and began turning the other way. The great five-bladed propeller scooped holes in the water as its blades churned through the flow of water coming the wrong way. Every shaft, nut, and bolt was stressed a little beyond the point where the designer's slide rules said they would break. But good designers always put in a little extra, and the *Nemo*'s were the best in the business. Nothing broke.

"Engines backing full speed, sir," said Murphy.

"Blow ALL ballast—full up angle on sail planes," said the Captain.

The lad on the sail-plane control, blood streaming from cuts by flying glass, spun his big wheel back against the stop.

"Rudder room shift to manual control on stern planes," said the Captain over the battle circuit. "Put them full up."

"Rudder room, aye aye. Shifting to manual control," came the groggy reply.

There was nothing more that anyone could do. The fate of the ship now hung in the balance as the churning propeller struggled to check the downward momentum of eight thousand tons. High-pressure air was blasting water out of the ballast tanks and making the ship buoyant. The sail planes were digging through the water trying to lift.

By now the ship was twenty degrees nose down from the jammed stern planes, and the angle was getting steeper. Men had to hang onto something to stand up.

A submarine with a lot of headway and a big down angle is in bad trouble, like an airliner that gets pointed down close to the ground. An airliner that can't pull out in time gets smashed into small pieces. A submarine that goes down below its pressure depth gets crushed like a beer can run over by a truck.

"Flippers are jammed," said the rudder room. "We can't move them."

"Keep trying," said the Captain.

With jammed flippers, the *Nemo* couldn't pull out of her dive as an airplane does. She had to check her headway before it took her too deep. She was already at a thousand feet, was thirty degrees nose down now, and was still forging ahead at fifteen knots. She was going deeper at the rate of seven hundred and fifty feet a minute. Even backing at full power, it would take a few more minutes to kill the momentum of eight thousand tons. And the nose was still going down.

By now emergency lights had come on, and throughout the ship, all hands were doing what they had been trained to do.

The battle circuit came alive with tense reports: "Small leaks in torpedo tubes–torpedo room tight" . . . "Missile section undamaged; no water" . . . "Engine room okay–need stretcher for injured man" . . . "Rudder room undamaged but flippers still jammed." Nothing vital had let go yet.

In the control room, as the down angle increased, everyone hung on to whatever they could and watched the three gauges on which their future depended: speed–angle–depth. The speed was down to ten knots. The angle was steady now at forty-five degrees. But the moving pointer in the depth gauge was only a hundred feet from the red hand marking crushing depth. It was still going down.

It soon became obvious it would go beyond the red hand.

"That red hand is just the builder's guarantee," said the Captain coolly. "You can always go deeper than that."

Three hundred feet beyond the red hand, the moving finger of the depth gauge stopped going down as the speed gauge finally registered zero. The speed gauge doesn't work going astern, but the laboring propeller soon started dragging the ship astern, and up. When the moving hand of the depth gauge again passed the red hand, going up, the pressure inside the boat may have gone up a little, too, as all hands let out the breath they had been holding.

The *Nemo*, like many other subs, had a St. Christopher's medal in a small glass case near the attack periscope. Polaris sailors are not superstitious or conspicuously religious, either. But like all gamblers who play for high stakes, they believe in working all the angles.

When the depth gauge started up, Chief Murphy shot a glance at the medal, which was certainly logged in heaven as a prayer of thanks.

"I think we've got her under control, Cap'n," he said.

"Not yet," said the Skipper. "We'll broach like a porpoise if we surface with any speed and this much angle on her."

When the depth gauge got to a thousand feet, the Skipper said, "Engines ahead one-third speed."

The rate of ascent began decreasing with the screw driving ahead again. As soon as the hand of the speed gauge started to lift off its peg and show headway, the Captain said, "Engine stop. From here on we'll float up." The depth gauge said three hundred feet.

A minute later the ship, still angled down thirty degrees, poked its stern up out of water. As more of the ship reared itself out of the depths, the stern fell into the water with a great splash, and the bow heaved up with white water cascading off its sides.

Nemo was surfaced, on an even keel, and in one piece.

The Captain took a quick sweep around the horizon with the periscope. "What the hell," he muttered, and took another slower sweep all the way around. Then he snapped down the handles on the scope and said, "Open the hatch. I'm going up. You come up too, Murphy."

As the Skipper and the Chief emerged from the hatch, an awesome sight met their eyes. Two miles to the south, where the Russian destroyer had been, there was a towering column of white stuff half a mile wide, reaching from the water up to about ten thousand feet. There it spread out into the familiar mushroom cloud of an atomic explosion. The top was boiling and billowing upwards.

The sea was confused and heaving. Large bubbles were coming up and bursting all around. A school of dead fish floated belly up nearby.

Great swells were rolling out from the bottom of the column as if a huge meteor had hit there. A deep growling noise came out of the north as the swells rolled under the icecap, lifting it, and breaking it into huge floes which ground against each other.

"Holy Mother of God," breathed Murphy.

The Captain stared wide-eyed at the cloud for a moment and then yelled down the tube, "Tell Commander Parker I want him up here right away."

"Do you think the Russian is behind that pillar of stuff, Cap'n?" asked the Chief.

"No. He's part of it."

As the Exec's head came up out of the hatch a minute later, the Captain said, "Why did you do it, Joe?"

"Do what, Captain?" asked the Exec, clambering out of the hatch.

"Why did you shoot?"

The Exec gaped at him in astonishment. "I didn't shoot."

"Go below, Murphy," said the Captain.

"Look," said the Captain, pointing to the south.

"My God," said the Exec.

"I gave you specific orders not to fire," said the Captain.

"I swear to God, I didn't fire, Captain!"

"Who the hell did, then?"

"Nobody, Captain! Our fish are still in the tubes. I was standing right there alongside the firing key all the time. Nobody touched it."

The Captain set his jaw, stared at the cloud for some moments, and said, "Thank God for that. But what the hell *did* happen?"

"I don't know . . . I thought we had been hit by his torpedo."

"We wouldn't be here now if we had," said the Captain.

"Yes. I realize that now. . . . Maybe he had a premature . . . or a circular shot . . . ?"

"Possibly."

"Do you think that thing ahead of us is what hit us, Cap'n?"

"I'm sure of it. The last range we had on him before the explosion was three miles. That's awfully close to fatal range for an underwater atomic blast. That's one reason why I held off firing. I was afraid we would take ourselves with him."

"He almost did take us with him," said the Exec.

By this time the mushroom cloud was extending overhead and rain began to fall.

"Let's get down out of here," said the Captain. "This stuff is probably radioactive."

As they climbed down the ladder into the control room, the O.O.D. said, "The torpedo room wants you and Mr. Parker to come up there, Cap'n."

As they went forward the Exec said, "It's probably about the tubes, Cap'n. That blast started leaks in both of them and we couldn't get the doors closed. If we had gone any deeper the leaks might have gotten away from us."

The Chief Torpedoman and four of his gang were standing alongside the tubes with grave faces. "We've lost both torpedoes, Cap'n," the Chief said.

The Captain leveled a cold look at the Exec. "Well?" he said.

"Captain, I swear to God we didn't shoot," protested the Exec.

"The retaining locks are broken in both tubes, Cap'n," said the Chief. He reached over and flipped a lever on the tube back and forth. "You can feel there's nothing in the tube on the other end of it. It's broken clean off. Same way on number two. Both doors are jammed open, sir."

"How did the torpedoes get out?" asked the Captain.

"We had a forty-five-degree angle on the boat," said the Chief. "With the locks broken there's nothing to hold them in. They just fell out of the tubes."

The Captain walked over and fiddled with the levers on both tubes. "When did you find this out, Chief?" he asked.

"Right after you sent for Mr. Parker," said the Chief. "After we got hit we were so busy with leaks and trying to close the doors that we failed to check on the fish. We just found out they're gone."

"Did we fire those torpedoes, Chief?" asked the Exec.

The Chief looked at him in amazement and said, "No, sir. You know we didn't, Mr. Parker. You were standing right here all the time."

"Don't you believe it, Captain?" asked the Exec.

"Yes. I believe it," said the Captain. "But the big question is, will they believe me when we get home and I tell this story? . . . Would the starting lever trip on those fish when they fell out?"

"No, sir."

"In that case they would sink. Right?"

"That's right, Cap'n."

"Also—if they don't start they don't arm. Do they?"

"Nosir. Both those fish are on the bottom of the ocean. Unarmed."

"Well . . . that's a new piece of gear for Davy Jones to put in his locker," said the Skipper. "Let's go aft, Joe. I want to cruise through that explosion area and see what we can see."

Half an hour later they were cruising slowly through the area where the white column had been. The Captain was at one scope, the Exec at the other. The white column was gone, and the great mushroom cloud was trailing off downwind.

By now everyone on the ship knew what had happened.

"I don't see a thing," said the Captain.

"Me either," said the Exec.

"Of course, you wouldn't expect to. Everything on that ship became radioactive particles in a millisecond."

The Doctor, who was standing nearby, spoke up and said, "Speaking of radioactive particles, I think you probably got some of them on you. I don't like the looks of your radiation badge."

"What's the matter with it?" demanded the Captain.

"It's changing color. You've been exposed."

"We got rained on a little bit, up in the sail."

"That's what did it, then. You've got to take a warm shower right away with lots of soap—and throw those clothes overboard."

"Wait a minute, Doctor. I wore this jacket on the *Nautilus* when we went over the Pole."

"It's got to go, Cap'n."

"Okay. Commander Parker and Chief Murphy got rained on, too."

"How about a message reporting what has happened, Cap'n?" asked the Exec.

"Yes," said the Captain. "As soon as we change clothes, come into the cabin and we'll draw one up . . . just the bare bones of what has happened. And I don't want to send it while we're still in this area."

13

At the time when the *Nemo* was emerging from under the ice-cap, the Security Council met in the Cabinet Room of the White House. Seated at the long table, awaiting the President, were the Vice President, Secretary of State, Director of the Office of Emergency Planning, the President's Special Assistant for National Security, and the Executive Secretary of the Council. These were the regular members who attended every session of the Council. At each meeting, other high officials having an interest in the subject matter were summoned to attend. This morning, the head of the CIA and the Vice CNO had been called in.

No aides or secretaries of the garden variety were present. Each place at the table had a mike in front of it, hooked to a tape recorder. A technician from the White House staff sat at a control console near the end of the table to flip switches and record what was said at each mike. The only figure in Washington with a better security rating than his was the marble statue of Admiral Farragut in the square next to the Army-Navy Club.

In the passageway outside the Cabinet Room were several dozen top-flight aides, special assistants, and technical experts brought along by the actual members of the Council. All were important officials who had plush reception rooms outside their offices where other pretty big wheels could wait their turn to get in. This morning, it was their turn to stand by. They might be called into the Cabinet Room briefly if their principals needed to consult with them. But they didn't stay after answering questions.

Also in the passageway was the Army captain in civilian clothes who carried the black brief case with the atomic code authenticators for the day chained to his wrist.

There was no small talk around the table in the Cabinet Room while waiting for the President. The makers of national policy had their morning papers open to their favorite columnist, trying to find out what the pundits were saying this morning about the war in Vietnam, the situation in South Africa, or anything else on which they needed guidance about world opinion.

In the Executive Office next to the Cabinet Room the President and Secretary of Defense were having a cup of coffee before the meeting.

"Mr. President," said SecDef, "I have decided I've got to get another CNO."

"Oh?" said the President. "What's the matter with Baker?"

"He's insubordinate," said the Secretary. "I can't depend on him. He didn't want to wait for this meeting before taking action on that Polaris business. . . . I've got him at home now—awaiting orders."

"All right," said the President. "Have you picked your new man?"

"Not yet. I've got several in mind, but I want to check their past performance before I make up my mind."

"There must be plenty of up-and-coming admirals who

would be glad to get the job," observed the President. "Pick a good one."

"I will," said SecDef. "But the way things are shaping up now, the right type for CNO is not too easy to find. Too many of these young admirals think that as long as they know how to handle a fleet of ships without causing collisions, they are qualified for high command. . . . And, of course, in this atomic age, the CNO doesn't really have to know anything about running a fleet."

"Nothing?" asked the President.

"Well—very little, anyway. The people at sea have to, of course. But the CNO is just a logistics man and an administrator these days. Naturally, he'll know something about ships from his background. But when he gets up on this level, dealing with billions of dollars and matters that affect the national economy, this is apt to be a handicap rather than a help to him. That was one of Baker's main troubles. He didn't see the broad picture."

"Is Admiral Baker going to go quietly, or will he raise a fuss about it?" asked the President.

"I can't tell yet. So far, he hasn't shown any signs of making trouble—except for being insubordinate about the *Nemo*."

"The Navy has powerful friends in Congress," observed the President. "Some of them would be glad to embarrass the Administration, you know. So make sure you keep this on the right level . . . civilian control of the military. . . . The press will back us up on that score."

"Yessir. That's exactly the level I've got it on now. That's where I'm going to keep it."

Soon the door of the Cabinet Room opened, and the President and SecDef entered. Everyone dropped their newspapers and stood up.

"Good morning, gentlemen," said the President.

"Good morning, Mr. President," came the reply, and everyone remained standing till the President took his seat at the head of the table.

"All right," said the President to the Director of the CIA. "What secrets have you got for us today that aren't in the morning paper yet?"

The CIA Director read through two pages of bulletins from all over. One reported a secret deal being made by Saudi Arabia to get twenty MIG airplanes from the Russians in exchange for oil. Another told of an impending coup by the military in South America which would throw out a pro-Communist regime. The Director added an aside, saying that although CIA thoroughly approved, they were not promoting this coup. Heads around the table nodded knowingly. A third item was about a stormy meeting of the Politbureau behind closed doors in the Kremlin where two high party officials were accused of high crimes against the party. CIA said that their transfer to minor jobs in faraway places would be announced soon. And so on through a dozen brief items, all loaded with hot information.

Some of these items came from good legwork and alert observation which could have been done by any well-trained reporter on the scene. Some came from wire taps and bugs in unlikely places, some from double agents, and some were bought for cash on the line. All had been well cross-checked and verified before they got into the White House bulletin. Some items were of such nature that obviously cloaks, and maybe daggers, were involved in getting them, but everyone around the table had sense enough not to ask questions about that. The National Security Council has a much higher regard for CIA's reliability than the general public has. CIA's rare bloopers like the Bay of Pigs are its only activities that get into print. And all present knew that CIA could, but wouldn't, prove that everybody in the government, except the JCS, had a hand in the Bay of Pigs fiasco and were at least as wrong as CIA had been.

When the CIA finished, SecDef gave a brief summary of the latest action reports from Vietnam—so many U.S. casualties

–so many enemy, by actual dead count–so many bombs on military targets near, but outside, Hanoi–so many planes shot down and so many air crewmen missing. SecDef summed up his report by stating, "All military operations are proceeding as planned, we are winning the military war on all fronts, the increase in draft calls next month will be only slightly larger than we had anticipated.

"Now, gentlemen," he continued, "a new matter in another area has just come to my attention which may affect the combat readiness of our retaliatory forces in the cold war. I have asked the Vice Chief of Naval Operations to brief you on it. . . . Admiral Homer."

"Mr. President and gentlemen," said Admiral Homer. "Up to now, we have regarded our Polaris weapons system as invulnerable. Until a few days ago, no one had ever succeeded in finding and tracking one of our Polaris submarines. On our own exercises, where we set things up so our destroyers would find a Polaris boat, the sub always succeeded in shaking them off without any trouble. Last week, we got a report from the USS *Nemo*, patrolling in the Arctic Ocean, that a destroyer–identified as Russian–had picked them up and tracked them closely for three days. Despite all the evasive maneuvers they could take, the destroyer stayed on top of them until they finally got rid of him by going under the Arctic icecap. Our captain reports that he thinks that his atomic reactor is what enabled the destroyer to track him. We do not see how this is possible, and he didn't explain it. We ordered him to return to Holy Loch, and sent our top experts up there to meet him and examine his records and his plant. Meantime, we thought it advisable to recall . . ."

"I'll take over now," interrupted SecDef. "The Navy has sixteen other Polaris submarines patrolling in the Arctic. These are an important part of our deterrent force. The Navy thinks it advisable, until we find out more from the *Nemo*, to redeploy these ships in the Atlantic west of Scotland. This will move the ships a thousand miles back from their targets, and some of the assigned targets will be out of reach. The Air Force has offered to take over these Navy targets. The Joint Chiefs have considered this reassignment of targets and have approved. The Navy wishes to redeploy right now. However, I see no urgency about redeploying, and prefer to wait until the *Nemo* gets into Holy Loch and we have a chance to analyze and evaluate her data."

"When will the *Nemo* arrive at Holy Loch?" asked the Secretary of State.

"The day after tomorrow. After she gets in, if we still can't put our finger on what has happened, I intend to redeploy the other ships until we do find the trouble. Since this involves our readiness to retaliate, I felt it advisable to bring the matter up before the Security Council."

"Will the strategic targets still be adequately covered if we redeploy?" asked the Sectretary of State.

"Quite adequately," said SecDef. "Even allowing for a fifty-percent loss of our delivery vehicles by a sneak attack."

"In that case," said SecState, "and since we will be doing this on our own initiative, secretly, and setting no international precedent, I see no objection to it. . . . I must say, though, that if I were in your shoes, I think that just to be on the safe side I'd redeploy right away, until we find out more about this thing."

"There are many factors involved in this," said SecDef. "And after considering them all, I think it best to wait a day or so."

"All right," said the President. "You have our approval to handle this matter as you think best. . . . Anything else on the agenda?" he asked of the Executive Secretary.

Before the Executive Secretary could answer, Admiral Homer spoke up. "Sir, don't you think we should mention the *Nemo*'s request to return over the Pole?"

SecDef frowned and glanced at the President. The President shrugged his shoulders and then said, "Yes. Let the Secretary of Defense tell us about that."

The Secretary thought for a moment, and said, "After we

ordered the *Nemo* to Holy Loch and while under the icecap, she sent a message requesting permission to return to Alaska via the North Pole. The message said they were afraid that if the Russian destroyer found them again, it would attack them. No reason was given for this apprehension. I was reluctant to approve this, because it would take eight to ten days longer to return that way, and I feel it is urgent for our technical experts to get aboard the ship and analyze their data. However, I did give the Captain authority to decide for himself. We told him that if he had solid reason for thinking he would be attacked, he could return via the Pole. We have no further word from him, so I assume he is carrying out his original orders. He should arrive at Holy Loch the day after tomorrow, and then we will decide what to do about the other ships."

The Secretary of State had been frowning and studying his fingernails closely. When SecDef finished, he squinted one eye, leveled a sharp glance at Admiral Homer, and said, "Admiral, I know very little about submarines, but I see you wear the submariner's insignia. I want to ask you some perhaps foolish questions."

"Yessir," said Admiral Homer.

"If the Russians decided to attack our boy, what chance would they have of sinking him?"

"An almost sure chance," said Admiral Homer. "The *Nemo* would be a sitting duck. His only chance of survival would be to shoot first."

"I assume you have not authorized him to do that?"

"Nosir."

"Suppose the Russian did attack our ship. How would we find out about it?"

"She would simply turn up missing. We would never hear from her again."

"Would she be able to tell us she was being attacked?"

"Probably not. Almost certainly not."

"Would there be any survivors—or perhaps floating wreckage?"

"No, sir. There might be an oil patch on the water for a few days, but that's all."

"Thank you, Admiral," said SecState. He resumed his study of his fingernails for a moment, and then said, "Mr. President, this situation is made to order for the Russians. They can destroy our ships without trace and we'll have no way of proving it."

"I thought you said last week that relations with the Kremlin were getting better," said the President, "that they were showing signs of becoming friendly. Why should they attack one of our ships?"

"The Russians can change tactics overnight, if they think it's to their advantage. This is a chance for them to hurt us at no risk to themselves. We would never be sure what happened to our ship. You know of course that they have no morals. They are cold-blooded, practical, and ruthless. I think if we give them a nothing-to-lose chance like this, they'll grab it."

"You really think they would destroy our ship?" asked the President, incredulously.

"I certainly do."

"I must say I agree with the Secretary," said the CIA Director.

"Now," continued SecState, "at the present stage, this is really Defense Department business. Our ships have a legal right to be where they are—they have been there for some years, and the Russians have never said anything about it. So State really has no responsibility in this matter yet. . . . But if one or more of our ships disappear, then State and everybody else will be in it up to their ears. I gather from what has been said that the *Nemo* has already started back to Holy Loch, so there's no use discussing that part of it. But I do feel that we ought to get the rest of our ships out of the Arctic right now—for the time being."

"What do you think, Admiral?" asked the President.

"I agree with the Secretary," said Admiral Homer. "As things stand now, our ships are vulnerable to being sunk without trace; they can't fight back; and I recommend pulling them back until we find out more about this."

"Mr. President," said SecDef, "if our ships are vulnerable in the Arctic, they are just as vulnerable anywhere else. If we are going to pull them out of the Arctic, we should logically pull them all the way back to our own shores. I want to wait until we know more about this before taking such a drastic step."

"All right. I agree to that," said the President. "In the present stage, this matter is primarily Defense Department business. I'll let you handle it your way."

As they were leaving the Cabinet Room after the meeting, the Secretary of State said to the Vice CNO, "Where is Admiral Baker this morning?"

"Oh . . . uh . . . he's on leave, sir," said the Vice CNO.

"Hmmmm," observed SecState.

14

Soon after secure from General Quarters, the boys began gathering in the crew's lounge. Almost all had been thrown flat on their faces or slammed up against something by the first impact. There were many bloody shirts, faces with cuts and bruises, and numerous black eyes. They looked like a bunch of sailors who had just been in a waterfront barroom brawl. All were well aware that the *Nemo* had come very close to joining the *Scorpion*, and that they were lucky to be alive.

"I take it all back what I said about the Marines the other day," announced Miggs. "I think maybe I will ship over with them next time, after all."

"I don't see what you got to bellyache about," said a pal. "I don't see any cuts or bruises on you."

"No. I was lucky," said Miggs. "Johnson was standing right in front of me when we got hit. He got slammed into the bulkhead and I got thrown into him."

Johnson had two big black eyes to confirm this story. "Yeah," he said. "Just getting slammed into the bulkhead would of been bad enough. But then this guy comes into me like a blitzing linebacker."

"That was a hell of a wallop we got," said Miggs. "I wonder how close they came to really getting us?"

"Aw, it didn't do much real damage. It busted a lot of glass. It started some small leaks in the torpedo tubes and jammed the doors open. But it didn't do any damage at all to the pressure hull."

"Well, it felt like the Empire State Building fell on us. These boats must be built like a concrete craphouse."

"They are. But of course you gotta remember that explosion was damn near three miles away from us. I got a ping on him just before it hit us," said a sonar man.

"Holy cow! Three miles!"

"Yeah. They say that's just about the edge of the blast area. In an airburst everything out to three miles from ground zero just disappears. But we had three hundred feet of water over us, so it was like being in a deep bomb shelter."

"Except that it wasn't an airburst anyway. You could feel the whole ocean quaking for half a minute afterwards. It must of been right on the water."

The lad who had been on throttle watch in the engine room spoke up: "I took off from my stool like a guy being shot out of a cannon, and smacked into the instrument panel. It knocked me as silly as a gooney bird. While I was still trying to figure out what happened, I heard the backing bell, so I got up, flipped the handle on the telegraph to full astern, slammed the ahead throttle shut and spun the stern throttle wide open."

"How the hell could you see to do that with all the lights out?" demanded a listener.

The engine man regarded him scornfully. "Hell, I was seeing so many stars it lit up the whole engine room. And besides, every time I come on watch, I practice finding all the controls with my eyes shut. I don't need no lights to do my job. I could feel the pointer on the telegraph was at full astern. I knew you don't go from full ahead to full astern just for the fun of it, so this was a real emergency. But I thought those turbines were going to tear right loose from their moorings when I shot the astern steam to them. The whole engine room shook like a mixmaster."

"Hunh," observed another. "If you think you got shook up, you should of been back in the rudder room where I was. When that big propeller started churning the wrong way and tearing the ocean apart I thought I was inside a dice box. I heard the flipper motor going full blast, and then it stopped with a bang and blew the fuses . . . flippers jammed up against the stops. We had a hell of a time getting them loose and connecting up the hand gear."

"What are you looking so sad about, Joe?" asked one of the boys of a reactor man who had said nothing, so far. "Where were you when it happened?"

"I had been playing chess with that wardroom mess boy," said Joe. "I been playing him ever since this cruise started, and the best I've been able to do is get two draws out of about a dozen games. But today I had him beat cold–checkmate in two more moves, and he knew it. He was just about to give up and concede when General Quarters went . . . then WHAM . . . The whole game got knocked to hell and gone, and we'll never be able to set it up again. I guess I just ain't living right."

"Well, I'll be gahdam," said his friend. "The whole bunch of us almost got knocked into Davy Jones' locker, and you're bellyaching because it broke up your chess game. Ain't that the iron knee of fate!"

At this point, Chief Murphy entered, and all eyes centered on him. "What did you see up there on deck, Chief?" asked one of the lads.

"Boy, it looked like the end of the world. Just like the picture of the Bikini explosion, except this one was live, and in color. Just looking at it scared the hell out of me."

"What happened to the Russian?"

"He just disappeared off the face of the earth—atomized. Not a thing left of him."

"Gawd almighty! How do you think it happened?"

"He must of blew himself up. He shot at us and hit himself."

"Are you sure we didn't let him have it?" asked the lad from the reactor room.

"Hell no—we didn't let him have it," said a torpedoman indignantly. "I was standing between the tubes all the time. We had 'em loaded and ready, but never fired. Both our fish were still in the tubes when we got hit. But that wallop busted the locks, and they slid out after we got that big down angle on the boat."

"Hell," said a sonar man. "If they had fired one of our fish, we would of heard it in the sound room. The only thing we heard was the Russian torpedo."

"How could you tell it was a Russian fish and not one of our own?"

"By the sound, for one thing. I know what our fish sound like, and this wasn't one of them. It was a different pitch, and a four-bladed prop. Ours are two. And if we had fired one of our own, we would of heard it and felt it when it left the tube. And besides, we got a tape of the whole business. From the time they fired the fish to the explosion was thirty-five seconds. The range was six thousand yards. No torpedo ever built can go three miles in half a minute. So it was his own fish that got him. You can bet your ass on that."

"I was standing right next to the Captain," said Murphy. "Just before we got hit, and after we heard the Russian torpedo, he told the torpedo room to open the doors, but not to fire. I heard him."

"Do you think they'll believe that when we get home and tell them?"

"They better believe it," said Murphy. "They won't know a damn thing about this except what we tell them."

"That son-of-a-bitch tried to sink us, didn't he?"

"Well," said Murphy, "I think he did. But when you come

right down to it, we don't know. All we know is he put something in the water that made noises like a torpedo and soon after that there was a hell of an explosion and we didn't see him any more. You can do a lot of supposing about what happened, but those are the only things we're sure of."

"Does this mean we are at war with Russia now?"

"No. I wouldn't say so. After all, the Russians don't know what happened—never will, unless we tell them. And they probably wouldn't believe us if we do."

"What are we supposed to do if another Russian comes along? After all, this guy tried to sink us. He must of had orders to do it."

"The answer to that question is very simple, son," said Murphy. "We just do whatever the Captain tells us to. That's all. This is a hell of a risky game we're playing with all those atom bombs we've got aboard. And one thing is for sure. The country has got to be able to depend on us to do just exactly what we are told. No more—no less."

There was a pause while the boys digested that bit of wisdom. Finally one of them spoke up: "How did this compare with some of those depth charge attacks you were telling us about, Murph?"

"That first wallop was much worse than any depth charge I ever felt. It would have split the hull of any of the old boats. But ours is twice as thick as they were. . . . I never felt anything before like the way the ocean shook. TNT doesn't do that. But in a way, this wasn't as bad as depth charges, because they keep slugging away at you for maybe an hour or more, and the air gets foul and full of chlorine gas. This one was just one big wallop and it was all over."

"The hell you say. I didn't figure it was over till the hand on the depth gauge quit going down. But I began to think it would be over soon when we went right on past the red hand! You mean to say you weren't worried when we were pointed at the bottom with all that headway on?"

"Well, yeah," conceded Murphy. "That was a kind of itchy

five minutes right after we got hit, when we had that big angle on the boat. And I hope you guys all know that the Skipper did a big-league job of ship handling to get us out of that. It's easy enough to look back now and say, 'Hell, he did the only thing that could be done.' But he did it before anyone else even knew we were in trouble. If he had taken as much as twenty seconds to make up his mind, it might have been too late. If we had gone a couple of hundred feet deeper, it could of been the end of us."

"I don't ever want to be any closer to an atomic explosion than we were to that one," observed one of the boys.

"Hunh," said another. "When the big blitz comes, if it does, I'd just as soon be at ground zero. It will be a pretty grim world to live in afterwards—won't it, Murph?"

"I don't know," said Murphy. "Before World War II, if anyone had predicted what was going to happen to London, Hamburg, and Tokyo and had said people could live through it and go on about their business, everyone would have said he was crazy. Human beings can survive some gawdawful punishment if they have to. Personally, I do want to survive the big blast—just out of morbid curiosity to see how the hell it all comes out."

While this was going on in the crew's lounge, the Captain and Exec were showering and changing clothes. Then the Exec came into the cabin to help frame a dispatch to CNO.

The Exec was still shaken from their narrow escape, from learning that the torpedoes were missing, and from the Captain's jumping to the conclusion that he had fired them.

"Captain," he said, "—are you satisfied now that I did not fire those torpedoes?"

"Yes, I am, Joe," said the Captain.

"I'll admit my finger was pretty itchy, and I wanted to," said the Exec.

"I understand that, Joe," said the Skipper. "So did I. But some good angel kept me from doing it."

"I think we should have fired," said the Exec.

"Maybe so," said the Skipper. "But there's no use in debating about that now. We didn't. Thank God."

"That son-of-a-bitch deserved exactly what he got," said the Exec.

"He sure did," replied the Skipper. ". . . Now, let's rough out a dispatch to CNO. I'm not going to put too much in this dispatch, because there's always one chance in a million the Russians may be reading our codes. I'll give the gory details to CNO by word of mouth."

"It's going to be pretty hard to tell the story in a short dispatch," said the Exec.

"Yes. I know. But the only thing that's urgent is to tell them we've been attacked. The rest can wait. We'll be at Holy Loch in two days."

A few minutes later, after several rough drafts, the Captain took a new dispatch blank and wrote:

> Destroyer identified as Russian in Lat. 70–15, Long. 02–10W at 1000 made sounds indicating he had fired torpedo. One minute later *Nemo* thrown out of control by tremendous blow. Recovered control just before reaching crushing depth. Upon surfacing noted mushroom cloud as from atomic explosion where DD had been. No trace of destroyer or wreckage. Believe he blew himself up. Continuing to Holy Loch.

"I think that tells them all they need to know until I can give them the rest in person," said the Captain.

"You don't want to mention our torpedoes?"

"No."

"Shall I send it now?"

"Not yet. I want to get out of this area before I do. I don't want to send a radio that Russian direction finders can pick up and put us at the scene of the crime. And I also don't want to get another Russian on our back. So I'm going to keep radio silence until we get nearer England, where they won't be able to sort us out of the other traffic."

"It will delay getting word to Washington," said the Exec.

"Yes. I know. But it will take the Russians a couple of days to realize their ship is gone. I don't think getting word to Washington is urgent enough to break radio silence . . . and, Joe, get the crew together in the lounge room. I want to cut them in on what's happening."

"Aye aye, sir," said the Exec. "I'll have them there in about ten minutes . . . and just one question, Captain."

"Yes?"

"What are you going to do if another one of those bastards gets on us?"

"I can't tell you ahead of time, Joe. We'll just have to play it by ear and cross that bridge when we come to it."

"It seems to me we're at war now, and we ought to act accordingly," said the Exec, and he strode out of the cabin and went forward to assemble the crew.

While the crew was assembling, the Doctor dropped into the cabin.

"Well, Captain," he said, "it looks like the good Lord was guiding you today when you held off on firing our torpedoes."

"I doubt if the good Lord Himself has time to bother about the things we do down here on earth," said the Skipper. "But my guardian angel was sure on the job."

"So what's the score now in the mutual coexistence business?" asked the Doctor.

"The score is one Russian destroyer is missing. They'll never know what happened to her unless we tell them. If we do tell them, they won't believe it. The Russians will probably always think that we did it."

"You know," said the Doctor, "if the Russians try to make anything of this, we might fire a countercharge back at them and say, 'One of our subs is missing. We think you did it.'

We might claim the ship and the sub destroyed each other. They would never know the difference."

"Hmmmm. That's an idea. It would work for the Russians, if they were in our shoes. But we can't lie well enough with a straight face. Remember how we got tagged out on the U-2 when we tried it?"

"Cap'n," said the Doctor, "I think this thing is going to be a blockbuster in the Pentagon. . . . We called the turn on what was going to happen too accurately. We said we thought we might be attacked if we returned to Holy Loch, and asked permission to return via the Pole. We got turned down. There may be some high-level scrambling now, to cover up."

"Could be," said the Captain. "But I don't think it will be in the Navy. I'm sure CNO didn't originate that dispatch to us. It came from higher up. I doubt if the JCS would use the weasel words that were in it. It must have come from either SecDef or the White House."

"That makes it all the worse."

"Why?"

"I think if a military man originated the dispatch, he would take the rap for it. Politicians will try to squirm out of it. They can say, 'We gave you your choice as to which way to come back. You just made the wrong choice.'"

"I doubt it," said the Captain. "This thing will be too big for that kind of stuff. They will be too busy trying to figure out how to preserve the peace of the world to get into any hassle about who dropped the ball."

"I'm not so sure about that, sir," said the Doctor. "Politicians can always convince themselves that what's good for their party is good for the country. If this message originated on a political level, I think they will try to put the finger on you for not coming home over the Pole."

"Hell. They practically said, 'Don't get frightened, little boy.' Anyone who came back over the Pole after getting that message ought to be sent to some quiet ammunition dump in the backwoods where nothing ever happens for the rest of his naval career. He's got no business playing in a rough game like this one out here."

"I must say you played it real cool today, Cap'n," said the Doctor.

"Just between you and me, Doctor," observed the Captain, "I was mentally flipping a nickel to see whether I should shoot or not when we got hit. . . . I sometimes think man has damn little control over his destiny on this earth."

"I think it's about the same up on the summit level, too," observed the Doctor, "when you get into one of those confrontations like the Cuban Missile Crisis to see who blinks first. Chance plays a big part. Maybe Khrushchev blinked because he got a flea in his eye."

The phone buzzed. It was the Exec reporting the crew was assembled.

15

A few minutes later the Captain was addressing the crew in the lounge.

"I got you together," he said, "to tell you we are on our way back to Holy Loch, and to cut you in on what I know so far. Each of you knows your own part of this story, but I'm the only one who has it all."

The Skipper then ran briefly through what the reader already knows, but which each of his listeners knew only the way the blind men in the fable knew what the whole elephant was. At the end, he said, "Finally, I want to give all hands a 'well done' for the way you did your jobs today. As you all know, we had a very close call. If any one of you had made even a small slip, we might not be here now. I'm proud of you. . . . Any questions?"

"Yessir, Cap'n," said a torpedoman. "Are we at war with Russia now?"

"No," said the Captain. "We don't know whether he had orders to sink us, or tried to do it on his own hook."

"Do you think this is going to start a war, sir?"

"No. I don't think so," said the Captain. "They may never know what happened to their ship. They may even assume we blew it up, and that might help avert a war. I think it would make good sense to the Russians for us to blow up their ship, if we could do it without leaving any bloody fingerprints. That's the way they play the game. I'm sure it would surprise and shock them to think we had done it. It might even make them respect us more . . ."

At this point the phone from the control room rang. Murphy answered and handed it to the Captain.

"Captain speaking," he said. ". . . What's the range? . . . What is he doing? . . . Okay. Reverse course to north. Put on full speed. I'll be back there in a minute."

He handed the phone to Murphy to put back on the hook.

"We have just made a small change of plans," he said to the crew. "Another destroyer has turned up, heading this way. We have reversed course to go back under the icecap and return to the U.S. via the North Pole and Bering Strait. They want me up in the control room now. I'll tell you more later."

Back in the control room, the Captain scanned the compass, depth and speed gauges. They showed course north, depth six hundred feet, and full speed.

"What do you hear now?" he called over the squawk box to the sound room.

"Twin screws, three-bladed props, three hundred rpm. Bearing due south, range thirty-five thousand yards," came the reply.

"How far was he when you first picked him up?"

"Forty thousand yards."

"We reversed course a few minutes ago. Is he still closing?"

"Yessir. Coming right at us and closing about a hundred yards a minute."

"How far ahead is the icecap?" asked the Skipper of the Navigator.

The Navigator stepped off the distance while the Exec peered over his shoulder. "Twenty miles," he said.

The Captain did some mental arithmetic and said, "We'll be under the cap in less than an hour . . . he'll still be at least ten miles from us . . . he can't reach us with a torpedo."

"How about rockets?" asked the Exec. "We've got anti-sub rockets that will go over ten miles. They must have them too."

"I know we've got them," said the Skipper. "But I don't think the Russians have. . . . Otherwise, that other guy would have used them."

"Maybe. . . . Maybe not," said the Exec.

"Range thirty-three thousand, five hundred," said the sound-room squawk box. "Closing slowly."

"He won't catch us," said the Captain.

"No. But he'll get within rocket range," said the Exec, pushing the Navigator aside and bending over the chart board.

"He hasn't got rockets," said the Captain.

"I wouldn't bet on that," muttered the Exec, picking up the dividers and measuring the distances to the destroyer and the icecap.

"Range still closing slowly," said the sound room.

The Exec tapped the chart table a few times with the points of the dividers, then slapped them down, wheeled around, and said, "Captain–what do you make of this? How come this new guy found us so fast?"

"By coincidence," said the Captain. "I think he was on his way up here to relieve the other one. The other guy had been on us for over a week. Most of the time he was running at high speed. He must have been getting low on oil. I think this one was coming up to take over from him and got here just a little too late."

"Do you think he has orders to get us?" demanded the Exec.

"Of course he has–the same orders the other guy had. . . . But he won't catch us."

The Exec turned back to the chart table and stood with his feet apart, staring at the chart with an angry scowl on his face. His jaw was set and his hands gripped the chart board so hard his knuckles were white.

"That other son-of-a-bitch almost did get us," he said.

"Sure," said the Captain. "But he didn't. What else is new?"

"It was just the grace of God that saved us," said the Exec. "We're lucky to be alive."

The Captain shot a sharp glance at the Exec, and so did the Navigator. "Come up to the cabin, Joe," said the Captain.

In the cabin, the Captain closed the door and said, "What's bugging you, Joe?"

"This running away," said the Exec. "I don't like it."

"I hope you don't think I do either," said the Skipper. "But what the hell else can we do? Do you want to just plow ahead for Holy Loch and be a sitting duck?"

"No. I want to fight back."

The Captain looked puzzled.

"Sit down, Joe," he said, motioning to the transom and dropping into his swivel chair at the desk. The Exec remained standing.

"In the first place," said the Captain, "we can't fight back, and you know it. Our torpedo tubes are out of action. And even if they weren't, I wouldn't use them."

"Not even after that bastard tried to torpedo us?" demanded the Exec. "Why not?"

Very seldom in the U. S. Navy does an Exec confront his Captain with a question like this when the Captain has obviously made up his mind on an important matter.

"Sit down," said the Skipper rather sharply.

The Exec obeyed. The Captain took out a cigarette, tapped it down on his thumb, and lit it. He took a couple of deliberate puffs and was about to speak when the Exec blurted out:

"Captain, we've let these guys go far enough. Too far, in fact. They tried to torpedo us. That's an act of war—and we had done nothing to provoke it. Now we've got another guy on our back, hellbent to do the same thing. We can't let them get away with this. Goddam it, we fought the British in 1812, when all they were doing was shanghaiing our sailors. These guys are trying to kill us. I'm willing to die for my country in a fight. But I'm not willing to just keep turning the other cheek until these bastards kill us. That's what the *Pueblo* did. I–"

His voice had been rising all the time.

"Throttle down, Joe," said the Captain. "They can hear you clear out in the wardroom. The only thing we could have done with that other guy was to shoot first."

"That's what we should have done," said the Exec. "And I thought you were going to when you had us open the tube doors. We were all set for the order to shoot, but it never came. Now you turn tail and run. What's so different this time?"

"Joe," said the Captain, "you're getting yourself into deep water."

"I don't care if I am," said the Exec. "I don't know if I'll be alive an hour from now. I'm saying what I think while I'm still able to say it."

"All right," said the Captain. "I'll tell you why we're running. There's only one reason for us being out here. That's to prevent a war. If we take any action against these guys, it might start a war. We can't start one by running."

"Hell, it's already started. That other guy tried to torpedo us. Isn't that war?"

"Not the kind of war I'm talking about," said the Skipper. "I'm talking about a war with those things we've got in Sherwood Forest. Hell, a torpedo isn't even a fart in a whirlwind in that kind of a war . . . and even in the other kind of war, we couldn't hit back now if we wanted to. Our tubes are out of action. So there's no use talking about it."

"Yes there is," said the Exec belligerently. "We can hit back. And I think the time has come to do it. Instead, we haul ass."

"What do you mean?"

"Our missiles are still okay. . . . We can blast their naval base at Murmansk off the map. I think we should do it while we're still able to do it."

The Skipper got on his feet with his fists clenched. "Stand up," he said.

The Exec got up. The Skipper lashed out and hit him a sharp blow across the face with his open hand. The Exec recoiled, threw one hand up to his cheek, and stared wide-eyed at the Captain.

"Well," said the Captain, "what are you going to do about it?"

"Nothing, sir," said the Exec.

"Why not?" demanded the Skipper. "I have no more right to hit you like that than they have to shoot a torpedo at us. Are you going to just stand there and let me get away with it?"

"Yessir, Captain, I am," said the Exec.

"Why?"

"There's too much at stake here to do anything else. If you and I fight, this whole ship would be a madhouse."

"You've answered your question about why I'm running," said the Captain. "If we did what you just proposed, the whole world would be a madhouse."

The Exec sat down on the transom with his head in his hands. "All right, Captain," he said. "You're right. I'm sorry."

"Joe," said the Captain, "there's only one order I can give on this ship that you have any right to question. That's the one to fire a missile. They've set up an almost foolproof system, so that when I say 'shoot,' you can check up and be sure that order came from the President. You are the one the country depends on to stop me if I go round the bend . . . and now you are proposing that I shoot an unauthorized shot."

"All right, Cap'n," said the Exec miserably. "I was way off base. I guess I just blew my stack."

"I should relieve you from duty, and put you in your room," said the Captain.

"Yessir. I guess you should, Cap'n," said Joe.

"But I won't," said the Captain. "Go back to the control room and take us under the icecap. Let me know when we get under. I'll be right here if you need me."

The Exec looked up at him in amazement. He got to his feet, said, "Aye aye, sir," and opened the door. There he paused for a moment, and added, "I don't know how to say thank you the way I should, Captain—but the Lord was guiding that selection board when they picked you."

He closed the door and went forward before the Skipper could reply.

Over the Captain's desk there were a compass repeater, speed and depth gauges. He sat looking at them for a minute, thinking, I can be in the control room in ten seconds. This is just a gesture, letting Joe take her under. . . . But it's a safe one—he couldn't do anything rash even if he wanted to. I've got nothing to lose by doing this, and I may save the career of a good officer.

He flipped a switch that cut him in on the squawk box circuit to the sound room. "What's your latest range?" he asked.

"Nineteen thousand yards. Closing slowly, about seventy-five yards a minute."

I think we'll make it, he said to himself.

He reached for a pen and a dispatch blank, and began writing a new dispatch to CNO.

TOP SECRET

Have been attacked with torpedo by Russian destroyer. Torpedo apparently recurved and blew up own ship with atomic warhead. Shock of explosion threw *Nemo* out of control. Regained control just before crushing depth. No trace of destroyer left. Mushroom cloud over scene. Half hour later another destroyer appeared on scene giving evidence of hostile intentions. Withdrew under icecap. Am proceeding to Kodiak via North Pole.

The Doctor tapped on the cabin door and came in.

"Sit down, Doctor," said the Captain.

"This has been a rough day, hasn't it, Captain?" said the Doctor.

"Indeed it has," said the Captain. "In more ways than one."

"I hear we're on our way home over the Pole."

"Rumors sure get around fast on this ship," observed the Captain. "Drop a hint about something like that to the crew, and pretty soon even the Doctor knows about it."

"You don't seem to be worried much about that guy that's chasing us."

"I always try not to look worried, Doctor. Worry is a contagious disease, especially when the Captain catches it. And I'm doing everything I can to get away from that guy, anyway," he added with a glance at the gauges over his desk. "I can keep track of what we're doing just as well from here as from anywhere else."

"Range one eight seven five oh," said the sound-room squawk box. "Still closing slowly."

"We'll be under the icecap in another half hour," said the Captain. ". . . Then we've got about eight days of routine cruising ahead of us."

"Well, that will give everybody time to collect their wits a bit before we face the debriefers," said the Doctor.

"Ummmmm," said the Captain. Then, after a pause, he said, "Doctor, something just happened that you ought to know about."

"Yessir."

"This involves me and the Executive Officer. I don't want you to say anything to Joe about this unless he brings it up. But I want you to know what happened if he does."

"Yessir."

"The Exec and I just had a serious clash, and I took rather drastic action to straighten him out."

"Yessir."

"He proposed firing one of our missiles at Murmansk, and . . ."

"Good God," said the Doctor.

"I gave him a hell of a smack in the face with my open hand, and that seemed to bring him down to earth."

"I spoke to him in the control room just before I came up here," said the Doctor. "He seemed a bit preoccupied, but I had no idea anything like that had happened."

"If we were remaining on patrol, I would have to ask you to put him on the sick list, and would have to make him turn over his keys and his code book to the Navigator. But soon we'll be under the ice, where we couldn't fire a missile even if we were told to. Joe is a good officer—I don't want to ruin his career . . ."

"Do you think he's back on the beam now?" asked the Doctor.

"I don't know, Doctor. He got as far off as it's possible for any of us to get when he made that proposal. How long does it take to get back to normal after a thing like that?"

"It's hard to say—you can never be sure. From what you tell me, he must be pretty badly shook up."

"I'm sure he is. And he should be. . . . That was a hell of a thing for him to do. It brought the world close to the brink. All it took to shove us over was a nod from me. . . . Of course, he's got to get out of the Polaris program now. I have to make sure he'll never get a command. But I want to do it in such a way that he can still have a useful career somewhere else. So I'm letting him handle the boat now as if nothing had happened."

"That's good enough psychology," agreed the Doctor. "But aren't you sticking your own neck out?"

"I don't think so. I've got no right to stick my neck out, because I'd be sticking everyone else's out too, if I did. But once we're under the ice, nothing much can happen—at least nothing that I can't stop before it does any harm. . . . Anyway, you know what the score is now, and I've told you just for information, not action."

"I understand, Cap'n," said the Doctor.

The phone from the control room rang. The Exec's voice said, "The edge of the cap is a mile ahead, sir. We'll be under it in a few minutes. The destroyer is still ten miles astern."

"Very well, Joe," said the Captain. "After we get under the cap, find me a polynya. I want to surface there and get off a message to CNO telling him what happened."

"Aye aye, sir," said the Exec.

Half an hour later the Exec came to the cabin.

"No polynya in sight yet, Cap'n," he said. "But we're watching for one."

"Very well," said the Captain, and handed the Exec the dispatch he had written to CNO. "As soon as we find one, surface and get that off."

The Exec read the dispatch and observed, "This will jar their barnacles loose."

"It's urgent to get that off as soon as possible," said the Skipper. "We've got other boats in that area that we ought to pull out of there."

After a pause, the Exec said, "Captain–I don't know what to say about that business a while back–except I'm sorry. . . . I was terribly wrong, and I know it."

"That's just about all that can be said about it, Joe," said the Captain. "As long as you know this, there's no need for me to say anything more. I have told the Doctor about it, although we're not making it a matter of official record."

"Thank you, Captain. I'm glad of that."

"But, of course, you will have to request assignment to surface ship duty when we get in because . . . well, because if you had been in command a few hours back, God knows what would have happened."

Joe's face colored up and he stared at the deck.

"Sit down, Joe," said the Captain.

Joe sat down.

"I had my heart set on getting one of these boats some day, Cap'n," he said.

"You've got to forget that now, Joe," said the Skipper. "If I ever heard that you were slated for command, it would be my duty to object—and to tell them why. If you request other duty, it will save me from the nasty job of having to put this on record."

The Exec weighed these words for a moment and said, "You're right, Cap'n—and thank you."

16

An outsider visiting the wardroom that evening would never have guessed that the Grim Reaper had almost got the main hatch open that day. It was only five hours since they had missed being crushed by a narrow margin. But everyone had now filed this in the back of their minds as finished business.

Polaris sailors, like aviators, are fatalists. They live one day at a time. They know they are living dangerously, but each one figures he will die in bed.

At dinner that evening, table talk was all about the trip over the Pole. This wouldn't be a real first—because the *Nautilus* and *Sea Dragon* had already been there. But it would still be an adventure.

"How are you going to find our way to the Pole for us, pilot?" asked the Gunnery Officer.

"That's the easiest problem of navigation that there is," said the Navigator. "Any dumb cluck can do it. All you gotta do, no matter where you start from, is to just steer due north till you get there."

"But how can you tell when you're there, with this solid roof of ice over our heads?"

"Just watch the latitude dial on our inertial navigator. When it says ninety degrees–we're at the Pole."

"Sure. But how do we keep going north when you get near the Pole? Doesn't your gyro get confused about directions up there?"

"Yes. So you just watch the longitude dial on the inertial navigator. As long as you steer so as to keep the longitude constant, you're going straight up the meridian heading north."

"But isn't the gyro heading one of the inputs that your computer needs to figure out the longitude? If your gyro doesn't know where north is, how can it figure out your longitude?"

"The gyro input is only used as a check. You can get along without it as long as your accelerometers are working . . . and we play a trick on the gyro so we can use it even when it gets confused and can't settle down on north. We rig it to work like the gyro turn-indicator in an airplane. An airplane gyro doesn't know where north is. All it does is enable the pilot to steer a steady course. So a day or so before we get to the Pole, and while the gyro still knows where north is and the ship is headed north, you switch over to the turn-indicator mode. It won't seek north any more, but it will stay where you put it for several days and enable you to steer very close to north. But the accelerometers in the computer are what we really depend on."

"Captain," asked the Gunnery Officer, "how close did you actually come to the Pole in the *Nautilus?*"

"As close as you can get," said the Captain smugly. "We figured the axis of the earth went smack up the barrel of our attack periscope."

"That's mighty close," observed Guns.

"Well, when we shoot those skyrockets of yours, we've got to know exactly where we're shooting from if we want to hit a pinpoint target. The system that figures out your firing position and feeds it into the missiles works just as well at the North Pole as anywhere else."

"How much water is there at the Pole, Cap'n?"

"It's over two miles deep up there. Twenty-two hundred fathoms. So except for seamounts, we've got nothing to worry about on the way up there. Coming down the other side is a different story. You can't head directly for Bering Strait because it's shallow, and you might get pinched between the bottom and the icecap or hit a seamount that isn't on the chart. If that happens, you'll be there till the icecap melts, a million years or so from now. But there is a deep valley in the bottom running from the Pole to Point Barrow. So when we get to the Pole, we've got to head for Point Barrow, keeping in the valley till we get out from under the cap."

"How do you know which way to head when you leave the Pole, pilot?" asked the Gunnery Officer.

"That's kind of tricky. No matter how you head when you're at the Pole, you're going due south. You want to be sure you're going along the right south—on the correct meridian. This is complicated because all meridians meet at the Pole, and you are in all longitudes at once."

"We called this 'longitude roulette' on the *Nautilus*," observed the Captain.

"Good name for it," said the Navigator. "If we were on the surface and could see the stars, it would be simple enough to pick out the 'south' that leads to Point Barrow. But we've got to do it blind. So we fall back on our inertial computers again. Right at the Pole, even the computer gets confused when it tries to indicate all longitudes at once. So we just have to make the best guess we can as to which way to head. It will be about twenty degrees to the left for us, this time. After leaving the Pole, we watch the longitude dial. By the time we get about ten miles away, it will settle down again, and we can change course right or left to get right on the meridian we want."

"What does the ten miles have to do with it?"

"When you're close to the Pole, a small error in position makes a big difference in longitude. At the equator, for instance, an error of one hundred yards would only be three seconds of longitude. But half a mile from the Pole, it would be three and a half degrees. By the time you get ten miles away, one hundred yards is only ten minutes of longitude, and your computers are pretty well settled down again."

Later, the Captain stood at the chart desk in main control writing up the night orders. These instructions, written just before the Captain turns in each night, tell the O.O.D. the courses and speeds the Skipper wants during the night, and anything else he has on his mind affecting the safe navigation of the ship. The Navy Regulations require that these be written in the Night Order Book so that if the O.O.D. runs the ship aground while the Captain is asleep, the court-martial can determine whether he did it the way the Captain told him to.

Captain Banks wrote:

Course 000, speed 15, depth 150 feet.
The only known danger to navigation is getting pinched between the bottom and the ice. If this should happen to us—nothing else ever will.
Keep fathometer and sonar going continuously.
Call me if water shallows to 200 fathoms.
If sonar sees anything ahead, reverse course and call me immediately.
Keep a bright lookout for a polynya. I want to surface and send urgent message in first one we come to.

The Captain signed the book and handed it to the O.O.D. He stood behind the helmsman for a few minutes watching the compass, depth and speed gauges, then said good night, and went forward.

Polynyas occur more or less at random in the Arctic icecap. They are here today and gone tomorrow at the whim of wind and tide. When you don't need one, you may find lots of them. When you do want one, it may be hard to find. This was the case with the *Nemo*.

For the next few days, nothing but solid echoes came back off the bottom of the roof of ice above her. Her urgent news of the attack had to wait.

In Washington, they had gotten her report of starting for Holy Loch. She was expected there in about fifty hours. Admirals Radbury and Vickory assembled an array of technical experts and got ready to fly to Scotland and meet her on arrival.

The Navy, of course, was in a dither over the sudden downgrading in the status of its number one weapons system. Their best scientific brains burned the midnight oil in the back rooms of the Navy Department searching for a clue as to what had happened.

Meantime, business went on as usual elsewhere in the Pentagon, with Admiral Homer acting as CNO. Admiral Baker spent the day on the golf course.

All next day, the *Nemo* bowled along at fifteen knots to the north, keeping a sharp eye open for a polynya. She didn't find any.

That afternoon, when the Doctor came to the cabin, there were two paperback books on the Captain's desk. One was the World Almanac; the other, Documents of the Vatican Council.

"I see your reading covers a wide range," said the Doctor.

"Yes," said the Captain, picking up the World Almanac. "I've been doing some research–checking population figures on some of the big cities in our country and Russia. I was curious about how much it reduced our retaliation potential when this ship went under the ice."

"Is it very much?" asked the Doctor.

"Depends on how you look at it. Just one of these boats can all but destroy Russia. Each one of our missiles has a warhead several hundred times more powerful than the Hiroshima bomb. If we had hit Hiroshima with one of these things we would have really creamed it. Instead of just frying the center of the downtown area, we would have blown the whole city, suburbs and all, clear off the map. Just imagine what sixteen of these can do. If you flattened the sixteen biggest cities in the U.S., all of a sudden, you would kill perhaps fifty million people, destroy the U. S. Government and most of our industry. We might be in bad shape for a while—maybe a couple of hundred years. So when you take that much leverage out of action, you have certainly reduced our bargaining power."

"That's the understatement of the year," observed the Doctor.

"But look what we've still got left . . . fifteen Polaris boats on station and ready, plus twenty-five more on call at short notice. We must have over a hundred Minute Men in silos along the Canadian border. And SAC always has planes in the air, armed and ready to drop several hundred bombs on target—just waiting for the word to go. I'd say that if the President gave the word right now, within six hours over five hundred hydrogen bombs would be delivered on target—if we could find that many targets big enough to identify. When you get down to city number five hundred you're working on pretty small towns. So when this ship went under the ice, it only reduced our overkill ability a little bit. Instead of being able to knock Russia back into the Stone Age, maybe it would only be the Ice Age—or vice versa, whichever came first. Hell—between us and Russia we've got enough bombs now not only to devastate this planet, but to sterilize Mars and Venus, too."

"Of course, the official party line here on earth is that these bombs will never be used. An all-out atomic war would be so awful for both sides that neither of us will ever start one," observed the Doctor.

"Sure. We all know that bit by heart," said the Captain. "But it only makes sense up to a certain point. If my neighbor and I don't trust each other, and we go around carrying loaded shotguns, we will both be pretty careful about tramping on each other's toes. That's reasonable. Not very friendly—but reasonable. But if each one of us installs a sixteen-inch gun aimed at the other's house, people might say we're overdoing things. That's what we and Russia have done. At the end of the next war, one side or the other will emerge from the wreckage and say, 'We won.' But when they do, some cannibal nation in Africa will say, 'Just a minute, sahib—you're not strong enough to run this world any more. We are taking over.' And we won't be able to do a damn thing about it."

"Then you think an atomic war is inevitable?" asked the Doctor.

"I wouldn't say that . . . not right out loud anyway. Only two things on this earth are supposed to be inevitable, death and taxes . . . and if you've got a smart enough lawyer even taxes aren't. But if we all accept atomic war as being inevitable—it will be. And of course another sure way to bring it about is to just bury our heads in the sand and say, 'it can't happen here!' Don't ask me the answer to this dilemma . . . I don't know."

"Well," said the Doctor, "as of now, we are top dog in this world, anyway. Don't you think we can stay that way?"

"No, I don't," said the Captain. "This mutual terror balance of power can't last. We're debating now about whether we ought to sink X billion dollars into underground shelters and an anti-missile system that will enable us to survive an all-out atomic attack. The think factory experts say that on a cost effectiveness basis, it isn't worth it. They set the whole thing up on their computers, grind in fifty million lives and X billion dollars, and the answer comes out that it's not a paying proposition. I think the Russians know by now that they can do anything, short of actually dropping an atomic bomb on us, and we won't pull the plug. Look what they did to us yesterday—a flagrant, unprovoked attack on one of our ships. They knew they could get away with it. No matter how thin you slice it, and no matter how you twist things around and look at them, you always come back to the same dead end—the atom bomb is so destructive that it neutralizes itself."

"You just got through saying it will never be used," objected the Doctor. "At least we won't wipe out the race if we never use it."

"I didn't say we'll never use it. I agree that no sane head of state will start an atomic war deliberately. But there must be a thousand young majors and commanders on both sides of the iron curtain who could fire a missile if they went round the bend. One of them proposed doing it right here in this cabin yesterday afternoon. And no matter how many safety locks we put in a system that is constantly on a knife-edge alert, there's always the chance that a mechanical mishap will fire one. But actually, I think the chance that a head of state will start the atomic war is even greater than the chance that a mechanical failure or a crazy major will do it. I can name you half a dozen heads of major states in our lifetime who would do it—Hitler, Mussolini, Togo, Stalin, and Mao Tse Tung. And, of course, the only head of state who actually did authorize firing the bomb was our own Harry Truman."

"Actually," said the Doctor, "there's no sane answer to this. The decision to use the bomb will always boil down to the will of some one man—the head of some state. All history proves that among a dozen heads of state, there is always at least one fool and often, one maniac—and even in our recent history, we had a President who was completely incapable of carrying out his duties the last year he was in office, but refused to give up power."

"You mean F.D.R.?"

"No. Wilson."

"Besides," said the Captain, "it doesn't even require a fool or a maniac to set things off. A kindly old grandfather type with one too many shots of vodka under his belt, or too long a pull on his opium pipe, could do it. Actually, I think it's easier to guard against a crazy major than it is against the very top man going round the bend."

"I agree," said the Doctor. "Much easier."

"So what is your prescription for what ails the human race, Doctor?"

"I read a science fiction story once," said the Doctor, "that had the best answer I've seen yet. In it a smart scientist hornswoggled the whole world into believing that UFOs were real, and that an invasion from outer space was about to begin. As soon as the nations became convinced of this they stopped all wars on earth, pooled their weapons, pointed them to the skies, joined hands together to repel boarders, and we all lived happily ever after."

"Makes much better sense than the way we're trying to do it now," observed the Captain.

17

That evening, Admiral Baker got a phone call at home from the CNO Duty Officer. "I've got the editor of a big newspaper on the phone here, sir," he said, "and he insists on talking to you."

"What does he want to talk about?" asked Baker.

"He wants your comment on a story that you are being relieved as CNO, sir."

"Hah!" observed the Admiral. "My crystal ball was right. Okay. Put him on this line—and I want you to listen in and also to tape the whole conversation."

A moment later the editor came through. "Hello, Admiral Baker. This is Jackson of the Washington *Times*. Sorry to bother you at this time of night, sir, but we have a story saying you are being relieved as CNO. Would you care to comment on it?"

"What's the source?" asked Baker.

"Our man just says an unimpeachable source."

"He must have told you more than that."

"He did. But we have to protect our sources, you know."

"What else does he say?"

"He says you and SecDef have clashed on the matter of civilian control of the military, and that SecDef has decided to relieve you."

"That's very interesting," said Baker. "Anything else?"

"Is this true?"

"No comment."

"Our reporter points out that there have been differences between you and SecDef about the XFQ, but that these are of long standing. He speculates that some new matter has come up. Do you care to say anything about that?"

"No comment."

"The story also says that there was a meeting of the Security Council yesterday, and that the Vice CNO attended, but not you."

"No comment," said Baker.

"I gather that you do not deny our story?"

"All I'm saying is 'no comment.' Whatever conclusions you draw from that are your own. Not mine."

"This is a big story, Admiral, and we're going to feature it. We think it is only fair to give you a chance to tell your side of it. We would appreciate your comments."

"That's very thoughtful of you, and I appreciate it. But all I've got to say is 'no comment.'"

"Thank you, Admiral."

When the editor hung up, the Duty Officer came back on the line. "We've got it all canned, sir," he said.

"Okay," said CNO. "Lock it up for future reference. Now put me through to Admiral Homer."

In a minute Baker was telling Homer about the *Times* story. "So it looks like I'm on the way to the old sailors' home," he concluded.

"Did he give you any source?" asked Homer.

"All he would say was an unimpeachable one."

"Hunh. I guess that eliminates the President—the Constitution specifically provides for impeaching him."

"So that means it was you-know-who, and he'll probably make it stick. . . . I just want to put you on notice, so you won't be surprised by the morning papers."

"Well, thank you, John. You know—my mother wanted me to be an artist, and I sometimes wish she had got her way."

"Don't get too downhearted. The first forty years are the hardest. And this job gets you a nice set of quarters, with the best mess boys in the Navy."

Next day, the big topic of discussion around Washington was the *Times* story about the firing of CNO. The White House, SecDef, and Navy Department all refused to comment on the story, but this just fanned the flames of speculation.

Since the *Nemo* was due in Holy Loch next day, Admirals Radbury and Vickory and a planeload of experts took off from Andrews Air Force Base for Scotland. No one had yet come up with any reasonable theory as to what had gone wrong. Vickory still insisted it couldn't be his reactor.

At the White House that morning, SecDef said to the President, "The Navy is sending all their top experts to meet the *Nemo* at Holy Loch tomorrow."

"I'm a little worried about our other Polaris boats," said the President. "The Navy made a flat recommendation that we pull them back. . . . If anything should happen now, we would look pretty bad."

"Nothing is going to happen," said SecDef. "It's almost forty-eight hours now since the *Nemo* reported she was heading for Scotland. All that stuff about danger of an attack on her turned out to be a bunch of hobgoblins. Tomorrow she'll be in Holy Loch, and I think we'll know very quickly what she was doing wrong. If we had agreed to that wild idea about coming back over the Pole, it would have taken another week to find out."

"Well—I hope it turns out all right," said the President. "Do you still want to get rid of Baker?"

"Yes. More so than ever. He was one hundred percent wrong on this thing. He panicked over the idea that the Russians might attack us. We can't afford to have a nervous Nelly in that job."

"But wasn't your hassle with him really over the wording of a message? That seems like a small thing."

"That was just the last straw. There were a lot of other things. And on this one, the difference wasn't so much on the wording of the message as the fact that he simply refused to carry out my orders to send it."

"He didn't make any objection to it when I spoke to him on the phone about it."

"That's right. And if he had a reasonable case and felt so strongly about it, he should have told you so."

"Maybe you're right on that," said the President. "Have you picked a new man yet?"

"No. Not yet. I want to go over the field carefully and be sure I get a good one, this time."

"Is this where I'll find out who he is when you do?" asked the President archly—pointing to the front page of the Washington *Times* and its story on CNO.

"No, sir. Naturally I'll let your office release the news on that."

The *Nemo* ran north all day, watching for a polynya, but finding none. The Captain was edgy about the delay in getting this very important news to Washington. But there wasn't a thing he could do about it.

That evening, Ensign Gateau tapped at the open cabin door.

"Come in, Gateau," said the Captain. "Have a seat. What's on your mind, young man?"

"Well, Captain," said the Ensign, "I've got a personal problem to decide pretty soon, and I want to talk to you about it."

"Okay, son," said the Captain. "Glad to help you if I can. What's the problem?"

"My three years of obligated service will be up in a few

months. I've got to make up my mind whether to stay in the Navy or get out."

"Hmmmm," said the Captain. "Cigarette?" he asked, offering the Ensign a pack, and taking one himself.

"Thank you, sir," said Gateau, whipping out a lighter for the Captain.

"That depends on a lot of things," said the Captain. "Such as, what do you want to get out of life? Obviously, money isn't the main thing, or you wouldn't be up here asking me about it."

"Nosir. Money is not my problem. And I know all the usual pros and cons about security, home life, standing in the community, and so on."

"That just about covers the field, doesn't it?" asked the Captain.

"Not quite," said the Ensign. "Maybe I'm looking pretty far ahead, Captain . . . but when I get through with whatever line of work I take up in life, I'd like to be able to look back and say that I pulled my weight in the boat and contributed something—that I did more than what I just had to do."

"You can do that in almost any line of work you take up," said the Captain. "As for a military career—every other country in the world envies us. None of them love us. Russia is a dangerous threat to us right now. China will be soon. The way this world is run, we've got to be able to defend what we've got if we want to keep it. When you help to do that, you're making it possible for artists, musicians, writers, and teachers to do great things. Looking back on my twenty years in the Navy, I think I'm entitled to feel that I've helped a little to make this a better world—or at least to prevent it from being a much worse one."

"There's no doubt about that, Captain. . . . But most of the time you're just standing by, like a fireman—ready to do a job if you are told to. I think that later on I'd like to be able to look back and say I did this and that to help make it a better world. Isn't it true that for most of your military career you have to just do as you're told? . . . Can anyone except the few who get to be CNO really say that they did anything on their own?"

"Of course I'm a long way from being CNO," replied the Skipper. "But I feel I've done more than just carry out orders, so far. Even as an ensign, you can leave your mark on the men who serve under you. If you do your job well, they will be better citizens on account of you. . . . And one thing I can tell you for sure, command of a ship is a job you can look back on when you're through and say, I did this and that. In fact, whether you say it or not, others will. There's no other job like it in the world. Sure, you've got to obey orders. But up to a point you're still a king in your own right. Whatever the ship does, good or bad, is right smack in your lap. If it's good, you're entitled to be smugly modest in taking the credit. If it's bad and if you're worth your salt, you've got to step up and take the blame, even if you had no control over what happened. After all, the Skipper is supposed to have control."

"Yes. I know that, Captain," said the Ensign. "But when you go in for a military career, don't you give up a big piece of your freedom? I mean, you can't say what you think any more. You've got to carry out orders, even if you know they're wrong."

"Not always," said the Captain. "Nelson put his blind eye to the telescope when the admiral hoisted a signal telling him to do something foolish at the battle of Copenhagen. You give up a certain amount of freedom when you join any organization. If you can't abide by its rules, you are always free to resign. But I agree that as long as you are in the Navy, you commit yourself to obey orders. Very few of us are Nelsons—and in this atomic Navy, there's no place for them anyway."

"But there are some things," observed the Ensign, "that I don't see how you can commit yourself to in advance."

"For instance?"

"Suppose you get orders to fire our missiles and you think it will be the end of civilization if you do. How can you say in advance, 'I'll do as I'm told, no matter what I think'?"

"You're really getting down to fundamentals—aren't you?" observed the Captain. "The answer is that if I can't say it, I've got no damned business being out here. If I have any mental reservations about it at all, I have no right to accept command of one of these ships. Once I do—I'm committed. I've got to have confidence in my government and the President. That's the only way it can be."

"But Captain," said Ensign Gateau, "I've been reading some books lately about the Nuremberg Trials. Isn't this country officially on record now saying that a military man must not rely on blind obedience of his orders? In fact, that he has got to question them and even refuse to obey them if he thinks they are morally wrong?"

"Unfortunately, we are. But that is just for the history books —and for the lawyers when we get ready to hang the losers of the next war, if we win it. When we committed ourselves to keeping the peace by balance of terror, we repudiated Nuremberg, at least as far as our own military people are concerned. You can't base national policy on a system in which a couple of thousand young majors have a right to decide whether they'll obey orders or not."

"Then you agree with the Nazis' defense at Nuremberg that all they were doing was carrying out their orders?" asked the Ensign.

"I didn't say that. I don't agree with anything we did at Nuremberg. The whole thing was a travesty of what we call justice."

"It's hard for me to see it that way, sir. Don't you think justice was done at the Nuremberg Trial?"

"That word *justice* covers a lot of ground," said the Captain. "One meaning is 'fairness.' I think the Nazis got exactly what was coming to them—and that's fair enough. But it also means conformity to the law. In dishing out their just deserts to the Nazis, we made a mockery of law."

"Why do you say that, Captain?"

"We charged them under laws that we made up after the event to fit the crime. We made it 'illegal' for the accused to challenge the jurisdiction of a court of foreigners trying them for crimes committed in Germany. To top it all off, we spent a lot of time at the trial trying to pin the Katyn Forest Massacre on the Nazis. We did this with a Russian judge sitting on the bench who knew that it was done by the Russians. The whole thing was a flagrantly illegal kangaroo court and every judge sitting on it knew it. They were all supposed to be pretty good lawyers, too, including even a justice from our own Supreme Court, who was the prosecutor."

"Do you mean to say we should have let all the Nazi bigwigs get off scot-free?"

"Hell no. But we made a farce out of international law by going through a mock trial which violated all previous rules of law. We should have just lined them up against a wall and shot them—that is, all except Admiral Donitz. I'm never in favor of shooting or hanging admirals."

"But they claimed that all they were doing was carrying out their orders. You say that's what you have to do. But you would have shot them for it."

"I wouldn't shoot them for carrying out their orders. I'd shoot them for losing the war."

"But you can't just line the losers up against a wall and shoot them, without a trial—that's not civilized."

"Well now, son," said the Captain, "let's not be too hasty in saying things like that. When and if I ever pull the trigger on that missile we've got labeled Sverdlovsk, I'm not going to give the citizens a formal trial before doing it—and there are nine hundred and seventeen thousand of them, according to my World Almanac. Does that make us barbarians? . . . Maybe we had both better take the Fifth Amendment on answering that one."

"But, Captain, I've heard you say that the only way this Polaris system can justify itself is by never being used."

"Yes. I've said that."

"I think you've also said that since we'll only use it in retaliation after being attacked in a war that nobody can win, it will just be a matter of vengeance when and if we ever do use it."

"Perhaps I have said that, too," admitted the Captain soberly. "But it goes a great deal further than just vengeance. Even after an atomic disaster, I think there will still be some human life left on the earth. If we didn't shoot back when we're attacked, whatever is left of the human race when it was over, would have to live under the Communists. If we shoot back and blot out the Reds, the race may, in several hundred years, make the earth a fit place to live in again."

"You make it sound pretty grim and hopeless, Captain."

"It's grim all right, but I don't say its hopeless—at least not while only we and Russia have the bomb. But when enough others get it, I don't know what the answer is. Maybe it's something like this—suppose you were struck by a poisonous snake, and knew you were going to die from it. Would you kill the snake anyway?"

"Well, yes . . . of course."

"I think the two cases are roughly parallel. It's a hell of a way to run a civilized world, but that's just the way it is—you and I didn't make it that way. And don't blame the military for it, either. The decision to make and use the atom bomb was made by the highest civilian officials in our government. They claim it shortened the war and saved half a million American lives. Perhaps this is true . . . but only because until we dropped the bomb we were hellbent on invading Japan. By that time Japan was blockaded in her home islands the way Hitler tried to cut England off. She was hanging over the ropes and hopelessly beaten. All we had to do was wait a couple of months and surrender was inevitable. . . . But we're an impatient people and can't wait. Except for the bomb we would have gone ahead with a stupid, unnecessary, and costly invasion. That's the only ground on which you can justify using the bomb. Looking back now, with the wisdom of hindsight, it was probably the most foolhardy decision ever made in world history up to now."

"I guess you're right on that," said the Ensign. "It gives me a queer feeling when I go through the Sherwood Forest. It makes me think of the Devil's Workshop . . . and, Captain, I used to think some of my classmates in college who grew long hair and beards were nuts, but sometimes I wonder . . ."

"Of course they're right about the world being crazy," observed the Captain. "But they're sure as hell not going to cure it by growing beards and never taking a bath."

"That's about the way I felt about them, too," said the Ensign.

"Well, son," said the Captain, "I don't think I can advise you on whether to stay in the Navy or not. You seem well able to decide that yourself. But if you stay in–I advise you to get out of the Polaris program."

"May I ask why, Captain?"

"Yes. You think too much about things we can't afford to have our Polaris sailors thinking about."

The Ensign thought for a moment, then rose and said, "Thank you very much, Captain."

"Have I helped you any?" asked the Captain.

"Yes, sir," said the Ensign. "On everything except the Nuremberg Trials. I don't think we can ever look at that the same way. . . . You see, Hitler made soap out of my grandparents."

"Well!" said the Captain. "I didn't realize that."

"Yessir. The family name in Germany was Ginsberg until Hitler came along. My father changed his. But my grandfather didn't."

18

Next morning, the *Nemo* spotted a polynya, surfaced, and got off its message about the attack.

The Navigator was on deck, of course, with his sextant and stopwatch as soon as they surfaced. He found the stars right where his inertial computers had told him they would be. Although his gyro compasses were beginning to be a little confused about where north was, his computers still knew exactly where they were. His look at the stars enabled him to check this, and to nudge his gyros back to the meridian.

The Pole was now only thirty miles ahead.

There is a five-hour time difference between Greenwich and Washington. The *Nemo*'s dispatch about the attack, sent at 7 A.M., got to the Pentagon at 2 A.M. The CNO Duty Captain had the Vice CNO on the scrambler phone within the minute.

"I've got an urgent one here from the *Nemo*," he said.

"Okay. Read it," said Admiral Homer.

The Duty Officer read the dispatch.

"Call up Admiral Baker and give it to him," said Homer. "I'll be down to the office in twenty minutes."

Admiral Baker's reaction was the same: "I'll be right down to the office."

Half an hour later, Admirals Baker and Homer met in the CNO's office. "I've canceled my leave," said Baker. "Get CinC Atlantic on the hot line. I'm going to have him pull all the Polaris boats out of the Arctic."

Soon a voice on the command circuit to Norfolk said, "Admiral Mansen speaking, sir."

"Sorry to get you out of bed at this hour," said Baker, "but I want you to recall all Polaris boats from the Arctic, right away. Pull them back west of a line from Scotland to Iceland. You'll get a dispatch on this within the hour, but get your action started now."

"Aye aye, sir," said Admiral Mansen. "You didn't get me out of bed. The *Nemo*'s message did. We've got everything all set on the redeployment. I knew it was coming. Our dispatch will go out in a few minutes."

"Nice going, George," said Admiral Baker. "I might have known your crystal ball would be working."

"Any special instructions you want me to give the skippers?" asked Mansen.

"Yes," said Baker. "Tell them to take all possible evasive action if they meet unknown ships in the Arctic. In another message, I'll give you a minor reshuffling of strategic targets, because a few of them will be out of range after redeploying."

"All right, John, everything will be taken care of," said the voice on the phone. "And for your information, I've already alerted my fleet commanders on the situation. We are ready for whatever comes up."

"Okay, George. We'll keep you informed."

"Now," said Baker to the CNO Duty Officer, who was standing by, "pass that dispatch to the White House Duty Officer and then get SecDef on the scrambler phone."

"What do you think they'll do about this?" asked Admiral Homer.

"I think there will be a meeting of the Security Council this morning, maybe before breakfast. I'm sure they'll decide to pull our ships out of the Arctic. There's nothing else they can do. I'm not going to tell them I've already done it, unless they find out somehow that I have. No use getting into a hassle now about whether I had a right to do it on my own hook."

"What else should we do now?" asked Homer.

"I don't think we should do anything more until the *Nemo* gets in and we get more details. As things stand now, we know they tried to attack our ship. We know the Russian blew himself up. So far, we aren't hurt. This happened seventy-two hours ago, so the Russians must know by now their ship is missing. I think they will assume we did it. Whether they will want to make an issue of this or not remains to be seen."

"Do you think we should tell them what happened to their ship?"

"Hell no! We shouldn't volunteer any information whatever. If they ask for any, or accuse us of anything, then we can think about what to tell them. Meantime, we have a big advantage over them, because we know what happened, and they don't."

The Duty Officer stuck his head in the door and said, "The White House has the dispatch. We're getting through to SecDef now. He'll be on in a minute."

Admiral Baker picked up his phone, waited for a minute, and then said, "Admiral Baker, Mr. Secretary. We have another dispatch from the *Nemo* saying she was attacked by a Russian destroyer, that she came out of it unhurt, and is returning via the polar route."

"Well, that's all right," said the Secretary. "We gave him authority to come back that way if he wanted to in the first place."

"The *Nemo* also says that the ship that tried to attack her blew herself up. An atomic explosion destroyed it without trace."

"Does the President know about this?"

"Yessir. We just phoned the *Nemo*'s dispatch to the White House Duty Officer . . . and Mr. Secretary," said the Admiral, "I've canceled my leave."

"I see," said the Secretary. "All right. We can discuss that later."

"So?" asked Admiral Homer as CNO hung up. "What's the score now?"

"You heard me tell him I've canceled my leave. Until he tells me otherwise, I'm back on the job. This is going to be a busy day. Get our people down here to their offices as soon as you can. Get word to Scotland to send Radbury, Vickory, and their experts to Alaska. That'll take 'em across the Pole, and they'll probably fly right over the *Nemo* en route. Get Orlando and the boys to whip up some breakfast for us, and then we'll see what happens. It will be a hot session of the Security Council this morning, and I want you to come along."

"You'll have a grand chance to tell them, we told you so!" observed Homer.

"Not a very good way to win friends and influence people, if you ask me," observed CNO. "Two, straight up, with lots of bacon and toast, Orlando," he called to the steward, who stuck his sleepy head in the door at this point.

Just before 8 A.M., Vice Admiral Hawley, Commander Subs Atlantic, was conferring with Commander in Chief Atlantic in the headquarters at Norfolk.

"Admiral," he said, "I'm getting concerned about the *Lincoln*."

"How come?" asked the Admiral.

"Everybody except her has receipted for our message. It's five hours now since our first transmission. We've been repeating it every hour, and there is still no answer from the *Lincoln*."

"Five hours . . . is that cause for alarm, at this stage?"

"I'm afraid it is. Everybody gets a message like that on the first transmission. They can't always all answer right away. But five hours is a long delay in answering."

"When did you last hear from her?"

"Seventy-two hours ago. Everything was normal. Just a routine report."

"Where was she?"

"Two hundred miles north of Murmansk. She was the furthest boat to the east."

"Suppose somebody was riding herd on her like they did on the *Nemo*. Would she get our message?"

"Sure. She would get it, all right. It might not be convenient for her to answer right away. But I think she would have surfaced and answered within five hours, unless . . ."

"Unless what?"

"Unless she's in real trouble."

"She could be under the ice, you know. The *Nemo* went under to get rid of that guy."

"Yes. But even if she can't find a polynya where she could surface and transmit, she could always pop out from under the cap for the minute or so it takes to spit out a receipt. She'll get our message no matter where she is. And it calls for an immediate answer."

"Okay, Mike," said the Admiral. "When should we really begin to get worried?"

"I think right now. If she has been attacked like the *Nemo* was, we may never hear from her again."

"How much longer should we wait before telling CNO?"

"I would tell him now. I would say if we don't hear from her within forty-eight hours at the most, we'll have to write her off."

The Admiral picked up his hot-line phone to the Pentagon. "I want to speak to CNO," he said to the aide who answered. ". . . All right. Put me through to the White House. This is urgent."

The Security Council met in the White House at seven that morning. Before the meeting, the Secretary of Defense and the President had a brief session together.

The President was boiling mad. "Those Russian sons-of-bitches must be crazy," he said. "Where I come from, if someone shoots at you, you shoot back."

"Not completely crazy," said SecDef. "Except for a lucky break, they would have gotten away with it and we'd never know what happened."

"But we do know. And I'm not going to let them get away with it."

"If what they want is war, we are ready for it," said SecDef. "We can flatten their country in a few hours."

"Looking back at this thing," observed the President, "the Navy called the turn on it pretty accurately two days ago."

"Uh huh," said SecDef. "But they misled us very badly on the systems evaluation of Polaris. The only reason why we invested so heavily in that program was because they convinced us this couldn't happen."

"About that story in yesterday's *Times*," said the President. "Will Baker be at this Council meeting?"

"Yes. I sent him on leave the day before yesterday, but I've recalled him."

"Good," said the President. "It might be premature to make a change now."

All faces around the council table were serious that morning. Present were the same officials as were at the last meeting, plus Admiral Baker, the Chairman of the JCS, and the Chief of Staff of the Air Force.

"Gentlemen," said the President, "by now you all know why this meeting was called. One of our Polaris subs has been attacked by the Russians. I'll ask Admiral Baker to brief you on what we know so far. Admiral Baker."

"Gentlemen," said Baker, "all we know is what is in the dispatch which you have in front of you. There are several points I want to comment on. First, we are quite sure that it was a Russian destroyer that did this. Second, the *Nemo* reports that a torpedo was fired at her. We can't be certain of this. She must have been submerged, so the only way she could tell would be from sounds in the water. These give a pretty reliable indication, but not a certain one. I emphasize these things because so much is at stake here. . . . The dispatch indicates that no real damage was done to our ship. The destroyer was apparently wiped out by an atomic explosion. The *Nemo* is now returning to Alaska via the North Pole, under the icecap. We will be out of communication with her for at least three days, maybe more. Meantime, I recommend that we recall all Polaris boats from the Arctic immediately, and deploy them west of Scotland."

There was a pause, during which the President looked at the Admiral rather incredulously.

"Is that all you want to do, Admiral?" he asked. "One of your ships was flagrantly attacked. All you propose now is that we pull the rest of our ships back from a place where they have a perfect right to be? Is this the same Navy speaking that produced John Paul Jones?"

Admiral Baker colored up a bit and said, "That's just my first recommendation, sir. I don't want to leave the stage set for another attack, and no time should be wasted in debating about it. Our official reaction to the attack is another matter. It requires very careful consideration."

"This is the same situation as Pearl Harbor, isn't it?" demanded the President. ". . . An unprovoked attack without warning?"

"Well, sir," began the Admiral.

"Let me answer that, Admiral," interrupted the Secretary of State. "There are important differences between this and Pearl Harbor. At Pearl Harbor, the Japs deliberately committed themselves to war. They left a shambles behind them for all the world to see. In this case, the Russians didn't think they were committing themselves to anything. They thought we'd never know what happened—and the odds were all in their favor. . . . They don't want war. If they were ready to shoot the works on all-out war, they would attack our cities with A-bombs. After Pearl Harbor, we had no choice but war. We had our war, and almost thirty years have gone by. Both Japan and the United States have recovered from the war and are stronger and more prosperous than they were before it. But the situation is entirely different today. If we and Russia fight now, thirty years from now both our countries may still be radioactive ruins. We've got to avoid a showdown that results in all-out war. We must not back the Russians into a corner they can't get out of without war. We had better let our tempers cool before we do anything more than redeploy our other Polaris boats."

"All right, George, I agree," said the President. "You're right about a cooling-off period. . . . Admiral, I apologize for that crack about John Paul Jones."

"Another thing," continued SecState. "When we speak of pulling our ships out of a place where they have a perfect right to be, we've got to remember that this right was established back in the days of John Paul Jones and sailing ships, when the range of a naval cannon was three miles. I'm not so sure we can still live with that doctrine."

"Freedom of the seas is just as important to us now as it was in John Paul Jones' time," said the Admiral, bristling.

"Don't get your cocked hat and epaulettes ruffled, Admiral," said the Secretary of State. "I'm not enunciating any official changes in national policy to the rest of the world. I'm just discussing the facts of life in the Atomic Age within these four walls."

The President glanced at the serious faces around the table. "Any comments on redeployment?" he asked.

"I concur with redeployment," said the Chairman of the JCS.

"I do, too," said the Chief of the Air Force. "The Air Force will cover any Polaris targets that are out of range."

"Just how will this affect our readiness to retaliate?" asked the President.

"Actually, hardly any," said CNO. "Only four of the present Polaris targets will be out of range, and SAC will take care of them."

"I think that since the Russians have already committed an overt act, the Air Force should go to a red alert status," said SecDef.

The Chairman of Joint Chiefs of Staff frowned dubiously.

"We can't get any closer to it than we are now, except on a temporary basis," said the Chief of the Air Force. "At the present moment, SAC has as many planes airborne, armed, and waiting for the word to go as they can keep there continuously. And, of course, a part of SAC is committed now to tactical targets in Vietnam. This commitment can be changed very quickly if necessary, but I don't think it is necessary. We can deliver an . . . adequate strike without them."

"I recommend against any change in the Vietnam theatre deployment," said the Chairman of JCS. "We are fighting a major full-scale war out there now, except for the use of A-bombs, and there's no sign of any end to it yet. Our ground forces are so fully committed and we've pulled back so much out of Europe that any other war we get into has to be atomic."

"We will alert Continental Air Defense," continued the Chief of the AF, "and they will probably put more of their fighters on a red alert status. But any time you give the word to SAC, Mr. President, Russia will be flattened within a few hours."

"Suppose they get in a sneak attack first?" asked the President.

"No matter what they do, enough of SAC will get through to obliterate Russia as a major power. A sneak attack would just cut down some on the overkill. It wouldn't affect the end result."

"The word end is very well chosen," observed SecState, in an aside to the head of CIA seated next to him.

"And, of course, Polaris would not be affected by a sneak

attack," observed CNO. "Twenty minutes from the time you give the word, sir, over two hundred missiles will be on their way."

"I'm not as confident of Polaris reliability now as I was a week ago," observed SecDef.

"What happened to the Russian destroyer?" asked SecState.

"We think she blew herself up with her own torpedo," said Admiral Baker. "Torpedoes run erratically sometimes. They have been known to recurve and hit the ship that fired them. We had three known cases of this in our Navy during World War II."

"What are your standing orders to your Polaris captains in case they are attacked?" asked the Secretary of State.

"Our standing orders to them are to avoid contact. Until the *Nemo* incident, they've been able to do it. Up to now, the question of what to do if attacked has not come up. However, it is the right—in fact, the duty—of any military commander to defend his unit if attacked."

"Do they have specific orders on what to do if attacked?"

"No, sir. However, in the reverse situation, when one of our destroyers picks up one of their subs near our shores, which happens every month or so, our ships have orders to stay with them, track them until they surface, but take no action which might be interpreted as being hostile."

"In this case, what would you have done, Admiral," continued SecState, "if you had been in command of the *Nemo?*"

"I think that if I had been sure the Russian had fired a torpedo at me, I would have fired back."

"Do you mean to say that the captains don't have specific orders telling them what to do in a case like this?" demanded SecDef.

"No, sir, they don't. It's not practicable to foresee all the situations which could possibly come up and issue specific orders covering them. Our Polaris captains are mature officers, carefully selected, and we just have to rely on their good judgment."

"That's what we did when we told the *Nemo*'s skipper to use his own discretion about coming home over the Pole. In that case, his judgment turned out to be wrong."

CNO's face flushed and his jaw took a firm set. "I wouldn't say we sent that message to the *Nemo*," he shot back.

Now it was SecDef's turn to color up. "Well," he said, "the message told him . . ."

"All right now," interrupted the President. "Let's not argue about that. I accept the blame for that message. I think the only thing we have to decide right now is redeployment of Polaris. You can go ahead with that, Admiral. We'll have to wait till the *Nemo* gets in before we decide what else we should do. How long will that be?"

"She will be under the ice for about five days. It will take her another three days to get to Kodiak."

"And how long will it take to get all our Polaris boats pulled back out of the Arctic?"

"We are restationing them in the Atlantic between Scotland and Iceland. This will take about forty-eight hours–from now."

"All right. Get it started," said the President.

"Mr. President," said SecState, "I think it is important to hold this information very closely and keep it out of the papers. We may have some very delicate negotiations with the Russians about this, and a lot of sensational publicity about it would handicap us severely."

"You're a hundred percent right on that," said the President. "We've got a bad enough press right now on Vietnam. Many of the opposition papers would welcome a chance to embarrass us on something like this."

"Mr. President," said CNO, "there's a story in the Washington *Times* this morning which will stir up a lot of speculation that could lead a smart reporter onto this story. The *Times* called me on it early this morning, and all I gave them was no comment."

"All right, Admiral, I'll take care of that. . . . Anything else?" the President asked, glancing around the table.

"I think CIA may have something to contribute in a few days," said the Chief of CIA. "With help from the Atomic Energy Commission and the Air Force, we should be able to verify the location of an atomic explosion in the Arctic. And perhaps we can find out in a few days how much the Russians actually know about it."

"Is it permissible to ask how?" asked the President.

"Yessir. But I would rather give the answer to you alone."

"See me after this meeting," said the President. ". . . That's all, gentlemen . . ."

The President was about to add "meeting adjourned" when the red phone at CNO's place buzzed and Admiral Baker answered. The others were getting ready to leave when the Admiral held up his hand and waved, indicating they had better wait.

19

It was CinC Atlantic on the phone with the news about the *Lincoln.* Baker took his report, asked a few short questions, and hung up.

"Mr. President," he said, "on the orders to redeploy the Polaris boats, one of them doesn't answer her radio call. It's still too soon to be really alarmed about this . . . but it may mean trouble."

Everyone around the table looked puzzled at this statement. The President said, "We just decided to send that message a few minutes ago. Isn't it a little premature to be concerned about it?"

"I sent the message five hours ago, sir," said Admiral Baker. "All ships except the *Lincoln* acknowledged promptly. But we can't raise the *Lincoln.* We don't know that she is definitely in trouble, yet . . . but I'm concerned about her."

"By whose authority did you send the message five hours ago?" demanded SecDef.

"Never mind about that, now," said the President. "What kind of trouble do you think the *Lincoln* may be in, Admiral?"

"I think the Russians may have sunk her, Mr. President. Of course, it's too soon to say that now. But if they have, we know as much about it now as we're ever going to know."

"How long will it be before you are ready to declare her lost?" asked the President.

"I would say that at the end of forty-eight hours there will be no doubt about it."

"So we've got forty-eight hours to make up our minds what we are going to do about this?"

"I feel that forty-eight hours from now we have got to notify the dependents of the crew. That means we've got to make a public announcement that she's lost."

"And if we have nothing more to go on then than we have now," said SecState, "that's all we can announce. We can't publicly accuse the Russians of sinking her, because it could be another *Scorpion* case."

"We will know damned well the Russians did it," put in the Secretary of Defense. "Coming right after the attack on the *Nemo*, there can be no doubt about it."

"All right. *We* will all know it," conceded SecState. "But we'd never convince the rest of the world. All we know about the *Nemo* incident came to us through strange sounds that some young sailor heard in the water. . . . Now don't start getting your back up to defend your sonar operators, Admiral. I know they are the best in the world; and I believe them when they say a torpedo was fired at the *Nemo*. But we would appear ridiculous to the rest of the world if we charged the Russians with making an attack, based on that evidence, especially when the *Nemo* came out of it unhurt. If we tried to explain that the Russian blew himself up, everyone would laugh at us."

"What do you want to do? Be an eyewitness of the attack yourself, before you believe it?" demanded the President. "Nearly every decision we take on this level is based on second-

or thirdhand information from diplomats, CIA agents, and even newspaper reporters. Many of these people are nowhere near as expert in their fields as our sonar operators are. If one of our captains says he had a torpedo fired at him, I believe it, even if the report does depend on a young sailor's ears. And I propose to do something about it."

"All right, Mr. President," said SecState. "Let's take a quick look at some of the things you can do. You can order an atomic attack on Russia. I'm sure you don't want to do that. The name of the game we're playing is SURVIVAL, and so the only thing that can trigger us into using the A-bomb is an attack with A-bombs on our cities. This is one of the disadvantages of an absolute weapon. We couldn't use it even in the *Pueblo* case. The second thing you can do is get into a conventional war with Russia. You just heard the JCS say we've got all the conventional war we can handle on our hands right now, in Vietnam. We can't just send the Russians a note saying 'tut-tut.' If we take any official action at all, it has got to be pretty drastic."

"I can get on the hot line to the Kremlin," said the President, "and tell Kosygin some things he will understand very well, but which we couldn't put in a formal diplomatic note. What the hell have we got that hot line for?"

"Mr. President," said SecState, "in some situations the very smartest and most constructive thing you can do is–nothing. I think that for the present time at least, this is one of them."

"Do you mean that we just ignore the sinking of one of our ships?" demanded Admiral Baker.

"We don't know it's sunk yet, Admiral," said the Secretary. "When and if we do know it, we certainly don't want to destroy the whole world on account of it, but we do want to react in such a way that the Russians won't try to go any further. It could be that a good break in luck has already taken care of that for us. If the Russians think we sank their destroyer, they may figure the score is even, and that's enough.

I'm sure they will be surprised that we would take such action, and they don't like to be surprised any more than we do."

"Anyway," said the President, "we've got forty-eight hours to consider whatever we are going to do. I want all here present to keep themselves available on short notice."

"One more thing, Mr. President," said SecState. "In a thing of this kind it is of vital importance that the news be handled intelligently. If the *Lincoln* is, in fact, gone, the situation will be as follows:

"A–We will think the Russians know what happened to her. We won't be sure.

"B–The Russians will know that one of their destroyers is missing. We will know what happened to her. The Russians won't–but will blame us for it.

"C–We know the Russians tried to sink the *Nemo*. Presumably they also know they tried, but they won't know whether or not they succeeded.

"So as things stand now, we know more about this than the Russians do. We will have to announce the loss of the *Lincoln*. I'm very curious to see if they announce the loss of their destroyer. I think it is very important to release no more information than we have to, and to keep the Russians guessing, at least in the early part of whatever exchanges of diplomatic amenities occur."

"I agree with that," said the President. "My office will handle the press on this. That's all, gentlemen–meeting adjourned."

As the President was leaving, the Admiral said to him, "May I see you in private for a few moments, sir?"

"Sure," said the President. "Come into my office."

The head of the CIA said, "Mr. President, you said you wanted to see me after the meeting." And started to follow them in.

The President shot a quick glance at CNO, got a stony stare in return, and said, "Wait outside . . . I'll see you right after Admiral Baker."

"This must be pretty hush-hush if it's too classified to cut even the CIA in on it," observed the President when they got in the office, thinking to himself, *Now comes the showdown between the Admiral and SecDef.*

"It is," said the Admiral. "It's something that only the two of us should know about . . . I don't want to get into another impasse like the *Pueblo*, where we couldn't do anything."

"God knows I don't either," said the President.

"I want to do something which I feel, from a purely naval point of view, should be done in this situation. But the stakes are so high that I feel you should be in a position to disavow it if it turns out wrong. I also feel that it should not be done at all if you definitely disapprove of it. I therefore feel it should be done without your official knowledge."

"Sounds like you're trying to have your cake and eat it too, Admiral. You want to do something you think I should disapprove of, but you don't want to do it unless I do approve."

"That's about the size of it," said the Admiral. "I want to do something unless you forbid me to do it. To give you a chance to forbid me, I've got to let you know what it is. But after I've done it, if it turns out badly, I want you to be able to say it was done without your authority."

"Like the way you redeployed the Polaris subs?" asked the President, squinting quizzically at the Admiral.

"In a way," said the Admiral. "But in that case, I acted on my own because it was the only thing we could do, and I was sure you would approve. It couldn't get us into any international complications."

"What's this new one you're going to spring on me? Something like the U-2?"

"No, sir. That was about as secret as yesterday's baseball scores. Too many people knew about it, and besides, the Russians had our plane and pilot. President Eisenhower tried to brazen it out, but finally had to take the rap for it. This would be something that only you and I know about. I'm not asking you to authorize anything. I just want you to have a chance to forbid it."

"But you just said you're going to tell me about it. After you tell me, I can't deny knowing about it. Can I?"

"Depends on how strait-laced your conscience is, sir."

"Well now," said the President, "when the interests of the country are at stake, my conscience wouldn't bother me a bit about doing something that might not be considered cricket—especially by the Russians. But to protect the interests of the country, I'd have to be damn sure I wasn't caught lying about it."

"This is exactly what I have in mind, sir," said the Admiral. "We have a destroyer that has been riding herd on a Russian sub off Cape Kennedy for the past three days—just like the Russian did on the *Nemo*. I want to tell our destroyer skipper to . . . er . . . make that sub disappear. This is the sort of a reaction to destroying one of our subs that the Russians will understand and respect. They will never know any more about it than we will know about the *Lincoln*."

"No oil on the beaches?" asked the President.

"Very little. The water is deep there, and it would be thirty miles or more offshore, where the Gulf Stream is fast and deep."

"Wouldn't a large number of Navy people know about this? Navy Department aides and duty officers, coding officers, radio operators, and others?"

"No, sir. I can arrange it so my instructions will go direct to the destroyer skipper by hand in a sealed envelope. . . . Now I'm not asking you to authorize this. But if you should suspect that I might be thinking of something like this, and if you didn't want me to do it—you could specifically forbid it, and I wouldn't do it."

"I see," said the President.

"If by some mischance we get caught at this, all you have to do is publicly disavow it, and tell the Russians, 'sorry about that.'"

"What the hell? You don't think they'd let it stop there, do you?"

"Yes, I do. For one thing, it would surprise the hell out of them. They would never think of apologizing like that, and wouldn't know what to make of it. . . . Look what happened when the Israelis blasted the *Liberty* that was minding its own business during the Egyptian war. It was outrageous—inexcusable. They just said, 'Ooops! Our mistake. Pardon us,' and that was the end of it."

"By God, you're right about that," said the President. "Admiral, maybe I should switch you to the State Department."

"If it turns out the *Lincoln* is lost, we will have to announce it in about forty-eight hours. So if I hear nothing from you by the time we have to release this news, I would like to assume you are not worried about me taking ill-advised action, and I will do . . . whatever I deem appropriate."

"Hmmmmm," said the President. "And if I find it necessary to say that you acted without authority—you will confirm this?"

"That is correct, sir."

"I'd probably have to publicly disavow you and fire you."

"No doubt whatever about that, sir. But you can do that any time you wish, in any event. I never have regarded this job as a lifetime career."

"Admiral . . . if you were a politician, I wouldn't dream of making a deal like this. I'd want to know what your angles were."

"Not meaning to be dramatic about it, sir—my only angle is the welfare of the United States. If the Russians get away with sinking one of our ships, it could very well encourage them to go a bit further. If we let them go much further, there will come a time when we've got to say, 'Stop, or we will pulverize you.' After the way the *Pueblo* fiasco turned out, they may not believe us."

"Just one more angle, Admiral. Didn't we agree at the meeting that the Russians are going to assume we sank their destroyer? Isn't that enough?"

"I think the way the Russians play this game, it's better to be definitely ahead of them instead of just even with them. If you'll pardon my saying so, sir, that's the way John Paul Jones used to operate."

The President made a wry face, and said, "Okay, I asked for that one. . . . I take it, Admiral, it is not your intention to cut SecDef in on this?"

"No, sir. It is not. In a thing of this kind, the fewer who are in on it, the better. . . . And again, if you'll pardon my saying so, sir, SecDef's office is the next to leakiest spot in the whole government. No one but you and I will know what has passed between us here."

"Huh," said the President. "Only the second leakiest, you say? What's the first?"

"The office we're in now, sir, when your staff are in on the secret, too."

"Okay, Admiral," said the President. "I'm afraid you're right. . . . You don't see eye to eye with the Secretary on all things, do you, Admiral?"

"I have great respect," said the Admiral, "for the Secretary's judgment on matters involving the financial affairs of the Defense Department, and for his scientific management of its vast organization."

"You sound like one of my own press secretaries evading a tough question. I note that you fail to enthuse about his talents as a naval strategist."

"I am able to control my enthusiasm about that, sir."

"Admiral," said the President, "if these were normal times, I'm afraid I would have to get a new CNO."

"I understand, sir."

"But I don't want to do it at this time. I think your advice on naval matters can be helpful to me in this emergency."

"Thank you, sir."

"In regard to the proposition you have mentioned, I feel you will not take any ill-advised action. If I think of any specific things which I do not want you to do, I will issue instructions to you about them before we announce the news on the *Lincoln* –assuming that we will have to announce such news."

"Aye aye, sir," said the Admiral. "I appreciate your confidence, Mr. President."

The Admiral started to leave, but the President stopped him, got up from his chair, and stuck out his hand. The two men shook hands, looked each other in the eye, and the Admiral left.

Back in his office at the Pentagon, Admiral Baker was greeted by the Vice Chief. "You have the news on the *Lincoln?*" he asked.

"Yes," said Baker. "No answer from her. They got it to me at the White House just as the meeting was about to break up."

"So what do we do?"

"We wait forty-eight hours. Then we declare her missing, and decide on the next move."

"How did the rest of the meeting go?" asked the Vice Chief.

"All right. They approved redeploying the Polaris boats. But I goofed and let the cat out of the bag that we had already done it."

"How did that sit with them?"

"SecDef didn't like it. But the President took it in stride."

"Any developments in regard to your duty status?"

"Yes. I think so. I had a talk with the President after the meeting. I think we see eye to eye for the time being. I don't look for any changes till this present crisis is over. . . . Now . . . what's the name of that destroyer that's sitting on the sub off Cape Kennedy?"

"The *Mahan*–DD 782. Commander Jenkins is skipper."

"Know anything about him?"

"Sure. Know him well. He was on my staff when I had the Sixth Fleet. Good, solid citizen. He's no brilliant strategist. But a good operator. You can give him a job and depend on him to do it."

"Can he keep his mouth shut?"

"Never opens it except to eat."

"That's fine. I'm going to write him a note. I want it delivered as quickly as possible, by hand, via officer messenger. Fly him to the Cape and send him aboard by whirlybird."

"Aye aye, sir," said the Vice Chief. "I'll set it up. He can be on his way to the Cape inside of an hour. Shall I send a yeoman in to take the letter?"

"No. This will be in my own handwriting. The only copy of it will be in a sealed envelope in my personal safe over there behind John Paul Jones' picture."

"Aye aye, sir. The messenger will be ready by the time you get it written."

Admiral Baker sat down at his desk, got out a sheet of his four-star personal stationery, and wrote the following letter.

From: Chief of Naval Operations
To: CO, USS MAHAN, DD 782
Subject: Special Instructions

1. It may become necessary to terminate the hold-down operation which you are now conducting. If it does, you will receive a TOP SECRET message from me saying, "REQUEST DISAPPROVED." Upon receipt of this message you will proceed to destroy your target without trace, using homing torpedoes with non-atomic warheads. This must be done in at least 200 fathoms of water with no other ships in vicinity, and preferably at night. When target has been disposed of, make normal reports of losing contact and inform me by message saying, "WITHDRAW REQUEST."

Signed,
J. Baker

The Admiral read this letter over, weighing each word carefully. Then he wrote an exact duplicate of it, and stamped

TOP SECRET across the face of both copies. Then he took another stamp and under the TOP SECRET on one, he placed EYES ONLY ________ and wrote "Comdr. Jenkins" in the blank space. On the other, he wrote VCNO in the blank. He put the Vice Chief's copy in an envelope and locked it in the safe behind the picture. He put the other copy in an envelope addressed "Comdr. Jenkins, CO, DD 782," melted two gobs of sealing wax on the flap, and stamped the Navy Department seal onto the soft wax.

Then he buzzed for his aide, and said, "Ask Admiral Homer to come in."

When Admiral Homer came in, the Chief handed him the sealed envelope and said, "Get this to the *Mahan* as quickly as possible. In your outgoing correspondence log, call it 'disapproval of request.' In case something drastic should happen to me and you have to take over, there's a copy of it in the safe over there."

"It will be aboard the *Mahan* about four hours from now," said the Vice Chief. ". . . We just got word the Secretary of Defense wants to see you in his office."

20

When the Admiral was shown into his office, the Secretary of Defense said, "John, I had a talk with the President about you last night."

"Yessir . . ."

"I have decided to keep you on as CNO, for the time being. I told the President I didn't think it advisable to make a change at a time like this, and he agreed."

"Yessir."

"I've got my hands full right now with the Vietnam war and—with other things. So I'm going to let you handle the naval end of this Russian incident."

"Aye aye, sir," said CNO.

"There is one thing I'd like to ask you about this *Lincoln* business. Why did we put one of our subs right in there under the guns at Murmansk, when it could reach all its targets from much further out?"

CNO regarded SecDef with some surprise. It had been put there against the Navy's advice by the whiz kids in the Defense Intelligence Agency, like the *Liberty* and *Pueblo* were. "I thought you knew all about that, sir," he said.

"Well, I didn't. I wouldn't have allowed it if I had. Why was it in there?"

"It was snooping on Russian radio traffic . . . observing the electronic characteristics of their radars, sonars, etc., and . . ."

"They had no business in there jeopardizing their major mission for that sort of thing."

"But, sir! Your people . . ."

"Let's not argue about it. That's just basic military strategy —you don't endanger your major mission for side issues. . . . The press could make the Navy look very foolish if they got hold of that item."

The afternoon of the Security Council meeting, SecDef's Chief of Information was closeted with the boss in the front office.

"We got trouble, Mr. Secretary," he said.

"What's wrong now?" demanded SecDef.

"That story we leaked on CNO has backfired. The Washington *Times* featured it as a big scoop. Now the White House denies it, and the *Times* is burned up about it . . . says we made fools of them."

"I've got bigger problems than that to worry about this afternoon," said the Secretary. "And the *Times* knows damn well this isn't the first time the White House has denied a true story. The President himself gave me a green light on firing Baker. But he changed his mind this morning and decided not to do it right now."

"The same old story," observed the Chief. "You know how sensitive the President is about such things getting out before he announces them."

"Sure I do. But Baker has got to go and I'm sure he will go before long."

"That's good, Mr. Secretary. But meantime, the White House has made liars out of us with the *Times*, and we can't afford to get in their doghouse. We've got to do something to pacify them."

"The hell with them," said the Secretary. "Let them sweat it out for a while. Baker can't last much longer. He's beginning to think he's John Paul Jones or something. He even got insubordinate with me at the meeting this morning. When he finally gets sacked, it will make the *Times* look pretty smart."

"They're getting ready now to break another big story," said the Chief. "One that can hurt us pretty bad. The Navy's report on the XFQ."

"How did they get hold of that?" demanded the Secretary. "It's still supposed to be classified."

"The usual way . . . a leak from the Armed Services Committee–one of the Senators."

"Those bastards will break security any time they think it will do them some good," declared the Secretary. "I wouldn't tell them the time of day–if I could help it."

"I agree," said the Chief. "Anyway, the *Times* has got the whole report. And now they think you're trying to fire Baker because he won't go along with you on the XFQ. They figure you planted the CNO story with them to undermine him. They're pretty hot about it, and they're ready to put the blast on you, now."

"I can stop that," said the Secretary. "The publisher of the Washington *Times* is a personal friend of mine. I'll call him up."

"That's where the heat is coming from, sir. Gordon thinks you took advantage of his personal friendship, and tried to use him."

"I don't see what he's got to be so smug about," said the Secretary. "Unless he can use you, you're no friend of his. . . . What do you think we ought to do about this?"

"Well," said the Chief, "I think you ought to tell Gordon the real reason why you want to fire Baker, or else give him some other big story that will take the spotlight off his busted scoop on CNO."

"Okay," said the Secretary. "Maybe I can do both. The Navy

is getting this country into a hell of a mess. Things are happening now that make the XFQ a very small potato . . . and they all come to roost in Baker's lap."

That evening the White House got an urgent phone call. The publisher of the Washington *Times* wanted to talk to the President. The Duty Officer, thinking of the CNO story, tried to stall him off. When Gordon stated what he was really calling about, the President was on the line in short order.

Gordon told the President he had it from an unimpeachable source that there had been a sea battle between one of our Polaris subs and a Russian destroyer. He said his information was that our ship had sunk the Russian in self-defense, and asked the President to comment. He would not reveal his source.

The President declined to comment, but made an urgent request, in fact a plea, that Gordon hold this story top-secret as a matter affecting national defense and that he come to the White House at eight next morning.

Gordon, now sure that his story was correct, was reluctant to hold off on this sensational scoop. He asked if this had anything to do with the firing of CNO. The President informed him that CNO had not been fired, and urged that the story be held up until they could discuss it in the morning. Gordon finally agreed grudgingly after being assured that his exclusive scoop would be protected.

After hanging up, the President had the Duty Officer call all members of the Security Council and schedule a meeting for seven-thirty next morning.

In the sound room of the USS *Mahan*, cruising forty miles off Cape Kennedy, a new watch was coming on. At the sonar scope the operator was telling his relief, "The Roosian is still down there at about three hundred feet, two thousand yards dead ahead of us. He hasn't done a thing for the past four hours but just poop along at four knots. You got good isothermal water today, no layer, and you can even hear 'em playing Victrola records . . . some of 'em pretty good."

The new man put on the headphones and took his seat in front of the big display scope. He listened while a couple of sharp pings went out, and watched the sound wave spread out in all directions in an expanding circle on the scope. He heard the answering muffled echo come back from dead ahead a few seconds later. Listening carefully, his trained ear could hear the faint swish, swish, swish of the Russian's propellers turning over at slow speed.

"Okay, Mac, I've got her," he said.

Right behind him the new watch was also relieving on the attack director. This is a box of mechanical brains into which you feed the bearing and distance of a target, its depth, course and speed, your own course and speed, and the torpedo speed. The box then figures out where the torpedo must be aimed in order to hit the target and sends this dope up to the torpedo tubes on deck. Automatic relays adjust the torpedo and keep the brain box informed how the tubes are pointed. When everything checks all around, a green light on the brain box comes on and all the operator has to do is pull his trigger and the fish goes on its way. The *Mahan*'s torpedoes were all homers, so if they got anywhere near their target they would automatically correct any small errors in aiming, and follow the target no matter how it tried to dodge.

"It's a simple shot from dead astern," said the operator to his relief. "Range, speed, and depth have been the same for over three hours—just a straight no-deflection shot. Running time for the fish is forty-five seconds. Propeller locks are on."

"Okay, pal, I've got her," said the new man. "There's a hell of a football game on TV this afternoon—Packers leading the Bears thirty to twenty-eight with the fourth quarter just starting."

The *Mahan* had been riding herd on this Russian for three days now. It was an old-style diesel-driven sub with schnorkel. Each night after dark it came up near the surface and poked its schnorkel up to run its diesels for about four hours and recharge its battery. The rest of the time it just loafed along at slow speed a couple of hundred feet deep, back and forth, forty miles off Cape Kennedy.

She was obviously in this area to snoop on missile shots from the Cape. When first sighted by aircraft almost a week ago, she was lying to on the surface where she could see the tops of the missile towers and listen in on any radio traffic to or from the missiles. She had a good look at one Polaris missile shoot before she was spotted.

When the *Mahan* appeared on the scene, she submerged and for two days tried hard to shake her off with evasive maneuvers, deep dives, and noisemakers. But the *Mahan* was an expert at the ASW trade and the Russian, being an old-style sub, couldn't squirm as much or run as fast as a Polaris boat can. When the Russian found he couldn't shake the *Mahan* off, he settled down to simply patrolling back and forth as he was doing now. Staying with him was just part of a day's work for the *Mahan*, and she didn't even have to put on any extra watches to do it.

In the Captain's small sea cabin next to the bridge, Commander Jenkins was working on a big jigsaw puzzle of the *Constitution* under full sail. It was, as he informed himself quietly every so often, a son-of-a-bitch, of picturesque and improbable ancestry. Those were the kind he liked.

Jenkins was no great naval genius or global strategist. But he was a good operator and a fine destroyer skipper. When the *Mahan* got a job to do, it was done in a straightforward, efficient way. You never had to tell Jenkins how to do a job —just tell him what you wanted done, and let him figure it out. If unusual difficulties came up, he doped out unusual ways of licking them.

He often said he was a two-speed guy—full ahead or stop. If necessary, he could stay on the bridge for days at a crack, catching cat naps in the Skipper's chair on the starboard wing of the bridge. When he wasn't needed on the bridge, he spent most of his time in the sea cabin, putting together jigsaws or working crossword puzzles. He would have been perfectly happy to have a permanent job as a destroyer skipper for the rest of his naval career. He was never going to make admiral, but he was one of the best men you could have around when there was a tough job for a tin can to do.

As Jenkins was trying to find where a piece of the *Constitution*'s water line belonged, his Exec tapped on the cabin door and entered.

"Well . . . what's new, Number Two?" asked the Skipper.

"Nothing at all," said the Exec. "Steaming as before . . . no remarks."

"You know, we're really defrauding the government when we draw our pay for doing a job like this," observed the Captain.

"Sure, we are now," said the Exec. "But I think we earned it the first couple of days, when he was trying to shake us off."

"Yeah," said the Skipper. "The boys did a damned good job hanging onto him then. He's no slouch at evasive maneuvers. Reminded me of a greased eel in a bowl of gelatin at times."

"Why do you figure he's still hanging around here, Cap'n?" asked the Exec. "He can't find out anything running submerged like he has been the past three days. Why doesn't he shove off?"

"I dunno," said the Captain. "A case of red tape, I imagine."

"How do you mean?"

"He probably asked permission to go home three days ago. But you know how long it takes us sometimes to get an answer out of our Navy Department to a simple question. Probably some commander in Moscow is afraid to answer him until he finds out what the Politbureau thinks. Meantime, he doesn't dare leave his station without permission, so he's just marking time. It's the same way in the Army."

"Could be," said the Exec. "Are you coming to the movies tonight?"

"Yeah. I'll be there."

"Okay—see you later, sir," said the Exec. As he opened the

door of the cabin to leave, a messenger from the radio shack handed him a priority dispatch from the beach. It said, "Officer messenger from CNO will land on board by helicopter at 1800."

"What the hell have we done wrong now?" he asked as he handed the message to the Skipper.

"Hmmmm," mused the Skipper. "I wonder."

School boys when called to the principal's office review their conduct anxiously on the way there. Naval officers do the same thing when CNO suddenly focuses his eye on them.

"Well . . . we'll soon find out," the Captain said. "He'll be here within an hour. . . . We've got a pretty good roll on the ship today. Don't let this guy slam into too many things back there when they lower him aboard."

Helicopters do not land on destroyers. They have to hover and lower passengers aboard in a sling. If the ship has a lot of motion on her, this can be tricky.

An hour later the whirlybird came over the horizon, circled the ship once to get the wind, and then came fluttering up the wake and hovered fifty feet over the fantail.

"Aw right now, you guys," said the Exec to the sailors in the landing detail. "Don't be bashful about grabbing this officer. I want to catch him on the fly—not first bounce."

A small crane swung out of the side door in the helicopter, and a limp figure hanging from a horse-collar sling under his armpits was lowered toward the heaving deck. Two sailors grabbed his legs as soon as they were in reach and steadied him down to the deck, where he quickly squirmed out of the horse collar. The whirlybird hauled off on the port beam.

The Captain was waiting on the wing of the bridge when the Exec escorted the messenger up. The officer saluted and said, "Lieutenant Jackson, sir. I have a message for you from the Chief of Naval Operations," and handed the Captain a large manila envelope.

The Captain broke the seals on the envelope and drew out a

smaller one of the type used for personal rather than official letters. It was addressed "Comdr. Jenkins—EYES ONLY."

"Excuse me, gentlemen," said the Captain. "Wait here a few minutes, please," and he withdrew to his cabin before opening the envelope.

He read the handwritten letter through twice and sat for some moments in deep thought. Then he read it again, stuck it in his pocket, and returned to the bridge. "You want a receipt for this, I suppose?" he said to the Lieutenant.

"Yessir," said the Lieutenant, producing a receipt card and a pen.

The Captain signed on the dotted line.

"Any answer, sir?" asked the Lieutenant.

"No. That's all," said the Skipper. "We'll call your whirlybird alongside and you can be on your way."

As the Exec and the Lieutenant went aft, the Captain walked over to the chart desk and studied the soundings in the area where they were cruising. Not less than two hundred fathoms anywhere around them, he noted. Then he settled himself in his high swivel chair on the starboard wing of the bridge and sat squinting into the breeze with a faraway look in his eyes, obviously turning over weighty matters in his mind.

Getting off a rolling destroyer in a horse-collar sling is really a much safer business than getting aboard. As soon as you get your arms in the horse-collar, the whirlybird can lift you off and haul clear. So there is little danger of being slammed against things, like when you are lowered aboard. But the air over the fantail is usually turbulent from the wash of the stacks, and as soon as the whirlybird pilot sees your arms in the sling he wants to get the hell out of there. So he gives her the gun and climbs a couple of hundred feet before reeling in on the hoist. Meantime, there you are a couple of hundred feet in the air, with no visible means of support except a wire cable about as big around as a lead pencil. The cable usually has fingerprints in it by the time the passenger is hauled back into the whirlybird.

"I'd much rather deliver messages on a bicycle," observed

one of the sailors on the fantail, as they watched the Lieutenant get yanked up into the air.

"Well done, you men," said the Exec to the fantail party. "Didn't put a bruise on him, or break a bone."

When the Exec returned to the bridge, the Skipper was still lost in thought. The Exec retired to the opposite wing of the bridge and waited. Finally the Skipper got up, walked toward his cabin, and motioned for the Exec to follow.

"Ed," said the Captain when they were in the cabin, "I may have a job to do."

"Yessir."

"All I've got so far is a 'prep' message–execute to follow later . . . maybe. When and if I do it, the fewer who are in on it, the better."

"Yessir."

"Including you," added the Skipper.

"Yessir."

"Actually, everybody on board is going to know about it eventually. But what they know will be second- or thirdhand–and by inference . . . not the kind of stuff you can go into court and swear to."

The Exec said nothing.

"I think that's about all I've got to tell you right now," said the Skipper.

"Aye aye, sir," said the Exec. "You said you're coming to the movies, didn't you?"

"Yes. I'll be there."

21

It's an old seafaring custom when ships cross the equator to have a Neptune Party. This is a bit of horseplay run by old-timers who have crossed the line before. Neptunus Rex, Ruler of the Raging Main, comes aboard accompanied by Davy Jones and a crew of cutthroats and pirates who initiate the new-comer "pollywogs" into the Ancient Order of Shellbacks.

When *Nautilus* made the first polar crossing she had Santa Claus come aboard and conduct a modified Neptune Party. The *Nemo* decided to do likewise.

While the *Mahan* patrolled off Cape Kennedy, the *Nemo* was nearing the Pole. All officers and crew not on watch, except the Captain and Navigator, were assembled in the lounge. The loudspeaker was saying, "The Pole is one mile ahead now. . . . We have two thousand fathoms of water here. . . . The ice overhead is fifteen feet thick. . . . In a few minutes, we will be at the top of the world. . . . This is the Captain's second trip over the top. He was in the *Nautilus* on the first one. . . . Stand by-y-y . . . ten seconds–nine–eight–seven–six–five

—four—three—two—one—MARK! North Pole! Time twenty-five thirty-two Greenwich—December fifteen."

A yell went up from all hands as the lights began to blink, and "Jingle Bells" came out of the loudspeaker. The loudest yell was from Brown, the wardroom mess boy, whose number in the crossing pool was closest to the time on the clock. Brown had just won five hundred dollars.

In a moment there was a hammering on the door in the forward bulkhead. "Ho—ho—ho-ho-ho," came a deep voice from the other side. "Open up, you landlubbers, and let a real seaman in." They swung the door open and in strode the Captain, wearing a red coat, a set of bushy white whiskers, and a Santa Claus hat.

"Ten-shun!" barked Murphy—and all hands bounced to their feet.

"Are there any shellbacks present?" demanded Santa Claus.

Murphy, Nagurski, and a couple of others who had crossed the equator held up their hands.

"All right," said Santa. "You real sailor men come up here beside me and help me hand out the papers to these pollywogs. Where's my scribe? DAVY! —Get in here."

The ship's yeoman, dressed as Davy Jones, entered with an armful of diplomas. These documents, headed Lat. 90 N, Long. 0 to 180 E & W, were signed by Santa Claus as deputy for Neptunus Rex, Ruler of the Raging Main. They were dated Wednesday/Thursday, December 15/16.

When the last one had been handed out, the Captain removed his beard and Santa Claus hat and said, "Congratulations. You have just entered a very select company—only a few hundred others are in it. Now we have some official business to do . . ." He handed out the highly prized dolphin insignia pins to ten men who had passed their tests and qualified on this cruise.

After this came ice cream with strawberries from the deep freeze and a big round cake, proudly produced by the cooks. It was shaped like a slice off the top of the world, with the meridians marked in colored icing and a red candle stuck in the center where the Pole would be.

While they were eating, a sailor asked the Captain, "Why the double date on our certificates, sir?"

"Well, you see," said the Skipper, "we weren't officially at the Pole until the control room got there. By that time it was twelve hours later on Thursday up in the bow, even though it was still Wednesday back aft."

"I see," said the lad, exaggerating quite a bit.

"Time gets all mixed up at the Pole," explained Murphy. "When you're right smack at the Pole it's any time of day you want to call it, depending on which way you are facing, and you can say it's either one of two days. When the *Sea Dragon* crossed the Pole in the summertime, they surfaced through the thin ice and laid out a softball diamond with the Pole going through the pitcher's box. The Skipper claims he hit a fly ball at 4 P.M. on Wednesday that wasn't caught until 4 A.M. on Thursday."

"Well I'll be Gahdam," observed several.

The day after they crossed the Pole, the Doctor came to the cabin for his daily chat.

The Captain handed him a dispatch they had received from Washington that morning. It read:

> When you reach edge of icecap, surface and make homing signals. Helicopter will rendezvous to place Admirals Radbury & Vickory aboard and to bring back Cdr. Banks for transportation to Washington.

"Well!" said the Doctor. "Pretty soon you'll be up there rubbing elbows with the real big wheels who actually run this world."

"Do you really think they run it, Doctor?"

"Well, if the wheels in Washington don't, I don't know who does," observed the Doctor.

"I sometimes think nobody actually controls the course of history, Doctor. The statesmen seldom do. They are just carried along by events. They struggle with each crisis that comes up and get out of it as best they can. I read something about the British Empire in Queen Victoria's time that describes it very well. It said, 'Her Majesty's government is like a man drifting down a river on a raft. Every now and then problems come up—snags and obstructions. But all he does is fend off from them and drift further downstream.' That's what the world is doing now about atomic war. We should never have let anyone else develop an atom bomb. But when the problem came up, we just fended it off, and drifted further downstream toward the holocaust."

Each morning, CNO and his Deputies start the day with a briefing conference. It covers the highlights of the news for the past twenty-four hours on the waterfronts and oceans of the world. Some items are from the morning headlines, some in top-secret flashes from the commanders of our far-flung fleets. Some are from the cloak-and-dagger boys of ONI and CIA, some from the code breakers in the Black Chamber. Current scuttlebutt from the back rooms of the Pentagon and halls of Congress is, of course, aired, evaluated, and sometimes acted upon. Solemn-faced experts on all subjects likely to come up sit around the walls of the room, ready to answer any questions that the Deputies can't. This is where matters of high-level naval policy and global strategy are settled—insofar as SecDef still lets the Navy dabble in such matters.

For the past week, the *Nemo* case had overshadowed all else. It was the last thing on the agenda this morning. When they got to it, Admiral Baker said, "I want to emphasize that this news of the attack on the *Nemo* is TOP-SECRET-NEED-TO-KNOW. Premature release of any news about this thing can do great harm. I want to be sure that if any news does leak, it doesn't come from the Navy. There are now two quite different phases to this thing. The technical one is still the Navy's most urgent item of business. The other involves high-level national policy and will be handled by the Security Council.

"Our best technical experts are now in Alaska and will get aboard the *Nemo* by whirlybird tomorrow, as soon as she comes out from under the ice. We will pick up the commanding officer at the same time and fly him down here—arriving probably the day after tomorrow."

As Admiral Baker paused for a moment, Rear Admiral Tuttle, the Judge Advocate General and CNO's legal man, spoke up. "Admiral, this of course calls for a formal court of inquiry. I've already drawn up a precept for it. I'd like to send the court to Kodiak to meet on board as soon as the ship gets in."

"No," said Admiral Baker.

"I have the precept here," said Admiral Tuttle. "We can change it any way you want—but I thought Kodiak would be . . ."

"Admiral," said Baker, leveling a cold glare at the JAG, "you can take that precept, fold it up into a neat wad, and stuff it in your—wastebasket."

"But, Admiral," protested the JAG. "We've got to have a court of inquiry. The regulations say . . ."

"Young man," said Baker, "don't quote the regulations to me. The regulations were written for the guidance of people who wouldn't know what to do if it wasn't all written down for them in a book. The one you want to quote was probably written in the days of square-rigged sailing ships, and doesn't say a word about Polaris submarines. Your job now is to thumb through the book and find me a regulation saying it's okay to do it the way I want to. There will be no formal court of inquiry. I want our technical people to go over all the ship's data and records with a fine-tooth comb, talk to all her people, and to find out how in the hell those guys are tracking us. And I don't want a bunch of lawyers peeking over their shoulders and citing a lot of legal gobbledegook at them while they are doing it."

"Er . . . uh . . . Aye aye, sir," said the JAG.

"Now the rest of you get busy on your parts of this thing," said the Admiral. "I've got to get over to the White House for a Security Council meeting."

Half an hour later, the President opened the meeting of the Security Council.

"Gentlemen," he said, "the Washington *Times* has the story about the *Nemo* and the Russian destroyer. I have called the publisher down here to ask him to kill the story. He's waiting outside now. I want you to back me up that killing this story is vital to our national interests."

"How accurate is their story?" asked the head of the CIA.

"Quite accurate—except they say the *Nemo* destroyed the Russian."

"Good God!" said the Secretary of State. "This would be a windfall to the Russians. They can claim the *Nemo* made an unprovoked attack on their ship; and when we announce the loss of the *Lincoln* they can say it was retaliation. They won't have to say it—everyone will assume it!"

"Where did he get his story?" the CIA man asked.

"He won't say. He says he has a right to protect his sources."

"There are damned few possible sources for that leak. It won't be too hard to track it down," said the CIA man.

SecDef studied his fingernails carefully. All others around the table searched their memories for unguarded statements in the past twenty-four hours.

"We'll look into that later," said the President.

The Secretary of State came back to the point: "This is a situation where the way the facts come out may be more important than the facts themselves. It's also one where if both sides have all the facts, the Russians, with their control of the news, can make things look bad for us."

"So . . . what line shall we take with the *Times?*" asked the President.

"I recommend we ask them to kill the story," said the CIA

man. "We've got to announce the news on the *Lincoln* within another day or so. We should simply say she is missing—another *Scorpion*, so far as we know—and this would be the truth. Then we should sit back and wait for the Russians to make the next move. The whole thing may just go away. But if the *Times* story gets out, the news media will stir up a storm about the *Lincoln* that may get out of hand."

"I concur, Mr. President," said the Secretary of State. "If this *Nemo* story breaks in the press followed immediately by news of the *Lincoln*'s loss, the whole country will scream for satisfaction. It could result in a confrontation from which we will have to back down—or else."

"All right," said the President, pressing a button on his desk. "Show Mr. Gordon in," he said to the secretary who answered.

As Gordon entered, the President greeted him, introduced him to the others, and said, "I'm sure you know we feel the matter we want to discuss with you is of the utmost importance."

"Obviously," said Mr. Gordon.

"Before we get into it," said the President, "I must ask you for your promise that everything said here will be off the record, with the understanding that it will not be published or attributed."

"Now, wait a minute, Mr. President," said the publisher. "You're asking me to buy a pig in a poke. It's unfair to a publisher to call him in and ask him to tie himself up that way before he even knows what you're going to talk about."

"The matter I want to talk about involves national security —maybe even world peace."

"I can't judge as to that till I know more about it," said Gordon. "Suppose you tell me about something I already know. Is this agreement you want supposed to bar me from publishing it?"

"No—not necessarily," said the President. "Whatever you know now, or think you know, is not covered by this agreement—if you make it. After you hear what I have to say, it will be a matter for your conscience to decide. But the fact of this meeting, and anything you learn here, must be off the record."

"Suppose that after the meeting something that I learned here comes to me through another source—what about that?"

"Again, this will be a matter for your own conscience."

"I can't help feeling that you are taking advantage of me, sir. I have a big exclusive story here and I feel it's substantially correct. I don't know how much longer it will keep. You're asking me to make a blind agreement that may jeopardize my story, without even telling me why."

"It involves a matter that could be of the utmost importance to the national defense," said the President. "I don't know how I can make it more emphatic than that."

"Well . . . since you say national security is involved, I'll agree to your conditions—reluctantly."

"Thank you, Gordon," said the President. "I brought you here to ask you to kill that story about the Russian destroyer as a patriotic service to your country."

"That's exactly what I thought. Mr. President—I'm always glad to be of service to my country. But I don't see how suppressing that story will be of any service. It's true—isn't it?"

"No. The story as you have it is not true."

"I'll be glad to print your version of it, if you care to give it to me for publication."

"Of course you would. But I'm not giving you anything for publication about it. However, I am telling you that publication of your story may do grave harm."

"How?"

"Well, let's assume just for the sake of argument, that it is true. It happened several days ago, and the Russians have said nothing about it. If it were true—as you have it—and if they knew about it, they would have raised hell. If one of their ships is lost and they don't know what happened to it, your story will provide them with information they can use to embarrass us."

"I don't see how it can embarrass us, unless we blew it up without provocation. Is that what you're trying to tell me?"

"No, I'm not telling you that. But that's how the Russians will use your story."

"How can they do that if it isn't true?"

"Hell, Mr. Gordon, you know as well as I do that ninety percent of their stuff isn't true. Truth has nothing to do with whether they can use a story or not."

"If a story of this kind could be of any use to them, they could make it up and release it, couldn't they? They don't have to wait until they see it in my paper."

"Don't be ridiculous, Jim. You know very well that even your severest critics are more apt to believe a story like that in the *Times* than the same story coming out of the Kremlin."

"Well, Mr. President, my criterion for publishing a piece of news is simply—'is it true?' This is why people believe what they read in the *Times*. I believe this story about the destroyer is true."

"I've just told you it isn't. Don't you believe me?"

"Frankly—no. You could make that statement somewhat honestly if you find one minor detail in the whole story that isn't exactly right. You refuse to tell me anything I can use about this incident, and I'm convinced that the main facts are correct."

"Then why haven't the Russians announced them?"

"I don't know. I'm not adept at reading the mind of the Kremlin."

"One reason could be that they don't know the facts. In that case, it might be very useful to the Russians to learn them."

"Mr. President, let's quit beating around the bush on this. What you have said so far, together with the rumors that you are about to fire CNO, convinces me there's a lot more to this story than meets the eye . . . Admiral Baker," he added, "this is a Navy story. What have you got to say about it?"

"No comment," said the Admiral.

"And how about you, Mr. Secretary," said Gordon, leveling a steady eye at SecDef.

"I think in a matter of this kind," said the Secretary, "you should defer to the wishes of the President."

"Regardless of the source of my story?" asked Gordon pointedly.

"Yes."

"Mr. President," said the publisher, "what I get out of this so far is that there's a lot more to this story than meets the eye. But until you give me more to base a judgment on, I can't see any real reason for not printing it."

"I've told you it is against the national interests to publish it. Isn't that a good reason?"

"I'm in no position to judge how the national interests may be affected. But I do know that even the experts often disagree on what's in the national interest."

"Not in this case, they don't. Here are the heads of the State Department and the CIA. They both agree with me."

The Secretary of State and head of CIA both nodded gravely.

"Mr. President, a good politician can always convince himself that whatever is good for his party is in the best interests of the country. You obviously feel that suppressing this story is good for your party. But unless you tell me why you want it suppressed, I can't decide whether it is in the best interests of the country."

"Then let's put it the other way around. How can publication of this story possibly help the national interest?"

"Now you're asking me to go way beyond the field of an editor. We can't weigh each piece of news to see if it's going to help our government before we print it. Some news which must be printed may be against the interests of the government, from a short-range point of view. But one of the basic principles of our democracy is that freedom of the press and publication of the truth are always in the national interest."

"Oh hell, Gordon, come off it. You know damned well that isn't always true. Some items of government business that would make big headlines have got to be classified . . . most of the CIA's business, for example."

"Sure. But every now and then, our free press catches the CIA doing something which is not in the best interests of the government and exposes them—luckily for the country."

"I don't know of a single exposé in which this was true," said the head of the CIA, bristling up. "Don't you admit anything should be classified?"

"Of course he does," said the Secretary of State. "But he reserves the right to break the classification if he doesn't think it's justified. Mr. President, we've got to tell Mr. Gordon more about what's involved here."

"All right," said the President. "Gordon, your story is just one piece of a bigger one. One of our submarines is missing, and we think it is lost. We will probably announce this within twenty-four hours. So far as we know, it could be another *Scorpion* case. By itself, this announcement will just be a piece of sad news to the country. But if coupled with your story, it could stir up a storm in this country that would get out of control."

"Do you think the Russians sank one of our submarines?" demanded Gordon.

"I'm not saying that," said the President. "We don't know. But it can do nothing but harm to have the press of this country accuse them of it, which they are sure to do if this story about the destroyer gets out."

"Do you mean to tell me that one of our submarines is lost, and you are concealing the news about it?"

"As of now, she is missing," said the President. "We can't declare her lost the instant she fails to answer a radio call. If we don't hear from her soon, we will announce it. Meantime, we're asking you to hold that story on the destroyer, at least until the Russians announce it. We feel the stakes are so high in this thing the news should be handled from this office."

"By 'handled,' of course, you mean controlled—censored."

"Your story," said CIA, "hands the Russians information they could never get any other way. My people read *Pravda* every day, but we never get a windfall like this out of it."

"Do you want to censor what I print the way the Politbureau does *Pravda?*" demanded Gordon. "A free press is the cornerstone of our democracy. It's the bulwark of all our other freedoms. You are already violating it by withholding the news on the loss of our submarine. My paper has a clear-cut scoop on a big story of national importance, and now you want to censor that, too. I have already held up publication for twelve hours at your request. I don't know how much longer this scoop will keep."

The President almost said an unprintable word, but restrained himself and said, "Mr. Secretary, how does the State Department feel about this?"

"We are alarmed at the possible repercussions of this story if it originates in this country. We urgently request holding the story."

"Well, there you are," said the President. "I feel the same way, Mr. Gordon, and I'm asking you as a patriotic service to your country to withhold publication."

"Mr. President," said the publisher, "you are asking me to violate the code of my profession and to give up my independent editorial judgment on a big story. I'm not going to do it. I'm going to publish the story."

After Gordon left, the President said, "That hypocritical son-of-a-bitch and his ethics of the profession. The number one ethic of that profession is that a scoop justifies anything. He would print a story that his mother was head of a call-girl ring if he had an exclusive scoop on it."

"He's got two big scoops now," observed the Secretary of State. "I'm concerned about what he'll do with the second one. Those two together would make a hell of a story. I'm sorry now that I advised you to tell him."

"You don't think he will break the *Lincoln* story too, do you?" asked the President.

"Yes. I do."

"He gave me his word he wouldn't," said the President. "And you all heard him."

"Yes," said the Secretary of State. "But a big enough scoop takes precedence over a thing like that. He can always find ways of squirming out of his agreement and write smug editorials proving that freedom of the press demanded it. His promise, given grudgingly, was on the basis that it was in the national interest. He told you in so many words that he makes the final decision on whether things are in the national interest or not. He can break the *Lincoln* story and claim it was contrary to the national interest to hold it . . . freedom of the press, public's right to know, and all that stuff. It's a hell of a scoop, and I think the whole can of worms will be on the front page by this time tomorrow. You remember during the war we were reading the Jap naval codes—and winning battles on account of it. But one of our leading newspapers found it out and refused to kill their scoop on it. I recommend we announce the loss of the *Lincoln* right now."

"I agree with that," said the CIA head. "If we announce loss of the *Lincoln* now, it will be the big headline story. The *Times* exclusive on the destroyer will be an unconfirmed rumor and will get crowded into the background."

"But," objected the President, "the Navy isn't sure about the *Lincoln* yet. We can't tell all those families their men are lost before we are sure of it."

"Why not?" demanded the CIA man. "If we're wrong, we'll correct it as soon as we find out. If we're right, the sooner the news is released, the better—especially if we can smother the destroyer story with it. I'd call a press conference this morning, if I were you, sir."

"I'll look awfully foolish if I have to retract the story later," said the President.

"I don't think you'll have to take it back," said the Secretary of State. "I think the Navy is convinced now that the *Lincoln* is lost. And this thing is getting to the point where you've got to be willing to stick your neck out."

"Hell, my neck is out all the time," said the President. "But before I stick it out any further, I want to be sure it's worthwhile."

"The stakes here are the whole jackpot. If this thing gets out of hand and the press inflames the country about it, it could lead to a confrontation, and God knows what. This eyeball-to-eyeball stuff is desperately dangerous business in which rational human beings lose control of the outcome. Your neck is out as far as it can go in one of them. I recommend we announce loss of the *Lincoln*, for reasons unknown, and say nothing about the Russian destroyer. I don't think the Russians want a confrontation any more than we do, and will be content to leave it that way."

"Suppose they think this means they can molest any of our subs they find?"

"I don't think they will. We're pulling out of the Arctic, and they'll soon know it. I doubt very much that they would molest one of our subs anywhere else. If they did, we could knock off one of theirs that is lurking off our own coast. That's the kind of response they understand and respect."

"I couldn't possibly authorize a thing like that," said the President. Butter would have melted in his mouth.

"We can cross that bridge when and if we come to it," said the Secretary of State. "We should announce loss of the *Lincoln*, sit back, and see what the Russians do. I predict they'll do nothing."

"No," said the President. "I'm not going to do it that way. I'll call in the congressional leaders and tell them what the score is. But I won't make any announcements to the press about it. I think Gordon will keep his promise about the *Lincoln*, and he may even kill the *Nemo* story."

"I think you'll be sorry," said the Secretary of State.

"Hell, Gordon knows as well as we do what the stakes are in this thing," said the President. "He knows how easily the press can blow up a rumor and reap the whirlwind–in this case, maybe an atomic one."

"This thing can do you a lot of harm politically," said SecState. "And the *Times* would consider that a great public service."

"I'll take my chances on that. Gordon knows that in international affairs I've got to act for the best interests of the country."

"You heard what he said about politicians and the best interests of the country."

"Sure. And on internal political questions, the little bastard is right. I suppose that when we are talking about a new post office for Pottsville, I usually can persuade myself that the fate of the party and the fate of the nation are one and the same. But the fate of the party has no weight in deciding a thing like this."

"Not even if it meant losing the next election?"

"That's right. Who was it said, 'I'd rather be right than President'?"

"Henry Clay–and he never got to be President, either."

"Well . . . ninety-nine percent of the time a statement like that is a lot of horseshit–but in this case, it isn't."

22

Next day the Washington *Times* scored an historic scoop. It hit the streets with banner headlines, UNDECLARED WAR AT SEA, U.S. AND RUSSIAN SHIPS SUNK. It broke both the *Nemo* and the *Lincoln* stories, attributing them to an unimpeachable source. It stated the *Nemo* had been attacked by a Russian destroyer while on patrol in international waters and, in self-defense, had torpedoed and sunk the destroyer. The *Lincoln*, on patrol in the same area, was missing and presumed lost—probably sunk by the Russians. It said the Navy was expected to make a "delayed announcement" of the *Lincoln* news at any moment.

AP and UP picked up the story from the *Times* and sent it all over the country. Headline writers had a Roman holiday blowing it up into another Pearl Harbor and the forerunner of an atomic blitz. All radio and TV networks broke into their morning programs with flashes about it—repeated throughout the morning. By breakfast time, everyone who could read or hear knew all about the *Times* stories.

A story about the loss of a whole Marine battalion and six jet fighters in Vietnam got crowded off the front page.

Soon, wild rumors were flashing across the country about SAC alerts and incoming missile salvos. The networks interrupted programs to tell of these rumors, and broke in again a few minutes later to deny them. The stock market opened with a wave of selling that soon became a near panic.

By nine o'clock, the White House press room was a bedlam of frantic reporters demanding a statement from the President, and of harried press secretaries stalling for time . . .

"The President is now conferring with the leaders of Congress."

"Is he priming them for a declaration of war?"

"Certainly not. He will make a statement later this morning. . . . He will hold a press conference at noon."

"Are the stories true?"

"No comment."

"You don't deny them?"

"No comment." . . . and so on.

Reporters had no better luck with SecDef or the Navy Department. If they managed to get through at all on the swamped phone lines, they were told, "No comment–ask the White House."

At noon, the whole country came to a standstill as everyone gathered around the TV sets the way they had during the Cuban missile crisis.

Every nearby phone outside the press room had someone sitting on it holding the line open for a reporter. All TV networks had crews training their cameras on the podium like machine guns. In place of the noisy gabble which usually attends such a gathering, there was a tense silence, almost as if in a church.

On the stroke of twelve, the President strode into the conference room. His face was grave as he took his place at the dais. He squinted into the glaring lights and said:

"Gentlemen of the press–and viewers in the TV audience.

I have sad news to announce. One of our Polaris submarines, the USS *Lincoln*, which was on patrol in the Atlantic, is missing. We must presume it is lost. The Navy is now notifying the next of kin of all members of her gallant crew.

"We have no details as to what happened to this ship. It may be another *Scorpion* case in which we never will have. We would never have known what happened to the *Thresher*, were it not for the fact that it happened on a test dive when a mother ship was standing by. When the *Lincoln* was last heard from three days ago, she gave no indication of being in trouble. The Navy is investigating all phases of her disappearance, and you will be informed as to what they find out.

"Going on to another subject, there is a story in a leading newspaper this morning saying that another Polaris submarine, the *Nemo*, has been in a sea battle with a Russian destroyer, and that the *Nemo* sank the destroyer. This story has been broadcast all over the country as a fact, by now. The story is not true. There has been no battle. The *Nemo* is now returning from a regular patrol in the North Atlantic and will be back at a U.S. base in about a week. She is in no trouble.

"These two news stories, breaking together as they did, have started all sorts of wild rumors. There have been rumors that salvos of incoming missiles have been detected by the DEW Line, that all SAC is on an airborne alert, and that we are on the verge of an atomic war with Russia. There is absolutely no truth whatever in any of these stories. I spoke to Mr. Kosygin this morning over the hot line to Moscow. He assured me that there is no crisis of any kind there, expressed his government's sympathy over the loss of the *Lincoln*, and said no Russian destroyer is unaccounted for.

"Now—my fellow Americans, I appeal to you as urgently as I can to be calm and do not get excited by the wild rumors that you may hear. They are untrue, and can do grave harm to the causes of world peace and the safety of your country.

"I assure you that these two causes are uppermost in my mind as I try to discharge the heavy duties of the office to which you have elected me. I ask you to have confidence that, in matters of this kind, the safety and welfare of the United States are my greatest concern.

"You must understand that in situations like this, we can't always release news as soon as we begin to suspect that something unfortunate has happened. It grieves me to know that the families of the *Lincoln*'s crew found out about the loss of their loved ones through the newspapers. We were not trying to conceal this news—we were trying to wait till we were certain before announcing it.

"Now, my fellow citizens, I have taken an oath to defend this country, and I will execute it to the best of my ability. You can help me a great deal in doing this by refusing to believe sensational rumors. I assure you that our armed forces are alert, ready, and able to defend the country. There is nothing special about this . . . their job is to be always ready.

"There is no truth whatever in the wild rumors that have been flooding the country about SAC alerts, canceling of military leaves, or calling up reserves. These rumors, and the passions they arouse, can do grave harm by making foreign countries with whom we are at peace think that we have lost our senses.

"I therefore ask you as earnestly as I can to remain calm, go about your business as usual, and to have confidence in your government's ability to maintain peace and security.

"Thank you—and God bless you."

As the President finished, the floodlights went out and power was cut off from the TV cameras.

"Any questions?" asked the President of the reporters as the TV crews set up a vain clamor to get power back.

"Yessir," said a reporter down in front. "What do you think happened to the *Lincoln?*"

"I have already told you, we don't know. We can't raise her by radio. It could well be another *Thresher* disaster."

"Do you think the Russians sank her?" persisted the reporter.

"That is the sort of rumormongering I was just talking

about," replied the President. "There is no more evidence for accusing the Russians in this case than there was in the *Thresher* or *Scorpion* cases."

"Do you deny the story in the Washington *Times* that the Russians sank her?"

"How can you deny that some specific thing happened when you don't know what happened?" said the President with some heat. "I couldn't deny a story that she was struck by lightning. The *Times* story is just a wild guess. There is no evidence whatever to back it up."

Another reporter got the floor and said, "The *Times* says their story comes from an unimpeachable source. Will you comment on that, sir?"

The President regarded his questioner coldly for a moment, and then said, "I won't insult the intelligence of this audience by trying to explain that term to the people who invented it."

From the back of the room came the question, "How about the *Nemo* story, sir?"

"All I have to say about that story at this time is that it is not true. And harping on it can do nothing but harm, by inflaming public opinion against a country with which our relations at the present time are—normal."

At this time a dozen hands were up all over the room. A reporter near the front rose and said, "Mr. President, I don't think you've been frank with us. You haven't given us any real news at all. You've confirmed one Washington *Times* story. You deny the other. My question is, why were you suppressing the *Lincoln* story till the newspaper broke it?"

"I answered that while the TV cameras were on," replied the President.

Another reporter asked, "Did this have anything to do with the firing of Admiral Baker as CNO—reported in the *Times* yesterday?"

"Admiral Baker has not been fired as CNO. And I want you all to know I have complete confidence in him, and no intention of firing him."

"Mr. President," came another voice from the back, "you

just came from a meeting with the leaders of Congress. Can you tell us what you discussed with them?"

"Certainly. We discussed these news reports."

"Did you tell them any more than you told us?"

The President frowned, and took hold of the podium with both hands. His press secretary could see quite plainly that he was getting ready to answer it the way it deserved to be answered. Before he could, the press secretary nudged the dean of the press corps, who rose, said, "Thank you, Mr. President" —and the conference was over.

Right after this, Admiral Baker called the President on the scrambler phone.

"Mr. President, the other day you and I reached an understanding regarding certain possible naval operations off Cape Kennedy."

"Yes, I recall the conversation."

"I made arrangements based on that understanding which can be put into effect on short notice."

"I see," said the President.

"I intend to put them in effect tonight—but am calling to see if you have any special instructions for me at this time."

"No-o-o-o," said the President. "The understanding which we reached yesterday covers the matter."

"Thank you, Mr. President."

After the press conference, the President had the Secretary of Defense on the carpet.

"Louis," he said, "I'm not going to beat around the bush with you. There comes a time in this job I've got when national interest takes precedence over everything else, including personal friendship and party politics. That time is here for me, now."

"Yessir, Mr. President," said SecDef. "I'm sure you always do what you think is best for the national interest."

"I'm not so sure of that—and neither are you," said the President. "But that leak to the Washington *Times* was definitely not in the national interest. I've had my people do some checking on it, and I know where it came from. I won't put you on the spot by asking you about it."

"All right, Mr. President," said SecDef, "I gave them the story. I'm sorry now that I did. They thought I had given them a bum steer on the CNO story and were burned up about it. I felt it was important to keep our good standing with them, so I gave them the *Nemo* story—but not the *Lincoln* one."

"I suppose you mean that I leaked the *Lincoln* story. But there's no point going into that . . . or anything else about this thing that has already been done. It's the future that I'm concerned about."

"Yessir."

"Now, Louis, there's something you'd better get straight, and keep in mind from now on. You're a politician, and until a couple of days ago, I was too. But when this thing reached beyond our shoreline and the Russians got into it, I stopped being a politician. From here on, I'm doing what I think is best for the country—no matter who gets hurt. If this upsets any of your plans—you'd better change them."

"All right, Mr. President. I understand. . . . We'll know more about this whole thing soon. I'm having the Captain of the *Nemo* brought down here tomorrow. We're picking him up by helicopter as soon as they come out from under the ice."

"Fine. I want to have a talk with him," said the President.

When he left the White House, SecDef was in a cold fury. As he saw it, this whole mess was all due to bungling on the Navy's part. He had left the decision on which way to come home up to the Navy. The Navy had decided wrong. . . . It became more important every day to get Baker out of there.

The press conference did not stop the storm that was sweeping the country. The only hard news in the afternoon papers was the list of the *Lincoln*'s crew, plus the President's denial that there had been a sea battle. But sensational headlines, which everybody read, were spread over stories, which hardly anybody read, saying nothing to justify the headlines. The casualty list generated sob-sister interviews all over the country with stunned relatives. The President's plea to remain calm and disregard rumors got scare heads saying, "President Views Crisis with Alarm."

All papers featured the fact that the Navy and other usual news sources were saying nothing. Columnists and pundits, noted for their inside sources, hinted darkly that they knew a great deal more than they dared to tell. They said the government had tried to hold off on announcing loss of the *Lincoln* because of other bad news coming out of Vietnam, and said they might be concealing a lot more.

The bottom fell out of the stock market and the exchange closed an hour early because the ticker got so far behind the waves of selling.

The UN session that afternoon was a disaster for the United States. In a meeting televised by all networks, the satellite nations had a circus hurling charges that the United States had recklessly gambled with world peace and praising the Russians for their great patience in the face of unprovoked aggression. Delegates from countries that few people had even heard of crowded to the rostrum to bask in the world spotlight and condemn the imperialist bully. Delegates from nations which didn't even have a big river in them made fiery speeches about freedom of the seas. Others from countries where it is still customary to eat captured enemies lectured the United States on international law.

Our European friends and allies remained discreetly silent all afternoon. The only voice raised in defense of the United States was that of our own Ambassador. The Soviet delegate sat through it all with a smug smile, passing when his turn to speak came because his satellite nations were doing better than he could.

The European press headlined the crisis just as our own did, and by sundown the whole western world was gripped in fear that World War III might be near at hand.

In this brittle atmosphere, the Russian Ambassador, late that afternoon, requested a meeting with the Secretary of State next morning.

The Secretary of State was conferring with the President in the White House that evening, discussing what he should say in the morning. Just the two men were present in the oval room, and both had grave faces. Responsibility for . . . God knows what . . . rested heavily upon them.

"What line do you think the Russians will take?" asked the President.

"Injured innocence," replied the Secretary. "They will disclaim any knowledge of the *Lincoln* and accuse us of trying to stir up the world against them."

"Hell, it's the other way around," said the President. "They're stirring the world up against us–ably assisted by our own press. . . . I specifically said this morning we did not know what happened to the *Lincoln*. I didn't even imply that we blamed them for it. I denied the wild rumors about a sea battle."

"Sure. But they figure they've got us on the defensive now. And they have. They've got us denying things, and they'll try to keep it that way. They'll always come out ahead at that game."

"Why?"

"Because they control their end of the news, and we can't. Our freedom of the press is a fine thing–most of the time. In domestic politics it sometimes keeps our government honest when nothing else could. But when you're playing a no-limit game against a crooked dealer, it often makes us look stupid to the rest of the world . . . especially the backward nations that we're trying to educate to our way of life."

"Well–what will they want tomorrow?"

"Propaganda material, I think," said the Secretary. "They've had little to brag about to their own people recently. They hit the jackpot in New York this afternoon. So they'll play this up big in Russia. They can also use it to gain face in the Far East, where their stock isn't very high now."

"You don't think they really want a showdown over this?"

"What do you mean by a showdown?"

"So far as I'm concerned, there's only one real showdown that I worry about . . . atomic."

"I don't think that's coming. They don't want that any more than we do. They're not crazy."

"But," observed the President, "when you stir up a crisis like this, there's always a chance it will get out of hand. They may start something they can't stop, or get so far out on a limb they can't back down."

"There's less chance of them doing that than there is that we will. They can turn things on and off at will. We can't."

"What do you mean, we can't? I'm the only one in this country who can start an atomic war. And I'm not going to do it unless they bomb us first."

"That's fine, Mr. President, and I agree that's the only sane way it can be. But we can get thrown out of office–the Communists can't."

"The hell they can't," said the President. "They got rid of Khrushchev a lot quicker than I can be got out of office. And I'd rather be ridden out of town on a rail than go down in history as the man who started the atomic war–if any histories are written after it's over."

"We see eye to eye on that," said the Secretary, "and I'd be on the rail with you. Now . . . I think they'll be fishing for information tomorrow. Trying to find out what happened to their destroyer."

"And what do you propose to tell them?"

"I don't think I should tell them a damn thing. Matter of fact, we don't know very much ourselves. If I told him what we know, or think we know, from the *Nemo*'s sketchy reports so far, they could twist it around and make us look real bad."

"Our own people are doing a pretty good job of that for them, right now," observed the President.

"They sure are," said the Secretary. "I think what we've got to do is stand on your statement today. . . . We don't know what happened to the *Lincoln.* The story about a sea battle is untrue. Period."

"How good a poker player are you, George?" asked the President.

"I used to do all right in my younger days," replied the Secretary. "But the stakes were a bit lower then than the ones I'll be playing for tomorrow."

"Well . . . play them close to your chest tomorrow," said the President.

23

That morning the Exec and a dozen officers on the *Mahan* were having breakfast in the wardroom, listening to the radio news. Suddenly the program was interrupted by a flash from Washington announcing the loss of the *Lincoln.*

Forks and coffee cups had stopped in midair at the start of this bulletin and remained there till the end.

"Holy cow," observed a lieutenant, "the *Lincoln.* I know Skinny Wicks, and he . . ."

"Shut up," said the Exec, holding his hand up as the radio went on . . .

"New York. In a copyrighted story, the Washington *Times* says an unimpeachable Pentagon source states that the USS *Nemo,* another Polaris submarine, was attacked by a Russian destroyer in the Arctic Ocean, and, defending itself against attack, it torpedoed and blew up the Russian. There were no survivors. The Pentagon and White House both refuse to comment on this story."

"Gawd almighty," said several officers at once.

"That goes for me, too," said the Exec, leaving his breakfast half finished on the table and heading for the bridge.

He found the Captain in his cabin, carefully moving the unfinished jigsaw puzzle to the back of his desk.

"Have you heard the radio news, Cap'n?" he asked.

"Uh huh," said the Skipper. "Just did."

"What do you make of it?"

"Don't like it," said the Skipper.

"I wonder where the *Lincoln* was when she was last heard from," said the Exec.

"You notice they were careful not to say," replied the Skipper. "Missing on patrol in the Atlantic is all the Navy release says about it. I'll bet she was up in the Arctic off Murmansk."

"Do you think the Russians did it?"

"Sure. I've been expecting this to happen for about a year."

"How about the *Nemo* story? What do you make of that?"

"I dunno. You'll notice there's nothing official on that. It's just a press report."

"They said it came from a reliable Pentagon source."

"Yeah. But that could be anything from a scrub woman to the SecDef himself. I have no doubt something happened involving the *Nemo* and a Russian can. But it's hard for me to imagine it the way this press report has it. The *Nemo* would have to shoot first."

"Unless the Russian shot first and missed—which is about what the story said," objected the Exec.

"Those guys wouldn't miss if they shot first," declared the Skipper. "And even if they did, I can't imagine the *Nemo* shooting back if she wasn't hurt. How could she be sure if she wasn't hurt? And she couldn't be hurt just a little bit. If she got hurt at all, it would be the end of her."

"There's apt to be a hell of a rhubarb over this," said the Exec.

"You can say that again. The newspapers will whip up a

storm. That's what started the Spanish War after the *Maine* blew up in Havana."

"Do you think this will affect us? After all, that guy we're sitting on could easily take a pot shot at us."

"Yeah—he could. But I doubt if he will. Sinking the *Lincoln* without trace off Murmansk is one thing. Blowing up a destroyer right here off our own coast is something else. I don't think they'll try it."

"Probably the *Lincoln* didn't, either."

"Uh huh. . . . Well, CNO knows what the situation is down here just as well as we do. He knows a lot more about this other stuff than we do. If he wants us to do anything different from what we are, he'll tell us."

"So meantime we just keep on as before?"

"That's right. Except I'll be out there in that chair on the bridge from now on," said the Skipper, sweeping the unplaced pieces of the jigsaw into the drawer and reaching for his cap.

That afternoon the Exec came to the bridge of the *Mahan* and handed the Captain a TOP-SECRET dispatch just received from CNO. All it said was "Request Disapproved."

"I don't know what this is all about, Cap'n," said the Exec. "But I suppose you do."

"Yeah, I do," said the Skipper. "Come in the cabin with me.

"Bill," said the Skipper, "you're a torpedoman from way back, aren't you?"

"Yessir. I've been around them a lot. I was Gunnery Officer of a ship like this one for two years."

"Okay. Tonight I want to fire a live shot with one of our fish—with a non-atomic warhead. I want to do it in such a way that the minimum number of people have any active hand in it."

"Yessir."

"So. . . . I'm going down to the sound room and man the director myself. There will be no one else in the room when I pull the trigger. Do you see any bugs in that?"

"Nosir," said the Exec. "Not if you've got a steady solution on the director and everything is holding constant."

"Okay. Now as far as I can see, I've only got to have one man up on deck at the tubes to do this. I need him to remove the propeller locks just before firing. . . . Right?"

"Yessir. That's right. Except for the propeller locks, those fish on deck would fire live right now if you pulled the trigger on the director. If you took the lock off now, you wouldn't need anybody on deck later on."

"I don't want to do that," said the Skipper. "I don't want any possibility of a live shot by accident. . . . Can you take a propeller lock off later on—without any help?"

"Sure. No problem."

"Okay. Then I can do this job so that I'll be the only one on board who knows what I've done. You'll know I've fired a live shot, but you won't know what I've fired at."

"Yessir. I guess that's right. But of course the torpedomen will find out soon that a fish is missing."

"Sure. And before long everybody on board will know it. They'll all have their own opinions about it, too. But none will have had any part in it, and they won't know—any more than you will know," he added, squinting narrowly at the Exec.

"Aye aye, sir. I understand. Let me know just before you go to the sound room and I'll have it fixed so all you have to do is close the contact in the firing circuit."

"Okay, Bill . . . about one o'clock tomorrow morning."

At twelve forty-five next morning the Exec came up to the bridge. The mid watch had settled down for their four-hour vigil and everyone not on watch was in his bunk asleep. The Russian had finished charging his battery, with only his schnorkel sticking out of the water, just before midnight and had gone back down to three hundred feet.

The Exec walked over to the starboard wing of the bridge

and said to the figure seated in the chair and peering out ahead, "Morning, Cap'n."

"Morning, Bill," replied the Captain. "We've got a nice night for it," he said, looking up at the brilliant star-studded sky.

"We sure have," said the Exec.

"You know, Bill," said the Captain, "I'd rather be sitting in this seat than in the CNO's, or the President's. All I gotta do is just carry out my orders. They gotta decide to give the orders."

"Yep. That's right," said the Exec.

"And I'm going to do this job in such a way that I don't have to issue any orders and nobody else has to do a damn thing. . . . After you get that propeller lock off, you have nothing to do with what happens from there on."

"I understand, Cap'n," said the Exec.

They spent the next five minutes observing the sky in silence. Then the Skipper said, "Okay, Bill. Let's get on with it. I'm going down to the sound room now."

"Aye aye, sir," said the Exec. "I'll go back to the tube now and remove the lock. As long as I've got the door open, the ready light on the director will show red. As soon as I get the lock off and close the door the light will go green and we're ready."

The Captain walked over to the O.O.D. and said, "I'll be down in the sound room for the next fifteen minutes or so. You just keep steering the courses generated by the director, the same as you have been."

"Aye aye, sir," said the O.O.D. "We've been steady on one-eighty degrees for three hours now."

The Captain took a quick squint at the chart, noted they were in 250 fathoms–and went below.

A minute later the Captain pushed open the watertight door of the sound room and came in. "Ten-shun!" barked the man on the director as soon as he saw who it was. The sound man looked over his shoulder in some surprise, but of course he remained seated at his set. The electrician on watch dropped his paperback book and bounced to his feet.

"Carry on—carry on," said the Skipper, waving his hand in a deprecating manner.

"How are we doing, Ski?" he asked the director operator.

"Okay, sir. Steady solution. Nothing happening except we got a red light on number one tube a minute ago. They must be making some adjustment."

The Skipper walked over to the sonar scope, peered at it for a moment, and then said, "Let me have your phones, son."

The operator handed the Captain his phones. The Captain listened for a moment, watching the scope. Then he said, "Cut in your tape recorder."

The sound man flipped a switch and started the recorder.

The Captain, still wearing the phones, stepped back to the director. "Let me have your stopwatch," he said to the operator.

Somewhat puzzled, the man handed over the stopwatch and said, "Fifty-five seconds is the running time for this solution, sir."

"Okay," said the Skipper. "Now, everybody out of the sound room. Close the door and just stand by outside till I call you back."

The men filed out and closed the door. The Captain stood watching the dials on the director and listening to the sonar. Soon the red light on the director changed to green.

The Captain took a firm hold on the pistol grip with his right hand, squeezed the trigger, and started the stopwatch with his left.

The ship gave a barely noticeable shudder as compressed air ejected the torpedo from its tube. The shrill beat of small high-speed screws immediately came in loud and clear on the sonar—as the light on the number one tube went back to red. For twenty seconds nothing changed except the decreasing sound level of the high-speed screws as the fish went on its way.

Suddenly there was heavy cavitation noise, the unmistakable

sound of a big propeller churning the water as it does when a sudden burst of power urges it to go faster—much faster!

The Captain had his eye glued on the stopwatch now. The hand swept past fifty-five seconds, and nothing happened. It was just coming up to sixty and the Captain was making up his mind to fire another fish when he got a shattering blast in both ears from the sonar phones.

The men outside the sound room felt the ship quiver a little, as she does when she hits a medium-sized wave, and heard a low rumble as of distant thunder.

The Captain shook his head to clear it, and kept on listening. The ocean was rumbling and burping now as the explosion reverberated off the bottom and re-echoed from the surface and from the violently disturbed water where it started. There were no more propeller noises, but you couldn't have heard them, anyway.

A minute later, as the sweep hand of the stopwatch passed 1–40, new noises came in. The first were high-pitched sounds like tires screaming when wheels are locked at high speed—steel plates tearing apart. Then rumbling crushing sounds like a huge beer can being mashed by a giant—or a pressure hull collapsing under the enormous weight of water as it fell toward the bottom. A few more decreasing rumbles—and then silence. Except for the outgoing pings from the sonar.

"Okay," called the Captain. "You men can come back in now."

As the three wide-eyed watch standers came back in, the Captain handed the phones to the sound man and said, "I've lost him. See if you can pick him up again. . . . Cut that tape off and give me the reel."

The sound man obeyed.

The Skipper punched the crown of the stopwatch, flipping the hand back to zero, and handed the watch to the director operator. "Much obliged, Ski," he said. "Good night, boys."

He shoved the small reel of sound tape in his pocket, turned on his heel, and strode out.

As the footsteps on the ladder receded, the sonar man and the electrician both looked at the director operator and said in awed voices, "Son-of-a-*BITCH*."

"All right now, you guys," said the operator—who was a senior petty officer. "You didn't see nothin', you didn't hear nothin', you didn't do nothin', you don't know nothin'. Keep your mouths shut."

As the Captain returned to the bridge a minute later, the O.O.D. said, "Sonar reports they've lost contact, sir."

"Yeah. I know," said the Captain. "I want you to increase speed to ten knots and go into a standard expanding search pattern. Zero time one minute from now."

"Aye aye, sir," said the O.O.D. ". . . Cap'n—I think we may have run over a large piece of driftwood or something a few minutes ago. I felt a bump—but didn't see anything. I've got the boatswain's mate down looking at the bow now."

"I thought I felt a bump a few minutes ago, too," said the Captain. "Let me know what you find out. I'll be up here in the cabin."

The Captain retired to his cabin, opened the drawer, and started fishing out the pieces of the jigsaw puzzle.

When the Exec looked in a minute later, the Skipper said, "I've just told the O.O.D. to start a standard search pattern . . . this may last several days. . . . Now I want you to send a priority to CNO, 'Request withdrawn,' and another to CincLant making a routine lost-contact report."

"Aye aye, sir," said the Exec. "Anything else?"

"No-o-o-o," said the Skipper. "I think it will be a quiet night now. . . . You can turn in when you get those messages off."

24

The same morning that the *Mahan* was eliminating hazards to navigation off Cape Kennedy, the *Nemo* reached the edge of the ice. As she emerged from under the icecap, she surfaced and began beeping a homing signal. This was picked up at Point Barrow and soon a big twin-rotor helicopter took off and headed north.

An hour later, Admirals Radbury and Vickory were on board the *Nemo*, and Commander Banks was in the helicopter heading back to Point Barrow.

There he transferred to a jet transport and was soon en route to Washington.

At the CNO conference that morning, Admiral Baker said, "Well, gentlemen. The stuff is in the fan now. I don't think the Navy had anything to do with the leak on the *Lincoln* and *Nemo*—and I want to keep the Navy out of this. Let SecDef and the White House handle it."

Rear Admiral James, Navy's Chief of Public Information,

spoke up. "I'm sure it wasn't a Navy leak, Admiral. But I'm having a hell of a time now. Every reporter in Washington is on my neck. I'm making myself look awfully stupid just saying I don't know and no comment."

"I'll have the Chief of Chaplains issue you a sympathy chit," said Admiral Baker, "and give you the key to the weep locker, because you're in for a lot more trouble. We're flying the Skipper of the *Nemo* down here from Point Barrow today. He'll be here in a couple of hours. I don't want the press to get anywhere near him. I'm going to put him up in my quarters while he's in town. He will be brought direct to this office from Andrews and the President wants to see him. Whether we can keep that visit under wraps remains to be seen."

"Oh my gawd," said Admiral James. "On top of that, I think the press already knows the *Nemo* is returning to Alaska. The Washington *Times* man is asking the clearance to visit Point Barrow."

"How the hell did he find that out?" demanded Baker.

"Maybe from the *Times*' unimpeachable source–maybe from Andrews Operations. A planeload of well-known experts left there for Scotland and wound up in Alaska. Any smart reporter can figure that one out."

"Well, you get busy and figure out how we're going to keep the press away from the *Nemo* in Kodiak," said Baker.

"There will be an awful uproar about that," said James, shaking his head sadly. "This is the biggest story of the year, so they'll be over at the White House screaming about the public's right to know and accusing us of censoring the news."

"Yeah," said Admiral Baker. "And don't forget freedom of the press takes precedence over everything else, including home, mother, the American flag, and the national defense. But I'm sure you'll know how to handle it."

"Speaking of that," said James, "there's one member of the press who is very insistent on seeing you . . . Pat Dugan of AP. I've been stalling him off."

"Old Pat Dugan?" said Baker. "Sure I'll see him. He was in VF Six in the *Enterprise* with me at Guadalcanal and Midway."

"But, Admiral," protested James. "If I let him in, there are a couple of dozen others I can't keep out."

"Oh yes you can. You just tell 'em I'm strictly impartial. Anybody else who was in VF Six back in '42 can come right in with Pat."

At the meeting between the Secretary of State and the Russian Ambassador that morning, the two diplomats were indeed like a pair of poker players. Each one knew certain things which might, or might not, be known to the other. Before committing himself to anything, each wanted to find out what the other knew without giving away what he knew.

The Secretary's ace in the hole was that he knew what had happened to the Russian destroyer. Presumably the Ambassador didn't. They hadn't even admitted officially that anything had happened. We had denied a newspaper report that there had been a naval battle. So, unless the Russians saw fit to bring it up—we knew nothing about any destroyer.

The Russians' hole card was full knowledge of what had happened to the *Lincoln*. Or at least the Secretary assumed that it was.

So far, nothing was really in the pot. The hands had been dealt and the betting—if any—was about to begin. The Russian had opened the pot, as it were, by asking for this meeting. He might pass—as the opener often does after the draw. Or he might shove in a stack of chips that involved the peace of the world.

At nine o'clock, the Russian Ambassador was shown into the Secretary's office accompanied by his interpreter. The Secretary also had an interpreter present.

The Ambassador assumed, correctly, that the room was bugged, and that the interview would be taped. As soon as he entered the room, the Secretary's security men knew from their bug detectors that his brief case had a tape recorder in it.

"Good morning, Mr. Secretary," said the Ambassador in English. "My government presents its compliments and hopes that you and your President are in good health."

"Good morning, Mr. Ambassador," said the Secretary. "My government returns the same good wishes to yours."

"My government also presents its condolences for the sad accident to your submarine *Lincoln.*"

The Secretary bowed slightly, paused a moment, and said, "Thank you, Mr. Ambassador."

"Unfortunate accidents of that kind happen," continued the Ambassador. "We have them, too," he added, watching the Secretary's face closely.

The Secretary nodded gravely and said, "Yes . . . I suppose so."

The Russian waited to see if the Secretary intended to amplify. When it was plain that he didn't, the Ambassador said, "My government is concerned about the stories in your press on the *Lincoln*—which state she was probably sunk by Russia."

"So is my government," said the Secretary. "We are doing all we can to stop these dangerous rumors. As you know, the President went on the air yesterday to tell the whole country they are not true. We deplore them just as much as you do. But as you know, Mr. Ambassador, we cannot control the press in this country. And sometimes the press acts irresponsibly."

"But some of their stories," persisted the Ambassador, "are attributed to government officials, and have caused great concern in my country."

"Mr. Ambassador," said the Secretary, "no government official has actually been quoted. All stories have simply implied or suggested that the information came from official sources, and I'm sure you know how little that means. The only government official who has actually made a statement is the President—and you know what he said."

"But your press has convinced a great many of your people that you sank one of our destroyers, and that we sank the *Lincoln.*"

"Unfortunately, what you say is true, Mr. Ambassador. But I assure you, my government does not accuse yours of sinking the *Lincoln.* We are trying to make our people understand this. In regard to the alleged battle between one of our submarines and your destroyer, we have categorically stated that this report is not true."

"Of course, Mr. Secretary," said the Ambassador, "a lot depends on what you mean when you say a story is not true. This can be said about a story which is wrong in only one very small detail."

The Secretary pondered that statement carefully before replying. "Is that what you are saying about the destroyer story?"

"No, Mr. Secretary, I'm not saying that. You and I both know that in affairs of state, some things which may be true are often better left unsaid." The Russian squinted and peered over his glasses at the Secretary.

"I won't dispute that, Mr. Ambassador," said the Secretary, and added, "and perhaps what you just said is one of them."

"In the present situation," continued the Russian, "my country is leaving certain things unsaid, for the time being, because we think the cause of world peace may be helped by it. Yesterday, at the UN meeting, we exercised great forbearance, and said nothing."

"Your motive is a very fine one, Mr. Ambassador. We noted the forbearance of your delegate yesterday. I assure you that my country's greatest desire is also to further the cause of world peace."

"Very well, sir," said the Ambassador. "The real purpose of my call this morning is to present a proposal to your government which we think would do a great deal to promote the cause of world peace."

"I shall be very happy to hear it," said the Secretary.

"For some years, a dangerous situation has been developing between us. You have had your atomic submarines patrolling close to our northern coast. The chance of an unfortunate accident, such as the one to the *Lincoln*, is always present. When such an accident happens, it can give rise to grave misunderstanding, as this one has. When coupled with reports of an unfriendly act by another of your submarines in the same area, it could endanger the peace of the world."

"I have already stated, Mr. Ambassador, that we are doing our best to refute the incorrect reports."

"My proposal," continued the Ambassador, "in order to prevent this dangerous condition from coming up again, is that our countries issue a joint declaration saying that it is an unfriendly act for submerged submarines to operate within five hundred miles of the shoreline of another country. My government proposes that we both file announcements with the United Nations that we will not permit this."

This was a lot more than the Secretary had bargained for at this meeting. He was taken aback by it for the moment. But he soon recovered. "I will convey this proposal to my government," he said. "And I appreciate your motives in making it. But I'm sure you know it is perfectly legal for warships, including submarines, to operate on the high seas outside territorial waters. Your submarines have often been close to our shores, too."

"This does not alter the fact that such operations can cause dangerous misunderstandings," said the Russian. "To promote world peace and prevent future situations like the present one, my government is willing to give up its right under international law to operate off your coasts."

"This is an interesting proposal which may have some merit," said the Secretary guardedly. "But," he added, "I think there would be more chance of getting an agreement of this kind if it were a private understanding between our governments, rather than a public declaration."

"My instructions specify a public agreement to be filed with the UN," said the Ambassador.

"Yes. I realize you must follow your instructions," said the Secretary. "And I also think our naval advisers will say that your proposition is a rather one-sided one."

"There is nothing one-sided about world peace," said the Russian.

"Quite true," admitted the Secretary. "I am merely anticipating what our naval people will say."

"This would apply to our submarines as well as to yours," said the Ambassador.

"I understand that. And again, speaking for the naval people, they will probably say we are . . . giving up a great deal more than you are."

"Perhaps your military men are not as concerned about peace as you and I are," observed the Russian.

"I can't agree to that," said the Secretary. "I think they feel their greatest duty is to preserve peace."

"Perhaps they sometimes conceal things from you which they have done that might endanger peace," said the Ambassador.

"Are you charging them with doing that in this case?" asked the Secretary.

"Not at this time," replied the Russian. "However, my government considers the present situation to be dangerous to world peace. We feel our proposal would remove that danger. We therefore consider this matter to be one of the highest urgency."

"I will convey this information to my government. I agree it is important. But I don't see why you suddenly consider it urgent. This has been going on for years."

"Your President thought it urgent enough to address your whole country about it yesterday. I fear that if the rumors your press is circulating get out in my country, there will be unfortunate consequences."

"I'm sure your country is capable of preventing that—if it wishes to," said the Secretary.

The Ambassador considered for a moment, then rose, bowed, and said, "Mr. Secretary, I have presented our proposal. I will inform my government of what you have said. I will await further word from you. Thank you for your courtesy—and good morning."

While the Russian Ambassador and the Secretary of State were meeting, Commander Banks, in civilian clothes, landed at Andrews Field just outside Washington. He was met by one of CNO's aides and whisked in to the Pentagon.

He was shown up to the front office immediately, where Admiral Homer took him in to CNO.

"Hello, Banks," said Admiral Baker. "We're sure glad to see you. Coffee?"

While Orlando was bringing the coffee, the three officers seated themselves at a table and Baker said, "Now—what happened up there?"

"Well, sir," said Banks, "I'm convinced that the Russians have found some way of detecting our reactor. I tried every trick I know to shake that fellow off—and I think I know all of them. I couldn't get rid of him as long as the reactor was lit off. Whenever I shut it down, he seemed to lose us. I've got a great mass of data on this for the experts to study."

"We've sent the best talent we have in the country up there to analyze your data," said Baker. "I'm sure that end of it will be well taken care of. Now . . . the thing of immediate interest to us down here is this business of the Russian blowing himself up. Tell me about that."

Commander Banks ran through the story of coming out, the torpedo noises, and the explosion. When he told about getting a forty-five-degree down angle on the boat while making twenty knots, both Admirals observed in unison,

"Gawd ALMIGHTY!"

"When another destroyer came boiling up from the south," continued Banks, "I reversed course, went back under the ice, and returned via the Pole. I thought by then I had . . . er . . . solid reason for thinking I was in danger."

"You can put your mind at rest on that score, Banks," said CNO. "And I want you to know that that message about 'solid reason' didn't originate in the Navy."

"I guessed as much, sir."

"Why didn't you shoot back after you heard him fire at you?"

"To be perfectly honest, Admiral—I don't know. I was trying to decide when the explosion hit us. In another thirty seconds, I might have. All I can say is, something made me hold back. I'm glad now that it did."

"So are we all, Banks. I must say you did a fine job in very difficult circumstances," said Admiral Baker. "What do you think happened?"

"Circular shot."

"Quite possible, all right," said Admiral Homer. "I was on a boat that had one—with an exercise head, thank God. We even have 'em with missiles. They had to blow up a big rocket at Cape Kennedy last week when it began wandering off course."

"There is one more thing I must tell you about, Admiral," said Banks, "that I didn't want to put in dispatches."

"What's that?"

"I lost two torpedoes, sir."

"How did that happen?"

"The shock of that explosion was a tremendous one. Coming from ahead, with the tube doors open, it wrenched off the retaining locks that hold the torpedoes in the tubes. When we lost control, we got a forty-five-degree down angle on the boat, and the fish just fell out and sank."

"Hmmmmm," said Baker. "That could complicate things. I'm glad you didn't put it in dispatches. I'm sure you checked carefully to make certain those torpedoes weren't fired by accident?"

"Yessir, I did. That's impossible. I questioned everyone in the torpedo room, and also our sonar men. There is simply no possibility that it was our torpedoes. They sank to the bottom inert and unarmed in two hundred fathoms."

"What kind of warheads did you have on them?"

"Atomic."

"That does complicate things. We have to account for them to the Atomic Energy Commission."

There was a pause for a moment as Baker and Homer were mulling this over.

"Let's go talk to the Secretary of Defense about this," said Baker. Buzzing for his aide, he said, "Set up an appointment with SecDef as soon as you can."

25

Half an hour later, Baker and Banks were ushered into SecDef's office. There were a half-dozen young assistant secretaries there too, to listen in on the briefing.

Banks ran through his story again, the same as he had for CNO. Some of the assistant secretaries knew a little about atomic reactors and asked questions designed to impress SecDef with this fact, rather than to elicit information.

Admiral Baker assured them that the best reactor experts in the country had been sent north to meet the *Nemo*.

Banks then told the story of the explosion.

When he finished, SecDef said, "I'd like to hear your reasons for deciding to return to Holy Loch."

"Well, sir . . ." said Banks, "the answer I got to my request to return via the Pole didn't leave me much choice."

"It seems to me," said SecDef, "it gave you plenty of room to decide either way."

"It didn't seem that way to me, sir. I felt that I had stated my reasons for wanting to come back over the Pole and had been turned down."

"We said that if you had good reason for thinking you were in danger you could return via the Pole."

"We didn't phrase it anywhere near as permissively as that," objected Admiral Baker.

"We left the final decision up to you, Commander," persisted the Secretary. "I'm interested to know why you changed your mind and decided it would not be dangerous to return to Holy Loch—even after you came out from under the ice and saw that the destroyer was still on top of you."

"Well, sir—he had been on top of me for three days. He had many opportunities to attack—but didn't. I really had no 'solid reason' to think he would do anything different until he fired a torpedo at me."

"Perhaps not," said SecDef. "But you do admit we gave you authority to return via the Pole if, in your judgment, this was indicated?"

Banks looked at Admiral Baker before answering. Baker glowered and was about to say something.

"I'm asking the Commander," said SecDef.

"Well . . . yessir. But to me the message clearly indicated that you did not share my fears about what might happen."

"Of course," observed SecDef, "we have to leave tactical decisions to the commander in the field. You were on the spot up there and in a better position to evaulate local conditions than we were down here."

"Those are the very words I used in discussing that reply with you, sir," blurted Admiral Baker.

"All right, Admiral," said SecDef. "And that's exactly why I left it to his judgment. Now, Commander—answer my question. Why did you change your mind?"

"Mr. Secretary. To answer your question frankly—I didn't change it. I still thought it probable we might be attacked. But if I came home over the Pole, I would never be able to prove it."

"So you endangered your ship against your better judgment?"

"That's not a fair way to put it," objected Baker.

"I think it's an accurate way," said SecDef. "Let the Commander speak for himself."

"Mr. Secretary," said Banks, "looking back on this thing now, I'm afraid you're right. Events proved I did endanger my ship. And I must admit, I did it against my better judgment."

"In my opinion," said Admiral Baker, "that message gave him little choice. Unless he tried to get back to Holy Loch, you would have said he was a nervous old lady."

"At any rate," said the Secretary, "he was right about the danger and wrong in not taking the safe way out when we gave him a free hand."

Admiral Baker counted up to ten and decided not to answer that one. Then he said, "There is one more detail about this that doesn't change the broad picture at all, but which you should know about. . . . Tell him about the torpedoes, Captain."

Banks explained what had happened to his torpedoes.

When he got through, an assistant secretary nudged his chief and whispered in his ear. The Secretary nodded, and asked,

"Commander, has it occurred to you that it may have been one of your own torpedoes that destroyed the Russian?"

"That definitely was not the case, Mr. Secretary," said Banks, "although I was afraid some people might think so."

"How can you be sure it wasn't one of yours?"

"First of all, I specifically warned the man on the director not to fire unless I gave the order—which I never did."

"How do you know he didn't fire anyway?"

"From the testimony of five other men in the torpedo room who were watching him. Also from the sonar noises, which were entirely different from those made by our torpedoes. And finally, from the fact that when you fire a torpedo, you feel it all through the ship—everyone knows it. There is simply no possibility that our own torpedoes had anything to do with the explosion."

"Well, suppose your torpedoes did fall out of the tube," said an assistant secretary. "Wouldn't they explode when they hit the bottom?"

"No, sir. When they fall out of the tube, they came out unarmed. They can't explode, even if you dropped them on concrete. And besides, they didn't fall out until we got the big angle on the boat, and that didn't happen till after the explosion."

This reply brought on another whispered conference between the Secretary and his aides. Then the Secretary said, "All right, Commander. That's all. Thank you."

As Banks and the two Admirals got up to leave, the Secretary said, "Admiral Baker, I'd like you to stay for a few minutes."

After the others left, SecDef said, "Admiral, has it occurred to you that this torpedo business is suspicious?"

"No, sir. It hasn't. Why do you say that?"

"It's just too pat. Your skipper is obviously a nervous type. He was jittery about going back to Holy Loch. I think that when the Russian got on him again, his nerve failed him and he fired those torpedoes at the Russian."

"I don't believe it."

"Why not?"

Baker's safety valve was close to the popping point. "Mr. Secretary," he said, "there isn't much use trying to answer that question to anyone who would ask it. But the main reason—though not the only one—is that I know Banks wouldn't lie in a matter of this kind. I know Banks well. I know his father, too, and so do you—Admiral Banks in London. Young Banks is a responsible officer with twenty years service. You just don't accuse those kind of men of lying, Mr. Secretary. His shoulders are plenty broad enough to take the blame for any mistakes he makes. He simply couldn't lie. He isn't built that way."

"The story he tells," said the Secretary, "is just made to

order to cover up a mistake in judgment on his part and shift the blame to his superiors. I want to check it."

"Just how do you propose to do that, sir?"

"I want to give him a polygraph test."

Baker looked at the Secretary in amazement. . . . "You mean –give him a lie detector test?" he gasped.

"Yes. In plain words, that's what I mean."

"No!" said Baker. "I won't stand for it."

"Admiral, I'm giving you your orders. This is what I want."

"Well, I'm telling you, Mr. Secretary, I'll have nothing to do with it. I won't permit it."

"Not even when I order you to?"

"That's right."

"Then you'll get it from the White House. What will you do then?"

"I'll carry it out and resign my commission."

"I don't understand you, Admiral," said the Secretary. "What are you so afraid of on this thing, anyway?"

"I'm not afraid of a damn thing on it, Mr. Secretary, except destroying the base on which our whole Navy is built–confidence in the honor and integrity of our officers."

"This is no time for the old-school-tie stuff, Admiral," said the Secretary. "I'm afraid some of your old Navy ideas about officers and gentlemen may be out of date."

When Baker got back to his office, he was an angry man. He motioned to Homer and Banks to come into the inner sanctum with him.

"You know, Hank," he exploded when they got inside, "I had a chance once to take a good job as piano player in a high-class whore house. I sometimes wish I had."

"What's the matter now, sir?" asked Homer.

"It's the goddamdest thing I ever heard of in my thirty-five years in this Navy."

"What is it?" asked Homer.

"He wants to give Banks a lie detector test."

Commander Banks shook his head like a fighter who has

just had a sharp rap on the jaw. Then he said, "I have no objection to taking one, sir."

"Well, I have," stormed Baker. "And I'm giving you orders right now not to take one unless the order comes from the White House. And it won't come from there except over my dead body."

"I'm not afraid of their lie detector test, Admiral," said Banks.

"I don't give a damn whether you are or not. You are not going to take one. They're not going to start that kind of stuff while I'm CNO."

Soon after this, Admiral Baker's aide announced Pat Dugan, the AP man.

As he entered, Admiral Baker said, "Hey hey, Pat. Long time no see. How are you? What's the latest scuttlebutt?"

"That's what I'm up here to find out, Admiral," said Dugan.

"All you want is the latest top-secret war plans for Vietnam, I suppose?" said Baker.

"No. Only the straight dope on those two Washington *Times* stories."

"That's even more classified than the war plans, and I'm not going to tell you anything," said Baker.

"Now wait a minute, John," said Dugan. "This is no way to treat an old shipmate from VF Six."

"Pat," said the Admiral, "any time an old VF-Six pilot wants to borrow two bits, he's welcome to it if I've got it. But on that *Times* scoop—all of my shipmates went down on the *Maine*."

"Can't you even give me some background stuff on it—on a not-to-be-attributed basis?"

"No."

"What's the matter? Don't you trust your old pals any more?"

"Come off it, Pat," said the Admiral. "Don't give me that injured shipmate stuff. You know very well I've got to be impartial, and treat all you guys the same."

"True enough. But, Admiral, I think the Navy is handling this thing all wrong. You're being so mysterious that a lot of wild rumors are getting blown up into a dangerous crisis. Don't you have any confidence in the press?"

"You asked for this, Pat," said the Admiral, "so you're going to get it without gloves on. I know many reporters in whom I have a lot of confidence. I know some, like yourself, in whom I would have complete confidence that they would respect any pledge they give me. But, of course, it's a low-down unfair trick to give a reporter a big story and pledge him not to use it."

"Sure. I agree with that," said Dugan.

"But in dealing with the press as a whole," continued the Admiral, "I don't have one damn bit of confidence in them. With a group of reporters, I've got to figure the ethics of the group are the ethics of the worst crook in the group. You guys are in a cutthroat racket, competing against each other, where a big scoop justifies anything. If a dozen decent guys think one SOB is going to score a scoop by breaking a pledge they've all given, they've all got to break it, or else let the SOB make bums out of the rest of them."

"Hmmmmmm," said Dugan. "I've got to agree with you on that, too. Although if you ever quote me on it I'll do what you big shots are always doing to us. I'll claim I was misquoted."

At this point, Admiral Homer stuck his head in the door and said, "You're wanted over at the White House in ten minutes."

When the Admiral got to the White House, the Secretary of State was there too.

"Baker," said the President, "the Secretary has received an important proposal from the Russians this morning about a naval matter. I want to get your reaction to it. Tell him about it, Mr. Secretary."

"I can do better than that," said the Secretary. "I'll play him the tape recording of the whole thing."

At the end of the tape, Admiral Baker said, "Sure. They want us to give them something for nothing. Their subs are no real threat to us—yet. Polaris keeps them honest when nothing else would."

"This is exactly what I told him your reaction would be," said the Secretary. "It's right there on the tape."

"I'm against any such declaration," said the Admiral.

"Well now, look," said the President. "We are already pulling our subs back from their coast, even further than he wants. We are doing this with no commitment from them. So if we agree to his proposal, we'll be the ones who get something for nothing."

"Quite true," said the Admiral. "If this were a private understanding between governments, I might agree to it . . . but not at a public session of the UN."

"You're making me look real smart this morning, Admiral," said the Secretary, rather smugly. "I also told him that very thing."

"And what was his reaction again?" asked the President.

"Naturally he said he had his instructions, and they said 'public statement.' However, when he tells Moscow what I said, perhaps he'll get new instructions. I suggest we give him time to discuss this with his government, and then I'll call him in and tell him we're ready to agree to his proposition on a private basis."

"Okay, John?" asked the President of Admiral Baker.

The Admiral nodded yes.

"Of course," observed the President, "what we're doing now is playing the game of 'chicken'—except that instead of doing it with a couple of hot rods on the road, we're doing it with a couple of hundred million people. But . . . I'm not quite ready to give way yet. . . . All right, gentlemen, we'll proceed on that basis."

The Admiral stayed behind when the Secretary left.

"Mr. President," he said, when they were alone. "I just want to let you know that the matter you and I discussed privately a few days ago has been . . . uh . . . taken care of, down at Cape Kennedy."

The President looked at him gravely for a moment, and then said, "Okay, John. Thank you. Good work. . . . Maybe this will get the word to them that the *Pueblo* era has ended."

"New subject, Mr. President," said the Admiral. "The Captain of the *Nemo* flew down from the Arctic today. I assume you want to see him?"

"Indeed I do," said the President. "Let's set it up for tomorrow morning . . . and . . . uh . . . the Secretary of Defense told me he was in town."

"Yessir."

"He also told me about a difference of opinion that you two have had about how to proceed in his case."

"Yessir?"

"I discouraged him from pursuing the matter."

"Thank you very much, Mr. President. I appreciate that."

"You know, Admiral," said the President, "if our man *had* blown up that Russian, it actually would make things a great deal better for all concerned to have him deny it and lie like a trooper about it."

"This is quite true, Mr. President," said Baker. "But the trouble is that all the early training of our naval officers is to tell the truth. Our whole system of naval command is based on the knowledge that they do. This works fine as long as they are in the lower echelons of command. But of course, when they get up to the political level, especially in international affairs, it would be disastrous."

"Indeed it would," said the President. ". . . Er, Admiral, now that you're up on that level, how can I tell about you?"

"That's a fair question, sir," laughed the Admiral. "The rules of the game are that no matter how high you go, you must always tell the truth within the chain of command–which includes the Commander in Chief."

"Okay," said the President. "How about Congress?"

"You certainly can't always be frank with Congress. But by the time you get up where you have to appear before Congress, you should know how to evade unwise answers without actually giving untruthful ones."

"I think some of my press secretaries must have had naval training," observed the President.

"Well . . . I'll have Commander Banks here at ten tomorrow morning," said Baker.

26

Next day the chicken game came awfully close to a smash. The Washington *Times* stories on the *Lincoln* and the sea battle had been allowed to circulate in Russia, but with no official comment. After hearing from their Ambassador about his meeting with the Secretary, the Russians decided the Americans were not sufficiently impressed. So the Kremlin released a bulletin that one of their destroyers was missing, probably sunk.

Pravda headlined the story, saying that when last heard from, their destroyer had been peacefully following a U.S. submarine that was spying on the Russian coast in the Arctic. It said that their ship disappeared without trace the day after the U.S. announced that the *Lincoln* was missing. It did not directly accuse the U.S. of sinking their ship, but the implication was obvious.

On the heels of this news flash, a mob gathered in the streets of Moscow and marched in fairly orderly fashion to the American Embassy. There it broke into a riot that almost wrecked the place. They hurled insults, ink and paint bombs, smashed windows, and beat up the Marine guards. They tore down and burned the American flag. The Embassy staff barricaded themselves inside and got ready to fight for their lives. As the mob debated whether to storm the building or set it on fire, the Ambassador ordered the secret files burned and sent a frantic radio to Washington saying he feared they would all be killed.

News of the attack on the Embassy in Moscow fanned the flames of anger already blazing in the United States about the *Lincoln.* A crowd of indignant citizens formed in Lafayette Square and marched up Sixteenth Street to retaliate on the Russian Embassy. Many bearded beatniks and hippies who were picketing the White House for peace joined the mob intent on tearing down the Soviet Embassy and throwing it away.

There were several urgent calls that morning over the hot line from the White House to the Kremlin and vice versa.

The Washington police, who had been trying to handle the mob with kid gloves, as if they were civil-rights rioters, finally resorted to clubs and tear gas. Order was restored and the mob fled, with the hippies screaming "police brutality."

In Moscow, the police had looked on impassively as the mob stormed around the U. S. Embassy. At a last-minute word from the Kremlin they stepped in, broke it up, and the mob dispersed quietly.

Meantime, as TV programs were being interrupted by flashes on the riots, the early-warning radar scopes on the DEW Line in Northern Canada suddenly spotted a dozen fast-moving blips coming over the Pole toward the United States.

If a dozen such tracks suddenly appear at any time coming out of the polar regions toward our northern border, it will cause grave alarm in the underground HQ of Continental Air Defense Command in Denver. But if wild rumors have been sweeping the country, and if mobs are rioting around the Embassies in Washington and Moscow, the Air Defense controllers can't hem and haw about what to do.

From first sighting of a missile until explosion over target can only be fifteen minutes at the most. There is no time for a council of war and a formal estimate of the situation. Air Defense has to make up its mind—but fast!

If they go off half-cocked crying wolf when there is no wolf, a lot of taxpayers may die of fright. If they take too long to make up their minds, a dozen of our big cities may get flattened out of a clear sky with no warning.

The sharp young general on watch in the great underground command post has a number of things he can check very quickly when the DEW Line goes red. All polar air traffic is constantly plotted on his huge plastic board of the North American continent—on which one inch is two miles. So are the orbits of all man-made satellites and also the many pieces of space junk now flying around the earth. He has repeater scopes from the DEW Line on which he can actually see blip, speed of flight, and direction of approach of the bogie causing the alarm. He has an up-to-the-minute display board showing political factors which favor or discourage a sneak attack. Computers, programmed with vast memory circuits, stand ready to spit out the answers to complex questions if he punches the right buttons.

This morning all signs in HQ pointed to urgent danger.

The harried General on watch had no choice but to hit the panic button. Flash Red lit up in the Pentagon, in SAC Headquarters at Omaha, and in Fighter Defense Command.

In minutes, interceptor squadrons were scrambling from our northern air bases and streaking toward Baffin Bay. SAC bombers which had been waiting, manned, armed, and ready on the runways, roared into the air all over the country loaded with hydrogen bombs and climbed toward the holding points where they would circle till the President told them to strike. The General released the Anti-Ballistic Missile Batteries to their local commanders, who fired a salvo of anti-missile missiles, aimed to intercept the bogies high over Canada.

Air Defense HQ works fast. But their decisions are made by human brains, at something less than computer speed. When they do arrive at their verdict and flash it to Washington, there is even less time left for hemming and hawing. If Air Defense says, "This is IT—missiles are on the way here," no one in the Pentagon is in a position to dispute them. Denver can release anti-missile missiles, but the Pentagon still has to make up its mind about retaliation with intercontinental missiles.

The White House is on the DEW Line circuit and gets a Flash Red as soon as the Pentagon does. The Secretary of Defense didn't wait for any advice from the Joint Chiefs' war room. He told the White House Duty Officer by teletype to advise the President he should retaliate. Immediately!

Not long before this, Admiral Baker had brought Commander Banks to the President's office to tell him about what had happened to the *Nemo*. Banks' story had been interrupted several times by the Duty Officer sticking his head in to pass along urgent bulletins.

Banks had finally finished his story and the President had just asked him, "Why didn't you shoot back when you were sure he had fired at you?"

Before Banks could answer, the Duty Officer burst in with the teletype from SecDef in his hand, followed by the young Captain with the black brief case. He said, "SecDef has just recommended immediate retaliation!"

The Captain began opening the brief case.

"Keep that goddam brief case closed," said the President. "I won't fire until after a missile explodes over this country."

There was a tense pause while all hands stared wide-eyed at the President.

The President broke it by demanding, "Where is the Vice President?"

"He's in California, sir," said the Duty Officer. "Making a speech in Berkeley."

"Okay!" said the President. "The same bomb can't get him and me both. We've only got about ten minutes to wait."

Within five minutes Air Defense Headquarters canceled the Red Alert. The blips on their early-warning scopes were from a flurry of meteors coming at the earth from the direction of Polaris. A dozen meteors on a radar scope look for some minutes exactly the same as we think a salvo of missiles coming over the Pole will look.

The President and Admiral Baker had gone to the White House war room when SecDef's message came in. When they came back, the President said to Commander Banks, "Where were we when we were interrupted?"

"You had just asked me why I didn't shoot when I thought the Russian had fired at me."

"Yes. Well, why didn't you?"

"I've been trying to think of a good answer to that for the past five minutes," said the Commander. "And the best one that I can think of, sir, is—for the same reason that you didn't fire a few minutes ago."

"That's good enough for me. I know just exactly what you mean, son," said the President.

News of the Red Alert and the firing of the anti-missile missiles generated a flash, interrupting even the TV commercials, that we had fired a salvo of Minute Man missiles at Moscow and World War III had begun. The flash was corrected by the Pentagon within ten minutes, but it took hours for the correction to catch up with false alarms which swept around the world like a blast from Gabriel's trumpet, getting wilder as they went.

In Europe, enough older citizens were left who had been through the bombings of World War II so that there was no panic. But this wasn't true of the United States. The few cities that had any civil defense organization at all soon found out that the one thing it couldn't cope with was the threat of an immediate atomic attack. Cars hastily loaded with terror stricken families poured out of the big cities headed for the open spaces.

Bumper-to-bumper traffic jams clogged the main highways. Citizens who couldn't leave town stripped the supermarkets of all the food they could lug into their basements. The churches were jammed with pious souls making peace with their Creator. The saloons bulged with others determined that if this was the end of the world, they would at least be in a state of bliss when they left it.

While this was going on, a SAC bomber carrying four hydrogen bombs disappeared over Baffin Bay. Hours later, the best guess as to what had happened was that it had been shot down by the anti-missile salvo turned loose by Air Defense Headquarters. This news leaked, and started more wild rumors on their way around the world.

For the whole world, that afternoon was a nightmare dragged out for quite a few hours. For years, everyone had accepted the possibility of an atomic war sometime in the future as simply being one of the facts of life in the 1970s. They had learned to live with it. But the possibility that it might burst on them this afternoon was a terrible shock.

It was a shock, too, for the top men on both sides of the Atlantic who held the fate of the world in their hands. Up till now, each side had figured—*We can go just so far to find out if the adversary is bluffing. If he isn't, we can always back down.* Now it had become plain that it wasn't possible to judge the point of no return with any accuracy. Each adversary had thought for a while that afternoon that the other had passed it and the die had been cast. The Russians had turned loose the mob on our Embassy feeling sure it would produce no more than a mild "tut-tut," as had attacks on United States Embassies in Cairo, Indonesia, and many other places. They had accepted the loss of the destroyer in the Arctic as the fortunes of war. But the disappearance of their sub off Cape Kennedy had been a rude jolt. They had done nothing to provoke it— They hadn't expected it— They feared it meant all-out atomic war was coming.

The President, too, was having second thoughts about how far he could go in the chicken game. After those five minutes that morning, he figured he knew what it would be like in hell, if he wound up there. His vast multi-billion-dollar defense setup, with all its electronic marvels and superhuman mechanical brains, had blared at him: "This is IT!" His top responsible adviser had told him, "You've got to shoot." But all they could do was advise. He had to decide.

It was just some stubborn streak in his make-up that held him back. And the thing that kept running through his mind during those five minutes was, Sinking their sub was too much—this is all my fault.

As panic mounted in world capitals, there were grave top-level meetings in Moscow and Washington. Although 4400 miles apart in distance and even more miles apart in outlook on life, these two gatherings were in emphatic agreement on one thing—neither one wanted war. Up to now, there had been hawks and doves in both Washington and Moscow. There were none now. There were only frightened men, groping for a way to avoid disaster.

Whatever it was that had started all this was no longer important. Both groups felt that whatever the "adversary" wanted, within reason, to avoid war was all right with them. The big problem was how to convey this idea to the other without seeming to make an abject surrender. Everyone was willing to meet the other's terms for the time being. Later—if necessary—they could try to squirm out of any bad bargain they had to make. But at any rate they would still be alive and able to squirm.

As the Politbureau met, reports were pouring in about the angry storm sweeping across the United States over the attack on the Embassy. The flash on the DEW Line alarm had reached them, and for a while they thought the rockets had been fired at Moscow.

The mystery of the SAC bomber's disappearance had leaked, and now, on top of all this, the Naval Commissar opened the meeting by announcing that their submarine off Cape Kennedy was missing—probably sunk by the Americans. This news, after all the other things, had everyone feeling that the next shock they got might be the blast of an atomic bomb.

The Naval Commissar was saying, "These are dangerous people we are dealing with. They are reckless gamblers. In the case of the destroyer, there may have been some excuse for what the American did. Maybe our ship made a clumsy attack. But in this new case, our submarine had no orders to attack. So we did nothing to provoke them. I can't imagine any destroyer captain doing this on his own authority. So it must have been ordered by the government. I now believe that they might even make an atomic attack on us."

The Prime Minister said, "It seems incredible that they would do that. I don't think they are crazy. They have as much to lose as we do in an atomic war. Even if they hit first, we will still have enough left to destroy them. Then the Chinese will take over what's left of the world. But this sinking of our submarine just shows that you can't tell about them . . .

"Now, comrades," he continued, "we can't waste time discussing this thing. We must decide what we will do while we are still able to decide things. In a moment we will vote, and the question will be very simple—war or peace?

"I will vote for peace. It has taken us over fifty years to build what we have now. We would be fools to lose it because of an argument about a few ships. We can live a while longer with the Americans—we can negotiate, talk, compromise. We can give them what they want now, and take it back later. But if the Chinese ever take over, that's the end of everything. I would rather live under the czars than under them. So, no matter what happens, I am not going to start an atomic war. If you want peace, I will do whatever is necessary to have it. If you want war, I will resign and you can get someone else to wage it. . . . Mark your votes now, and put them in the box."

When the votes of the Politbureau were counted a minute later, it was 9 to 0 for peace.

In the United States, waves of anger and fright swept after each other across the country as press, radio, and TV blared each new crisis or rumor of one. Decisions involving life or death for millions were being made by the government. Obviously the only sane decision was to stay alive. But the world was a madhouse this afternoon. Millions followed the news with the same helpless feeling as a gambler watching the ball take its final bounces on a roulette wheel.

The helpless feeling extended to Congress, too. A secret poll would have shown nearly all Senators and Congressmen in favor of peace—at almost any price. But things were breaking too fast today for the President to ask Congress for help in deciding them.

And the one big decision, overshadowing all others, was one that only one man would make . . . the Atom Bomb? There could be no Gallup Poll or vote in Congress about this. It was in the hands of the President alone—the fate of the nation, for better or for worse.

The BOMB hung over the world like the sword of Damocles.

The President called the Security Council to order and said, "Gentlemen. There comes a time when the buck doesn't go any further. It winds up in my lap and I've got to make decisions that no one else can. Today is one of those times.

"I didn't call you together to ask for advice. I brought you here to tell you what I have decided to do—so that whether you agree with me or not, you will at least know why I'm doing it.

"I can't see how we can get any closer to war than we are right now, without actually shooting. That attack on our Embassy was obviously deliberate. We think the Russians sank one of our ships. They think we sank one of theirs. We had a false alarm on the DEW Line a few hours ago, and now one of our SAC planes with four atom bombs aboard is missing—possibly shot down by the Russians."

The President paused, and everyone braced himself for what might be the decision that would change history.

"There is a young officer outside that door at the end of the room," continued the President, "with a goddam black brief case. That brief case might just as well be hung around my neck like an albatross. . . . If I ever decide to open it—it will be.

"I'm not going to open it today. In fact, I'm never going to open it, unless Russian bombs explode over one of our cities. I hope the Russians feel the same way about this Thing as we do. Unless they are mad—they must.

"What we've got to do now is to be careful we don't make them think we are going to attack them. If they ever become convinced that we are on the point of doing it—they may attack first.

"So now, gentlemen, here's my decision. I'm going to ground SAC. I want every airplane with an atom bomb on board kept on the ground—armed and ready. But on the ground. I want all missile silos battened down, closed tight, and kept that way."

He paused to let this sink in.

"Mr. President," said SecDef, "this will delay our reaction time, in case you do have to shoot, by perhaps a couple of hours."

The Chiefs of Staff of the Air Force and Army nodded grave agreement.

"I know that very well," said the President. "But if I ever give the word to shoot, I don't see that it makes a damn bit of difference whether our world goes up in smoke at two A.M. or an hour and a half later."

"We could lose an important part of our striking force on the ground in their initial attack," persisted SecDef.

"So what?" demanded the President. "We've got enough to blow Russia off the face of the earth ten times over. If this thing breaks, what difference does it make whether we only kill one instead of two hundred million of them in our first attack? The ones that die right away from blast will be the lucky ones.

"So . . . get SAC on the ground right now. I want them dispersed as widely as possible. No matter how hard they hit us, we'll have enough left to blot them out, not even counting Minute Man or Polaris.

"From here on this is a diplomatic problem—not a military one. It's a job for me and the Secretary of State, rather than the generals and admirals. Now you people in the Defense Department go back to your offices and get going on what I've told you to do. I want the Secretary of State to stick around."

In the oval room, after the meeting, the President said, "Well, there you are, George. My job is to decide. I've made my decision, and now you're stuck with it."

"I think you decided wisely, sir," said the Secretary of State.

"Now. When you meet with their Ambassador in the morning, you must make it crystal clear to him that we want peace, not war. We do not accuse them of sinking our submarine. We will ignore their attack on the Embassy. If they bring up the subject of their destroyer, you can truthfully say that we didn't sink it—I talked to the Skipper of the *Nemo* this morning."

"Yes, Mr. President. I understand all that."

"The only thing they have asked for so far is this declaration about keeping our submarines five hundred miles away from each other's shores. I am willing to go along with that. Even by a public declaration, if we have to."

"I concur with that, too, sir. If necessary, I'll agree to a public statement at the UN. But I hope we won't have to."

"So do I," said the President. "But we almost passed the point of no return today. I didn't like the looks of things there. . . . And I don't want to get close to it again."

"I understand how you feel, sir. I'll do my best to keep away from it tomorrow."

"I wish you luck," said the President. "I'll even say a prayer for you. I found out today I still remember how to pray."

27

When the Secretary and Ambassador met next morning, it wasn't a chicken game any more. Although both still wore poker faces, it wasn't even much of a poker game now. Neither player was willing to call a big bet by the other. Each figured that, so far as this crisis was concerned, he himself held a small hand and the adversary probably had a straight flush.

They were playing for a huge pot. But neither wanted a showdown. Both would welcome an offer to just throw in the cards face down, split the pot, and go home.

Had either one suddenly snarled and shook his fist, he could have had the other's watch. But neither knew the other felt that way.

After the usual amenities, the Secretary said, "I want to make it clear that despite anything you hear on radio or TV, or read in our newspapers—the main objective of my government is to preserve peace."

"Our two governments are in complete agreement on that," replied the Russian.

"That being the case," said the Secretary, "we can certainly resolve our differences. At our last meeting, I told you we might agree to your proposal on submarines, except for the public announcement of it . . ." He paused for a moment, considering how best to say we would agree to it any way they wanted it.

The Russian thought it was his move, so he said, "In the interests of world peace we are willing to modify our proposal and accept a private agreement between our two governments."

"Then that matter is settled here and now," said the Secretary. "It is my understanding that we are agreeing not to operate our submarines submerged within five hundred miles of each other's coasts, and that there will be no public announcement of this."

"That is correct," said the Russian.

"I think perhaps we should have some record of this," said the Secretary. "I suggest we dictate a memorandum of this now. We can both sign it, each retain a copy, and the matter will be closed."

"I agree to that," said the Russian.

The Secretary buzzed for his stenographer and dictated a short memorandum, accepting a few minor changes in wording suggested by the Russian.

"How long do we want this agreement to last?" asked the Secretary.

"I think until denounced by either party."

"That is satisfactory," said the Secretary–and added a clause to that effect.

As the stenographer withdrew to type the agreement, the two men looked at each other in some surprise. They had met only a few moments ago feeling this might be a difficult and dangerous session–with world peace at stake. Now the mountain had turned out to be a molehill.

"We will issue instructions to our Navy today," said the Secretary.

"And we will do the same," said the Russian. "And now, what

about those recent naval—incidents? We are willing to consider them closed if you are."

"I presume you refer to the *Lincoln* and to your destroyer which disappeared?" asked the Secretary.

"Also to our submarine off Cape Kennedy."

The Secretary had no idea what he was talking about. "I was not aware that you had one there, Mr. Ambassador," he said. "I don't know what you refer to."

"Perhaps your naval people neglected to tell you about it. Just as mine have told me nothing about the *Lincoln*. But these two submarines disappeared under similar circumstances. We each feel that the other country's sub was the victim of an—accident. Perhaps it is best to let matters rest that way. We do not intend to announce the Cape Kennedy incident."

"Then I see no reason to pursue either matter any further," said the Secretary. "What about the destroyer incident?"

"Frankly, we don't know what happened," said the Ambassador. "Perhaps it's better for all concerned to just leave it that way. Our naval people, of course, have their own opinion. And a sudden disaster is less likely for a surface ship than for a submarine. But since your government has officially stated there was no battle, mine will say no more about this incident. I suggest it would be in the best interests of world peace if all these naval incidents were allowed to die with no further publicity."

"I agree. But you know, of course, we have no control of the press in our country. The government will say nothing more about this, except that we do not charge your government with any misconduct. But I'm afraid the press will keep this alive for some time."

Here the stenographer returned with the typed memos. The Secretary handed one to the Ambassador. They both read the documents carefully, signed their own copies, exchanged papers, and signed each other's copies.

As the Russian folded his paper and put it in his pocket, he let out a silly little giggle and said, "*Karoshy!*"

"I'm not sure what it means, but I think I agree," said the Secretary.

"It means—that's very good."

"Would it be proper for me to take off my shoe and hammer on the desk to show how much I agree?" asked the Secretary.

"No—no. Only Khrushchev did that—and he usually had too much vodka when he did it."

The Ambassador rose, the two men shook hands, and the meeting was over. World War III was postponed.

A little later the Secretary was reporting to the President. At the end of his report he said, "I've never seen him in such a co-operative mood before. The Russians seemed to be scared even worse than we were. I think if I had demanded that they get out of Berlin, he would have agreed to it."

"Well, why the hell didn't you?"

"I was caught flatfooted, to tell the truth. I thought *we* were going to have to make concessions—and was prepared to do it. He even said they had lost a sub off Cape Kennedy recently—but did not intend to announce it."

"He probably just made that up to show you what nice guys they are," said the President solemnly.

"Mr. President," said the Secretary, "we must persuade the press to drop these Navy stories. They are just waving a red rag at the Kremlin."

"No doubt about that," said the President. "They lit a fire that almost got away from us this time. But of course their version of it is that they just did their duty."

"By almost starting an atomic war?"

"Of course their story is that they don't make history—they just report it."

"They'll have a hell of a time reporting it after they get the atomic war started," observed the Secretary. "Can't we give them some other big story now to take the spotlight off this naval business?"

"I'm coming to that. I think we can. I'm going to make a

change in the cabinet. That ought to grab the headlines for a while."

"Hmmmm . . ." said the Secretary. "That depends. . . . I doubt if most editors even know the names of more than three or four cabinet members. . . . Are you looking at me, sir?"

"No. SecDef."

"They know him, all right."

"He stirred up this mess to begin with," said the President, "and then choked up on us when the chips were down. But I can't just fire him. I've got to find some other spot for him. One with a lot of prestige—but where he can't really do any harm . . . like maybe Ambassador to de Gaulle?"

"De Gaulle can do a lot of harm. I know a much better spot than that. Very great prestige—but no matter what he does or says, it won't affect the course of history one way or the other."

"I can't appoint him Vice President—what other job is there like that?"

"Ambassador to the UN."

"By God, that's it," said the President.

Later, the President had Admiral Baker in. "Baker," he said, "we've got to keep the press from getting any more on the *Nemo* story."

"Yessir," said Baker. "They haven't found out yet that Banks is in town. I'm keeping him at my quarters out at the Observatory. He's going back to Alaska tomorrow."

"Now, how about the ship itself? If they ever find out she's in Kodiak, every publisher in the country will be up there waving big checks at your young seamen for exclusive stories. If I were a sailor and somebody offered me more than the Navy will pay me in the next ten years just for using my name on a story, I'd think twice about saying no."

"That's right, sir. Out of a hundred and twenty on board, somebody might take it."

"All right," said the President. "It's in your lap, Admiral. I want you to keep the press away from the *Nemo*."

"Aye aye, sir," said Baker.

Back in his office, CNO was conferring with the Vice Chief, the Deputy for Operations, and the Chief of Information. They had just received a message from Vice Admiral Radbury on board the *Nemo*: "Have found radiation leak. All Polaris boats affected. Can fix."

"Okay. That takes one big load off our minds," said Admiral Baker. "Now . . . the President wants the press kept away from the *Nemo*—he's very emphatic about it. He thinks the Russians are pacified now, and he doesn't want to stir them up again."

"We're going to have a hell of a time keeping the *Nemo* under wraps now," said ChInfo. "Everybody and his brother knows she is coming into Kodiak. SecDef has cleared about a dozen reporters that I know of to go up there. If we try to bar them from the ship, they'll make an even bigger story out of that than they did about the sea battle. And SecDef is on their side."

"Where is the *Nemo* now?" asked the Admiral.

"She went through Bering Strait this morning. She'll be in Kodiak the day after tomorrow, sir," said OP-03.

"Okay," said Baker. "The best way to kill this story is to let it age and ripen awhile. We'll have the *Nemo* pass up Kodiak. I'll bring her back to the East Coast via Panama—hell, via the Cape, if necessary. We can keep her at sea another couple of months. By that time this will all be ancient history, instead of front-page stuff."

"You're right about that," said ChInfo. "But all those editors and publishers that have gone up to Alaska will . . ."

"The hell with them," interrupted Baker. "Your job is to pacify them. That ought to keep you busy for a while."

"We've got Vickory and Radbury and all those experts aboard," objected the Vice Chief of Naval Operations. "We've got to get them back here. And we've got to get the Skipper back aboard."

"Do it by whirlybird, the same as we did at the icecap."

"No strain," agreed OP-03. "We can do that."

"And the *Nemo* has been out two months now. She will be running short of food pretty soon," persisted the Vice Chief.

"Have a beef boat meet her at sea when she goes by Frisco. Give her all the food, mail, newspapers, and anything else she wants."

"Aye aye, sir," said Admiral Homer. "We'll get the dispatches out this morning and set it up that way."

28

The Naval Observatory is where they keep track of what time it is. Most people nowadays think this is done by Western Union, the phone company, or maybe NBC. But the time that they put out is secondhand. If you really want the most official time there is, you go to the Naval Observatory for it.

Checking up on time seems like an easy job, but it depends on how fussy you are. A wrist watch is good enough for most of us. To navigate ships you need fine chronometers. They have to be checked every day against the stars. For space travel, even the best chronometers aren't good enough. And when you start fooling around with the fuses that fire atom bombs, your timing has to be fantastic.

The Observatory grounds are a seventy-two-acre wooded tract two miles from the White House on Massachusetts Avenue just beyond Embassy Row. Back in the days of sail when life was simpler than it is now, all they needed was a small building in the woods with one telescope.

As the Navy went from sail to steam to Polaris, the Observatory kept up with it. It now has hot lines to branches on the West Coast and in South America, and an array of shops, offices, laboratories, and domed transit houses, with a large staff of atomic scientists, mathematicians, and astronomers. It has buildings full of mechanical brains, and its timepieces range from the sundial near the main gate to CESIUM clocks in air-conditioned vaults, that tick off microseconds. In the early days the astronomers checked our chronometers against the stars. Now they check irregularities in the motion of the stars by means of the CESIUM clocks.

The Observatory grounds are also the site of the seventy-five-year-old brick house where CNO lives. Mrs. Baker was out of town, so Commander Banks had the house to himself during the day—except for the mess boys.

He had a late breakfast the day after his visit to the White House and spent the morning writing a long letter to his father in London. In it he told the whole story of his brush with the Russian destroyer. He also told of a decision he had just reached. Then he wrote an official letter to CNO.

He spent the afternoon making a tour of the Observatory with Dr. Michelson, the head astronomer. The Doctor told him a lot of things about time, how it is measured, and how it varies, that even an expert navigator like himself never heard of.

Dr. Michelson took special pride in explaining the CESIUM clock. He said, "The stars gave us time as accurately as we needed it until the Atomic Age began. To control fission, we needed much more precise timers. So we developed the CESIUM-beam clock."

"How close does that give you time?" asked Banks.

"Plus or minus one microsecond," said the Doctor proudly. "One one-millionth of a second. The atomic second, which we determine here, is the most precise physical measurement which man makes—much more accurate than our measurements of mass or distance."

"That figures," said Banks. "After all, time is the most valuable quantity we have on this earth. . . . How much of it do you figure we've got left, Doctor?"

"Oh—quite a few million years," said the Doctor. "The earth's rotation only slows down a few seconds every decade. It will be a long time before it stops."

This didn't answer the question quite the way that Banks meant it. But he let it go. "How far back does time go, Doctor?" he asked.

"Most experts agree the earth is at least five billion years old."

"And how do you think it all got started?" asked the Commander.

"Well," replied the Doctor, "one school of thought says it all began with a lot of nebulous stuff that sort of congealed into atoms, molecules, and then stars, more or less by chance. Another says it began with a huge hunk of matter that exploded . . . the big bang, or expanding universe theory, and . . ."

"How long do you think it will be," interrupted Banks, "before we wind it up the same way with our hydrogen bombs?"

"Well, Commander," said the Doctor, "you're sort of overstating things a bit, aren't you? This world of ours is just a speck of dust in the whole scheme of things. Even if we blow it to smithereens with an atomic blast, I doubt if people on the nearest star would even notice it."

"You think there is a bigger scheme of things, then—do you, Doctor?"

"Yes. I belong to the old-fashioned school who think if you go back far enough, you find God behind it all."

"I don't see how anyone could look out at the stars every night as you do and not believe in God," said Banks. ". . . But if a great all-wise God did it, how do you explain the ungodly mess we've got here on earth now? Why does He tolerate man?"

"I don't think He pays any attention to what man does down here," said the Doctor. "He put all we need here on earth for man to use. He gave man a wonderful brain to figure out how he ought to use it. . . . And now, we can do as we damn please with it.

"You're getting way out of my field, now, Commander," added the Doctor. "I'm just an astronomer. I can tell you what the stars and planets will do for the next couple of hundred years. But God only knows what man will!"

At dinner that evening in the big brick house, Admiral Baker told Banks about the meeting of the Secretary of State and the Russian Ambassador, and of the secret agreement to pull all submarines back from each other's shores. He said, "So now the crisis has passed. We've had another confrontation on the brink—but there will be no war. This time, perhaps we both blinked."

"My God, Admiral," said Banks. "Isn't there any limit to what we've got to stand still for? They made an unprovoked attack on my ship; they sank the *Lincoln;* and so we agree to pull our ships out of waters where they have a perfect right to be. This would have been unthinkable only a few years ago when I was a kid."

"The atom bomb is a great equalizer," observed the Admiral.

"If we've got to put up with this when only a few of us have it, what the hell will we have to swallow when the underprivileged nations of Africa get it?"

"Keep your shirt on, Commander," said Admiral Baker. "There's a lot more to this than meets the eye; more than I'm at liberty to tell you. . . . But we gave them something to think about, this time. . . . What time are you shoving off for Alaska?"

"Four A.M., sir. I'll be leaving here for Andrews about two-thirty."

"And when will you be in Kodiak?"

"It's about an eight-hour flight, sir. There's a five-hour time difference, so I'll get in there about seven A.M. Alaska time."

"Have they told you about the change in schedule for the ship?" asked the Admiral.

"Nosir."

"The dope on it is being held very closely to keep it away from the press. The *Nemo* is not coming into Kodiak. We're going to put you back aboard and lift our people off by whirlybird. Then we will bring the ship back to the East Coast via Panama. We want to keep the press away from you as long as possible."

"Aye aye, sir," said Banks. "Of course, we'll be getting a little short on rations."

"All taken care of," said the Admiral. "A beef boat will rendezvous with you off San Francisco, and give you all the food and anything else you want. Just let us know what you need."

"Nothing but food, sir."

"Oh! By the way," said the Admiral, "I'm embarrassed that with so many other things happening, I've forgotten to congratulate you on being selected for Captain."

"Thank you, Admiral."

"I'm not always too sure about these early selections," continued the Admiral. "But in your case, I think it was well earned."

"I was very lucky, sir."

"Sure you were. You've got to be lucky to cash in on a hundred-to-one shot like that. But we need lucky people in this Navy. Those are the kind I like to have around me. If the selection boards would always pick lucky people who are going to stay lucky, I'd be well satisfied. . . . And now," said the Admiral, "I've got more good news for you."

"What's that, sir?"

"You'll be getting a new job as soon as you bring your ship around to the East Coast. . . . The President was quite impressed with you yesterday. He is due to get a new naval aide. He has asked for you."

Banks squirmed uncomfortably. "Admiral," he said, "there's something I've got to tell you—probably should have done it before this, but didn't have a chance."

"What's that?"

Banks reached into his pocket and pulled out the two letters he had written in the morning. "Here are two letters I would like to leave with you, sir," he said. "One is for my dad, and should go in the diplomatic pouch to London. It's got classified matter in it."

"Okay. I'll be glad to take care of that."

"The other is for you, sir. . . . It's my official request for retirement."

The Admiral looked at him incredulously. "Retirement?" he said.

"Yessir."

"But . . . but . . . WHY, for God's sake?"

"It's hard to explain, Admiral. But I'll try. On these Polaris patrols, you've got lots of time to think . . . maybe more than is good for you—and maybe I've been thinking too much. . . . But anyway—I love the sea. I love the Navy. I like doing dangerous things. I think fighting battles at sea—against other ships—is right down my alley. If you called for volunteers tomorrow to blast the Chinese atom base in Manchuria off the face of the earth, I'd be at the head of the line, asking for the job. And when I pulled the trigger on those missiles, I'd yell, 'Go, Baby, go!' Or if you want somebody to slip in submerged to the naval base at Murmansk, and mine the harbor—I'm your man. But my target now isn't ships. All my missiles on the *Nemo* are zeroed in on cities. . . . Sure, I know the point of aim is an airfield, or a munitions plant. But millions of people live within blast radius of ground zero. If I ever shoot, it won't be a battle—it will be a slaughter. I'm not a fighter now; I'm an executioner. I just stand by out there, perfectly safe, a hundred fathoms deep (at least until last week, I was safe)—and wait for a radio message telling me to shoot. When the message comes, if the authenticators check, I shoot. That's all there is to it. And make no mistake about it, Admiral, I'll shoot. I've got a good ship and a fine crew, so my missiles will all run hot and straight and hit their targets. Meantime, enough of their missiles will be hitting our cities so that there isn't much use coming home. We might as well open the scuttling valves after we have done our job. . . . This is a hell of a way to run the world, Admiral—and I don't want any part of it."

The Admiral thought for some time before answering. Then he said, "Son, what you're complaining about is just the way that life is on this earth. It's run by force and always has been. I learned this when I got blown up in the *Arizona* at Pearl Harbor. The force we've got today comes in megatons instead of thousand-pound bombs—but the idea is still the same. When the diplomats and politicians get things messed up bad enough they dump it in our lap. . . . I know what you mean about being a fighter. I was a Corsair pilot in World War II—and shot down my share of Japs. Anyone who says there isn't a hell of a thrill in hand-to-hand combat for your life is a damn liar. But when your dad and I took off from the *Enterprise*, we were on our own. It was us against any enemy we ran into, and no holds barred. But we only carried six fifty-caliber machine guns. The kind of power you pack in the *Nemo* has got to be controlled by the head of state. . . . You're wishing for the old days before even radio to come back, when a captain was on his own after he got out of sight of land. I'd like to have the old days back, too, when CNO used to command the fleets. But they're gone forever. We are more civilized now."

"Admiral," said Banks. "I don't think the head of state does control things any more. The bomb is so terrible it controls him."

"What you say is true to some extent of our government, Spike," said the Admiral. "If we were the only ones who had the bomb, I doubt if it would ever be used again. But the only chance for peace on earth in our time went overboard when the Russians developed their bomb. Now the only thing that keeps them from clobbering us is the fact that you are out there, cocked and ready to let them have it."

"That's the thing that bugs me, Admiral," said Banks. "The only times there have been long eras of peace in this world have been when one nation was strong enough and tough enough to beat the hell out of anyone who tried to disturb the peace. We were strong enough to do that at the end of World War II. But we didn't have the guts to take on the job of enforcing peace. We turned it over to a lot of starry-eyed idealists and look what they produced–the United Nations, for Gawd's sake! Where countries that I can't even find on the globe have one vote the same as we have–one nation, one vote. We should have forbidden anyone to monkey with the atom bomb, and made it stick. But we didn't. So now it isn't good for a damn thing except staving off an atomic war. Look what has happened since the Atomic Age began: the Berlin blockade–the Wall–Hungary–the Bay of Pigs–Korea–Vietnam . . . the *Liberty*, the *Pueblo*, now the *Lincoln*–and but for the grace of God, the *Nemo*. Look at the turmoil in Africa, Indonesia, and China. There's more fighting in the world now than there ever was. The bomb is just a millstone around our necks."

"This is all just crying over spilled milk," said the Admiral. "And whether the bomb is a millstone or not, it's the only thing that stands between us and slavery under the Reds. Your retiring won't make it a saner world. You've still got to live in the world whether you like the way it's run or not. You can't run away from it. . . . Have you got something good lined up for yourself on the outside?"

"Nosir. Maybe I'll go into a monastery. If I was looking for a good job, I can't think of anything better than aide to the President."

"Then this makes no sense at all," said the Admiral. "With an even break in luck you're headed for two stars, maybe more if you've got what it takes. You'll be closer to the President than I am. You may have a hand in helping to make history. This will break your dad's heart. He never ran from anything. But that's what you're doing–quitting–running away."

Banks colored up and said, "I think it's unfair to say that, sir. When war comes, you can recall me. If there's anything left to recall me to after the big blast."

"Hell, it's your duty to help prevent the big blast. If enough people quit on us like you want to, the peaceniks and flower children will take over and soon there'll be a Russian commissar in the White House. . . . Now look, Spike, you're going off half-cocked. I'm going to stick this damn thing in my bottom drawer and keep it there till you've had time to think this over. You go back to sea, and when you get to Panama, I want you to send me a message and tell me whether to tear this up or put it through."

"Aye aye, sir, Admiral," said Banks. "I'll do as you say."

"How about this letter to your dad?"

"Hold it till you get my answer, sir," said Banks.

When Banks was leaving at two-thirty the next morning, Admiral Baker was at the door to see him off. He stuck out his hand and said, "Good luck to you, Spike. You've done a good job in this Navy. You can do a lot more. Think it over—and God bless you."

"Thank you, Admiral," said the Commander. "God bless and guide you, too."

At 0400, a Navy jet transport roared off Runway Nine at Andrews, swung left, and headed northwest toward Alaska.

Nearly everyone in Washington was still asleep. Hardly anyone expected the holocaust to come in their lifetime.